THREE GUNS FOR TONTO
THE COMPLETE TALES OF
SHERIFF HENRY, VOLUME 7

THREE GUNS
FOR TONTO
THE COMPLETE TALES OF
SHERIFF HENRY, VOLUME 7

W.C. TUTTLE

PRIMARY ILLUSTRATOR
CARL PFEUFER

COVER BY
ARTHUR MITCHELL

POPULAR PUBLICATIONS · 2023

TABLE OF CONTENTS

THE SHAME OF ARIZONA

Alas for Wild Horse Valley and its amiable sheriff, Henry Harrison Conroy. The era of good feeling is officially over; and it is open season again for dry-gulchers, bank robbers, horse-thieves, smugglers—and critics of the local administration

1

LUKE-WARM HOTBED

IT WAS ALONG a far-flung stretch of the Mexican Border, south of Tonto City, where most of the terrain is on edge. Moonlight silvered the brushy, rocky hills, smoothing the rough edges. Here was the old barb-wire fence, which separated Arizona from the land of *mañana,* with its beaten trail where the Border Patrol rode, always alert for the *contrabandista.*

Two dim figures worked beside the fence, loosening staples from the weathered posts. One could hear an occasional *cre-e-eak,* as a staple was withdrawn. The two men worked slowly and carefully, alert for any sound, until they had dropped the wires from a number of posts. Then they went back, only to ride out of the brush a few minutes later and carefully work their horses over the down wires.

But one horse caught a loose wire across an ankle, picked up the slack, whirled and caught the wire across the heel of its shoe. The taut wire whined and hummed, as the horse reared backwards, trying to get loose, and the rider leaped out of the saddle, cursing aloud. Then the wire snapped, but the rider clung to the tie-rope and managed to subdue the animal.

Two of the Border Patrol, riding along the fence, had heard the wires, and were coming at a swift gallop as the unseated rider mounted his nervous horse. Guns flamed in the moonlight when the two men who had crossed the Border opened fire. It was like the popping of a dozen fire-crackers; then a complete silence.

The two men who had crossed the border moved in close to each other.

"Downed both of 'em, damn 'em," one growled. "You git hit?"

"Naw. Well, we won't have them two to bother about. Let's go."

SEVERAL HOURS LATER Ted Vickers and Jack Bennett, Border Patrolmen, rode into Tonto City on one horse. Vickers was unconscious, riding in the saddle, while behind him rode Bennett, badly hurt but able to keep Vickers upright. They found Dr. Knowles. Bennett was able to tell him that they had been ambushed near the Border, and that the dry-gulchers had gone north.

Danny Regan, the young foreman of the JHC spread, was having a poker session at the King's Castle Saloon, but offered to awaken the sheriff and deputy. Danny pounded loudly on a door in the Tonto Hotel, then invited himself in and lighted the lamp.

Henry Harrison Conroy, the sheriff of Tonto, short and fat, with the reddest nose to ever grace a vaudeville poster, sat up in bed and blinked thoughtfully at Danny. Rising to a corresponding position beside him was Judge Van Treece, the deputy: sixty years of age; tall, lean and gaunt, his scraggly gray hair standing on edge as he gazed at Danny through pouched eyes.

They were like a pair of suddenly awakened owls—one a

Wham! Oscar pulled the trigger, and the small
office shook with the concussion.

fat, round-faced owl, the other of the horned variety; very fierce, but slightly bewildered.

Danny proceeded to tell them about Vickers and Bennett. Henry doubled a fat fist and massaged his nose violently.

"Rub the thing off," advised Judge, "it's a nuisance."

"Eh? Oh!" Henry chuckled. "How badly are they injured, Danny?"

"Vickers got hit twice and Bennett got it once. Doc says they'll prob'ly live. Bennett says the smugglers came this way; he's dead shore of that, Henry."

"Hm-m-m-m," mused Henry. "Came this way. My goodness!"

"Well, suppose they did?" said Judge. "Tonto City has always been a hotbed of *contrabandistas*. Two more would not harm us. As far as that is concerned, it might be two of our very best citizens. You were about to speak, sir?"

"If given an opportunity," replied Henry dryly. "I rather resent that hotbed assertion, Judge. Unfortunately we are close to the Border, and also unfortunately there is money to be made in an illegal practice, such as smuggling drugs and jewels—not to mention the heathen Chinee. But this is not a hotbed, Judge."

"It is more than just luke-warm, Henry."

"Oh, possibly a degree or two—but not hot."

"We've got to move some horses pretty quick," said Danny. "Today I heard that there's a buyer in Agua Frio, offerin' a hundred dollars for horses. Looks like another move toward a revolution, Our horse herd is workin' too darned close to the Border."

"Might be well to put them on the north range," nodded Henry.

"Hmph!" snorted Judge. "Wake a man up in the middle of the night to report a shooting scrape, over which nothing will be done. This is a Federal case, anyway. Never mind the horses. Go home, Danny, and let us sleep."

"I could," suggested Danny, "get Zell Hork and Nick Balleau to help me throw them horses onto the north range."

Nick Balleau and Zell Hork worked for Steve Malloy's Quarter Circle M, lying close to the Border, and due south of Tonto City.

"Very well," agreed Henry. "I quite approve of that, Danny."

"If this business session is over, perhaps we might go back to sleep," said Judge.

"All right, Judge," grinned Danny. "See yuh *mañana*."

AS DANNY STARTED for the door they heard the unmistakable sound of two shots, spaced about a second apart. It was not unusual to hear shots fired in Tonto City, because cowboys are prone to salute the moon with a six-shooter during slight inebriation; but following so closely on the shooting at the Border, the shots seemed to signify trouble.

Judge groaned audibly. "And after all the nice things the Scorpion Bend *Clarion* said about the lack of crime in Wild Horse Valley," he said.

"I did not see the paper today," remarked Henry. "In fact, I never expected the editor to say anything nice about us."

"Rather premature, I am afraid," sighed Judge. "I have a feeling that something is wrong."

"Do yuh think I ought to go and see if anythin' is wrong?" asked Danny.

Heavy footsteps clattered down the hallway. Henry said, "No use, Danny—something *is* wrong."

It was Tommy Roper, the young man who operated the livery stable: an ex-cowboy with a noteworthy impediment in his speech. Danny opened the door. Tommy was hatless and coatless, breathing heavily.

"Sh-Sh-Sh-Sh—" began Tommy.

"Sheriff," prompted Henry. "No prefaces, Tommy; what actually happened?"

"Man," replied Tommy, "sh-shot and kuk-kuk-killed."

"Clear and concise," applauded Judge. "Name, Tommy?"

"St-stranger."

"No more at present, Tommy," said Henry. "We will dress."

"Fuf-fuf-fifty mum-men down there, and they had to pup-pup-pick me," complained Tommy.

"Judge," said Henry, "your pants usually button in front."

"To hell with precedents in an emergency!" snorted Judge.

"We'll wait for 'em downstairs, Tommy," said Danny.

"My feet are swollen," complained Judge. "Can hardly get my boots on."

"They would fit better, my dear friend, if you had them on the right feet. No matter now, except that you are more splay-footed than usual."

"Are you taking your gun?" queried Judge.

"Why, if I may ask, sir? The man is dead. Come on."

The man was indeed quite dead. He was lying in the dust near the King's Castle hitch-rack, surrounded by a number of men, while Doctor Knowles made an examination by lantern light.

He was a man of possibly forty-five, six feet in height and weighing about a hundred and eighty pounds. He wore a brown suit, brown shoes, brown shirt, with a brown and green necktie. A crushed, brown fedora hat lay on the ground near him.

"Shot twice," said the doctor. "Does anyone know who he is?"

No one replied, until a man said, "I think he came in on the mornin' stage, Doc, and went to the Tonto Hotel. I never seen him since then."

"I seen that feller early this evenin'," said another. "He was looking into the bank windows, and then he went on up the street. It was almost dark."

THE BODY WAS removed to Doctor Knowles' house,

where the clothes were searched; but his pockets were empty. There was not a single clue as to his identity. He had registered at the hotel under the name of John Jones, Chicago, Ill. It seemed that Mr. Jones had spent most of the day in his room.

"Mr. Jones," observed Henry, "traveled exceedingly light. Not a piece of baggage and nothing in his pockets."

"That's what whips me," declared the old hotel clerk. "That there feller had a fancy valise when I showed him to his room. When he went out this evenin', he shore didn't have it with him."

"Well, you lose a customer," said Judge.

"Paid up for five days. Yessir, I charged him four bits a night, and he paid me two and a half, right off the reel. Never even questioned the price, and didn't kick about the pitcher bein' cracked. He was a gent, if I ever seen one."

"Well, Judge," said Henry, "we may as well go back to bed and hope that no more killings disturb our rest."

"We ain't apt to git any more t'night," said the clerk.

2

COME TO A SHOOTING

THEY WERE A queer pair, these peace officers of Wild
Horse Valley. Henry Harrison Conroy was born in a back-
stage dressing-room, and for fifty years the theater had
been his home. For years he was a headliner in vaudeville,
known from coast to coast, a juggling comedian, with a
nose like a ripe tomato and the voice of a tragedian.

When vaudeville waned, and the theaters began
retrenching on the top salaries, Henry's act was canceled.
At the same time Henry received a letter from Tonto City,
saying that his uncle had died and left him the JHC cattle
outfit. With no knowledge of the cattle business or of the
range country, Henry came to Tonto City to claim his
inheritance.

The short, fat man with the red nose, immaculate garb,
even to spats and a gold-headed cane, amazed Wild Horse
Valley. His actions, speech and dress amused the cattle
people and appealed to their sense of humor; so at the next
election someone suggested writing Henry's name on the
ballot for sheriff. Started as a joke, it ended in grim reality.

Wild Horse Valley awoke next morning to find that they
had carried the joke too far. Henry realized the extent of
the joke, and in order to not be outdone by Wild Horse

Valley, he appointed Judge Van Treece, a derelict lawyer, as his deputy. Then, to complete what Judge dubbed "The Shame of Arizona," Henry appointed Oscar Johnson as his jailer.

Van Treece—tall, lean, dignified, and with a mile-long thirst—had gained fame as a criminal lawyer, and might have gone far in his profession, except for that thirst. Oscar Johnson, horse-wrangler on Henry's JHC ranch, was a giant Swede, with very little education and a thirst for battle.

But in spite of it all, the sheriff's office at Tonto City had been effective. Even Henry's bitterest enemies were obliged to admit that this roly-poly, red-nosed person achieved results—in his own way. Both Henry and Judge were atrocious revolver shots, and their horsemanship left much to be desired.

HENRY AND JUDGE did not arise early next morning, As they were eating breakfast in the dining room, the elderly clerk came to them and imparted the knowledge that a stranger had come in on the early stage from Scorpion Bend, and inquired about Mr. Jones.

Henry nodded gravely, and replied that as soon as possible he would have a conversation with this stranger.

But the stranger had not left his room; so Henry sauntered to the bank, where he admired the new gold and black lettering on the window. Frederick Hale, the new banker came out, smiling pleasantly. Hale was tall, slender and good-looking, slightly gray at the temples, and not the usual type of small town banker.

"Slightly overdone, Sheriff," he said smilingly, "but effective."

"Very pretty," said Henry. "Tonto needs new signs."

"It does," agreed Hale. "The place is rather weather-beaten."

Lawrence Eddy, the new cashier, came out to look at the sign. He was fairly young, with sleek, black hair, well-tailored clothes and a superior air. When he had gone back into the bank, Frederick Hale said:

"A very efficient young man, Sheriff."

"Time," said Henry, "will take off that gloss."

"Perhaps. But we believe in the future of Tonto City."

"Good, good," said Henry absently. "It may have a future, in spite of the fact that it has had mighty little past. I give you good afternoon, sir."

Henry bowed and went toward his office. Frederick Hale smiled thoughtfully and went back into the bank.

Judge Van Treece doted on Shakespeare, and just now he was in the office, tilted back in a chair against the wall, deeply engrossed in a paperbacked edition of the bard of Avon. Seated on an army cot, which groaned under his weight, was Oscar Johnson, nicknamed "The Vitrified Viking," cleaning a rifle. Oscar's button-like nose was streaked with gun-oil.

Henry came in and sat down at his desk, glancing keenly at Oscar, who was quietly humming a song.

"The newly-renovated bank is really a credit to our drab street," remarked Henry. Judge grunted. "Mr. Hale believes in the future of Tonto City," continued Henry.

"Yudge," said Oscar quietly, "do you know de best way to find out if a gon is loaded?"

"Pull the trigger," replied Judge absently.

Wham! The small office shook from the concussion, and a handful of shingles jumped off the roof.

"It vars loaded," stated Oscar blandly.

Judge's glasses had been jarred out to the end of his nose, and he glared angrily at Oscar. Henry stepped gingerly out of the office and looked around. Judge's brows lifted slightly, as he looked up at the hole in the ceiling. Henry came in, followed Judge's gaze and then looked at Oscar, who was calmly wiping his fingers on a rag.

"It vars loaded," repeated Oscar, "and Yudge told me to pull de trigger."

"I told you—Oscar, you seventeen kinds of a damn fool, I—"

"You said, 'Pull de trigger,' und I yust pulled de trigger, Yudge."

"You asked me—oh, what is the use?" sighed Judge.

"After all," remarked Henry, "it only means *another* hole in the ceiling."

JUDGE ADJUSTED HIS glasses and picked up a newspaper. "Henry, did you read the latest editorial in the Scorpion Bend *Clarion?*" he asked.

Henry sank down in his desk chair and rubbed his red nose.

"You know I never read that scurrilous rag, Judge. What does it say?"

"The editor compliments you, sir," replied Judge.

"Eh? Compliments me? Plain ink—no vitriol, Judge?"

"Change of heart, I suppose. However, here is the heading which says, 'Credit where credit is due.' The editorial follows:

" 'Feeling especially charitable today and with malice

toward none, we believe we should compliment the sheriff of Tonto on his ability and the efficiency with which
his office has recently functioned. Perhaps, in the past, we
have been unduly harsh in our criticism of the estimable
Sheriff Conroy and his queerly assorted crew; but if our
constructive criticism has borne fruit, we feel justified in
the manner in which the paper's editorials goaded the
Tonto peace officers into action. We do not want to pat
ourselves on the back—but.'"

Henry's eyes were closed during the reading, but now
he opened them slowly.

"The only good thing about it is brevity, Judge," he said.
"I do like that 'strangely assorted crew' idea. But I do not
like his unmitigated gall in claiming the credit for our
actions. Credit to him—indeed! The malicious little sidewinder will make us the laughing stock of Wild Horse
Valley. Goaded by a newspaper! Faugh! Judge, is there any
of Frijole's prune whisky left? I need something to remove
the taste of that egotistical editorial from my palate."

Judge turned to Oscar.

"Slave, fetch the demijohn."

"Yah—su-ure," grinned Oscar, and went back into the
jail.

Frijole Bill Cullison, cook at Henry's JHC ranch, spent
most of his spare time—and much of Henry's—concoct-
ing and distilling prunes, rice, raisins and any other fruit
or grain that might be handy at the time. No two batches
were ever the same, except that they were always potent.

Judge filled the three tin cups to the brim.

"Here is to law and order, my friends," he said grandly.
"For more than three months we have not even had a fist-

fight in Tonto—until this murder. Civilization has reached Wild Horse Valley; or can it be that the criminal element are afraid to enter our domain?"

"I believe that is it, sir," stated Henry soberly.

"Afraid of our unrelenting war against crime, Henry?"

"Oh, no—not that, Judge. Afraid of laughing themselves to death. Please do not interrupt. What I can see about me, I can see in my own mirror. To your health, gentlemen."

They drained their cups. Judge said to Oscar, "What is your opinion, my Viking?"

"Ay t'ink," said Oscar quietly, "that Frijole is getting vorse. He put too much hurse-liniment in de last batch."

"Hark!" exclaimed Henry. "Listen a moment."

There were loud voices on the street, and someone came running down the wooden sidewalk, making a great clatter.

"Bragging too soon!" snorted Judge.

The runner was the immaculate Lawrence Eddy, cashier at the new bank, entirely out of breath and slightly disheveled.

"Come to the bank—quick!" he panted. "Attempted hold-up, and a man shot!"

3

HORSE-THIEVES!

SHOWING SURPRISING AGILITY for their age and size, Henry and Judge ran almost a dead-heat to the bank, with Oscar thumping behind. Quite a crowd had gathered about the agitated Frederick Hale.

"Keep them back from the doorway, Oscar," ordered Henry. He and Judge went into the bank, where the banker led them back to his little private office near the rear.

The room was furnished with only a long table and several chairs. Between the table and the doorway sprawled the body of a man, face up. The fingers of his right hand still clutched the butt of a Colt .38.

"Someone has gone for Doctor," said the banker. Henry looked that man over closely. He was possibly fifty years of age, dressed fairly well. He wore a huge garnet ring on his right hand, but that seemed to be all his jewelry.

"Your cashier said it was attempted robbery," said Henry.

"That was his intention," said Hale. "He came in and asked about a Mr. John Jones. When I told him I'd never heard of Jones, he said he wanted to talk business with me; so I brought him back here. When we were inside the room, with the door closed, he drew a gun. He said, 'I want money and I want a lot of it.'

"Before I could explain anything, he said, 'You will go to the doorway and ask your cashier to bring you ten thousand dollars in currency. When he brings it, I shall lock you both in this room, until I can make a getaway. If either of you fails, I shall kill you both, if possible. I warn you that I am a good shot.'

"But he overlooked the fact that I was armed, Sheriff. As I stepped past him, going toward the door, I bumped him with my left shoulder, throwing him off balance, and before he could turn to shoot, I drew my gun and shot him."

Old Dr. Knowles came bustling in, ignored everybody and went to work on his examination.

"The man is dead," he said. "Shot directly through the heart."

"I am sorry," said Hale. "I had to do it."

"You were very fortunate, sir," said Judge soberly.

Dr. Knowles, being the coroner, assisted Henry in a search of the man. His trouser pockets contained a few dollars in silver, a knife, several keys and some matches. A search of his coat pockets drew a complete blank, until Henry dug deeply in one pocket and took out a sheet of paper, folded into a small size. One side of the sheet was covered with writing, which proved to be the chorus of an old Spanish love song, translated into English.

"I'll get some of the boys to help carry him away," said the elderly doctor. "Have you any idea who he is, Henry?"

"Not the slightest, Doc. Perhaps someone in town knew him. I have never seen the man before, I am very sure."

"Is there anything I can do?" asked Hale anxiously.

"Just be glad that you saved your money—perhaps your life," replied Henry. "The man must have been desperate."

Henry and Judge went back to the office, where they partook of Frijole's distillation again.

"Not even a fist-fight," remarked Henry sarcastically. "Perhaps the criminal element are afraid of our unrelenting war against crime."

"Our efficiency has spread to the banker, it seems," murmured Judge. "At any rate, Henry, the case is closed. That man attempted to rob the bank and was killed. One dead outlaw, and the money still in the bank. I drink to Mr. Frederick Hale, a welcome addition to our law-abiding community."

Henry pulled out a large drawer in his desk and removed a huge stack of reward notices, which had been collected for several years. Judge looked narrowly at Henry. Ever so often the rotund sheriff would go through that collection, slowly and seriously, scanning each picture and reading the text carefully on those which did not carry a picture of the wanted man.

Judge secured his old copy of Shakespeare, tilted back against the wall, and adjusted his reading glasses. Oscar came in.

"Das ha'ar man come in on morning stage from Scorpion Bend," he announced. "He told de hotel his name vors Tom Marsh."

"Anybody know him?" asked Judge.

Oscar shook his head. "Yust a stranger, Yudge. Hanry, you vant me to clean your seex-shooter?"

"If you please, Oscar," replied Henry, deeply engrossed in a reward notice.

Judge tossed his book aside, put his glasses in his pocket, and left the office hurriedly.

JOHN CAMPBELL, THE big, gray-haired prosecuting attorney, sauntered in and sat down. "I saw Judge hurrying away," he remarked. Henry nodded.

"Just one of his superstitions, John. He thinks it is bad luck to be here when Oscar is cleaning a gun."

John Campbell glanced up at the numerous bullet holes in the ceiling, and nodded slowly. "Few superstitious are as well founded," he said. "I was down at Doc's place, taking a look at the corpse. No one seems to know who the man was. Hale had never seen him before."

"His right name," stated Henry, "was Thomas Mitchell, alias Tom Miller, alias Tom Marsh, wanted for smuggling Chinamen and drugs from Mexico two years ago at El Paso. He has a crescent-shaped scar over his right eye, a scar on the left side of his nose, where a mole had been removed—and is said to have a very good baritone voice. Everything checks, except the voice, John; and I found the English translation of a Spanish song in his pocket."

"You found all that on a reward notice, Henry?"

"No reward," smiled Henry. "Merely a wanted man."

Campbell leaned back in his chair and lighted a cigar.

"Our new banker seems very efficient, Henry. A few more business like him, and we would not need a sheriff."

Henry nodded soberly. "And yet," he said, "it would seem that Mr. Mitchell, with all his aliases, was a careless man. He overlooked the fact that the banker was armed, and also gave the banker an opportunity to shoulder him off balance."

"You doubt the banker's story, Henry?"

"Of course not, John; I merely decry the mental caliber

of Mr. Mitchell. Would you like to sample some of Frijole Bill's latest distillation, John?"

"I would not!" replied the lawyer flatly. "The last time I tried that infernal concoction I mounted my horse backwards and came all the way home in a dazed condition. My wife swears that I forced her to sit in a straight-back chair and listen while I recited the Declaration of Independence."

"Quite possible," agreed Henry soberly. "Frijole tells some wonderful tales of what the mash does to William Shakespeare, the ranch rooster."

"I have heard some of them, Henry. By the way, have you seen Hale's daughter?"

"Who hasn't?" countered Henry, smiling. "When she walks down the street, John—*mm-m-m-m-m*. I would venture to say that every cowboy in Wild Horse Valley has washed his neck twice during the past week. Why, I caught Frijole Bill polishing his boots with stove polish, and even Thunder and Lightning are wearing their Sunday red ties every day."

"I suppose that Oscar is still true to Josephine Swensen."

Oscar looked up quickly. "To ha'al vit vimmin," he said.

"You haven't quarreled with Josephine again, I hope," said Henry.

"Yosephine is alvays talking about yentlemen dis and yentlemen dat, and den she vent to chorch vit a Yerman miner named Yoe. Ay ask her if Yoe is a yentleman, and she said he was porfect yentleman, 'cause he didn't ask to kiss her goodbye."

"What did you say, Oscar?" asked Henry.

"Va'al, Ay didn't mean it yust like it sounded."

"And now there is a rift in your lute."

"Yah?" Oscar looked up quickly. "Va'al, Ay don't know about dat, but dere vars a rip in my shirt. You vant me to load dis gon?"

"No thank you, Oscar," replied Henry huskily. "Just place the gun and cartridges on my desk. Thank you for cleaning it."

"You are velcome, Ay am su-ure."

OSCAR WALKED OUT, leaving Henry wiping his eyes. Josephine Swensen was waitress and chamber maid at the Tonto Hotel; a tall, lean, hard-featured woman, with a huge mop of colorless hair, a penchant for queer-looking clothes, especially hats, and the ability to swap punches with anyone. She had been Oscar's light o' love for several years, and their battles were proverbial.

"You will hold the inquest tomorrow, Henry?" asked the lawyer.

"A double bill," nodded Henry. "Did you hear how the two officers are getting along, John?"

"Very well. I dropped in at Doc's place a while ago. Two more of the Patrol were there. Usually those boys are pretty tight-lipped, but right now they're mad. Those men fired upon Vickers and Bennett without any warning. Bennett says they heard the sound of taut wires, as they were riding the trail, and when they rode to investigate, they were fired upon."

"After all," sighed Henry, "a *contrabandista* is a dangerous man, and those two boys could hardly expect abject surrender."

"That's true, Henry."

"Crime," remarked Henry thoughtfully, "was quiescent

for several months, but now it appears rampant. Is there any news of an impending revolution in Mexico, John?"

"Yes, there seems to be a certain talk of it, Henry. The usual thing, I suppose—a demand for horses and guns."

"That reminds me of something. I told Danny to hire Zell Hork and Nick Balleau to help him round up some young stock and throw them on the north range. We cannot tempt a horse-thief too much."

"That's right," said the lawyer. "I heard Steve Malloy wailing about living too close to the Border. He bought several hundred Mexican calves, and he's afraid of cattle rustlers, in case war breaks out down there."

Steve Malloy owned the Quarter Circle M, a small ranch, due south from Tonto City, and, right on the border. Nick Balleau and Zell Hork were his two punchers.

IT WAS LATE that afternoon when Danny Regan brought Nick Balleau and Zell Hork to the office. They had put twenty-five JHC horses in the home corral, instead of out on the north range. Henry paid off the two cold-jawed punchers from the Quarter Circle M, and they headed for the King's Castle Saloon.

"Some pretty good lookin' stuff in that herd, Henry," said Danny, "and I thought we'd break a few of 'em. Mostly three-year-olds, and some that might make polo ponies. Plenty speed, if yuh ask me. Why don't you and Judge come out to the ranch for supper?"

Judge groaned audibly. He hated horseback riding. Henry hated it as much as Judge, but was too proud to admit it. They saddled their horses, Judge complaining bitterly about his rheumatism.

"Growing pains," said Henry.

"Growing? At my age?"

"Growing old, Judge."

On the way to the ranch they met Thunder and Lightning Mendoza, two diminutive Mexicans who worked on the JHC for Henry. They were in the ranch buckboard, looking very important as they drew up. Except for Oscar Johnson, they were probably the worst drivers in the valley.

"It ees like these," explained Lightning. "Frijole ees ron out from flour in the brad. He ees saying that we don't need oatsmill, too—much. We have not got planty botter and the bacon ees fresh out tomorrow."

"I see," nodded Henry. "In other words, the larder needs replenishing."

"Sure," agreed Lightning. "We get lard too, I theenk."

"How is Frijole?" asked Henry.

"Frijole," said Thunder, "ees ver' sore."

"What is wrong with him?" queried Judge.

"Wa-a-a-al," drawled Lightning, "it ees like theese. Frijole make some new prune leeker. Oh, smals ver' good. Frijole tell Thunder to breeng the horse-leenement, wheech makes the firs'-class taste for the neck. Wa-a-a-al, Thunder mak' meestake and breeng the torpentine."

"And he put turpentine in it by mistake?" asked Henry.

"Oh, jus' leetle beet. Maybe two, t'ree quart."

"Merely a dash, eh?" smiled Henry. "You two better have Oscar come back with you."

"You theenk we can' drive good?" queried Thunder.

"How much money have you two?" countered Henry.

"I'm having one dollar and seex-beets," confessed Lightning.

"You better ask Oscar to drive back. A dollar and six-bits will buy a lot of tequila."

"I cross your heart, you hope I die," swore Lightning. "My leetle brodder and me are swore up on tequila."

"Swore off, eh?" queried Judge. "When did you swear off?"

"Las' Chreestmus."

"Last Christmas! You've been drunk fifty times since then."

Lightning shrugged his shoulders. *"Quien sabe?* Maybe we forgeet."

"Well," said Henry, "don't forget to ask Oscar to drive back to the ranch."

"We tell heem," agreed Lightning, "But jus' the same, I theenk we can drive worse than heem—I hope."

"I doubt it," said Henry, "but there is a chance that Oscar will be sober enough to make the curves. That is the only buckboard we have left—what there is left of it."

FRIJOLE BILL CULLISON, sixty, small, wiry, with a lean little face and whiskers like a bob-cat, greeted them soberly.

"I knowed yuh was a-comin' out."

"Second sight or a crystal ball?" asked Judge soberly.

"Huh? Oh! No, it wasn't that. Yuh see, I aimed to have some fried chicken for supper next time yuh showed up, and I says to m'self a while ago, 'Jist as shore as hell, they'll come t'day.'"

"Meaning that we will have fried chicken," smiled Henry.

"Yuh would have, Henry—except for Bill Shakespeare."

"That," declared Judge, "is a lie before you tell it, Frijole."

"Well, I tell yuh, it ain't no lie, Judge," protested Frijole.

Henry sat down on the porch and mopped his face with a handkerchief. "Proceed, Frijole," he said. "It sounds interesting."

"Thank yuh, Henry," said Frijole, glowering at Judge, who glowered right back at him.

"Yuh see," began Frijole, "I noticed Bill Shakespeare a-settin' on the corral fence, watchin' Danny and them two rannahans from the Quarter Circle M corral twenty-five broncs. That started it. Yuh see, Old Bill's been havin' trouble with a bobcat from Smoke Tree Canyon lately. Twice he done forked that cat, but got throwed.

"Well, I went out to the shop and I made Bill a pair of spurs. I strapped 'em onto his lean ol' shanks and I says, 'Bill, you jist sock these into that fuzz-tailed pussie, and yuh can ride him to hell and back.'

"This mornin' I done brought off a mess of prune whisky, and I'd plumb forgot' about Old Bill gettin' his beak into the mash. Why, he ain't been on a toot for three weeks, and I reckon he jist kinda let hisself go, 'cause the next thing I knowed I seen him staggerin' down to the stable.

"I figgered I'd take them spurs off him until he sobered up, but all to once I seen that bobcat circle the corner of the stable, with Old Bill a-ridin' him straight up. They cut around the corner, and the next thing I knowed, there goes every danged chicken on the ranch, strung out and goin' like hell toward Smoke Tree Canyon, with Old Bill a-rompin' along behind them on that bobcat, his new spurs socked to the shanks.

"Old Bill was shore a-rockin' and a-ridin', but guidin' the destiny of that scared bobcat. So, yuh see, there ain't a danged chicken left on the ranch."

"That's a lie!" snorted Judge. "A rooster riding a wild-cat—why, the idea is ridiculous."

"That's jist what I said, Judge," declared Frijole. "But after all, what's an idea to a rooster?"

Henry wiped his eyes and had difficulty with his voice. "The—er—liquor turned out all right?" he asked huskily.

"Prettiest stuff you ever seen, Henry. Yuh can stand six feet from a keg of it, and yuh can hear it moan."

"Moan?" snorted Judge. "Ridiculous! What makes it moan?"

"Gettin' old so damn fast," replied Frijole soberly.

"We understood," said Henry, "that Thunder made the mistake of putting turpentine in it, instead of horse-lin-iment."

"Oh, they told yuh, eh? Let 'em think so. I had to do somethin' to keep them two out of my private stock."

Henry chuckled at Frijole's scheme. "But why put anything in it?" he asked.

"Matter of taste and protection, Henry, horse-liniment gives it a tang, and—well, it kinda comes along behind and heals up anythin' the other stuff happens to bite into. Well, I better git busy on some supper for you boys. Sorry about the chickens."

OSCAR, THUNDER AND Lightning did not arrive for supper. The new batch of prune liquor met with the approval of Judge and Henry, and also the critical taste of Frijole Bill.

"She shore crackles to the taste," said Frijole, "and yuh don't need to be finicky. I tried a few drops on a flour-sack, and she reacted fine."

"I'll bet it cut a hole in the sack," said Judge.

"Oh shore it did. But I'll tell yuh this much: she never left no frayed edges."

After supper they looked at the twenty-five head of horses in the corral.

"What do yuh think of 'em?" queried Danny.

"As far as I can see," replied Henry soberly, "each has four legs and one tail. However, the colors vary, which is natural, I suppose."

"They're all partly broken," said Danny.

"Partly broken means what?" asked Henry.

"I know that one," said Judge soberly. "A partly broken horse only bucks when you mount him."

"I reckon that covers it," grinned Danny.

. . . Judge and Henry played cribbage and sampled Frijole's brew until nearly midnight; but Oscar, Thunder and Lightning did not come. Frijole slept in a little room off the kitchen. Danny gave up his room to Henry and Judge, and slept on a cot in the main room.

Henry and Judge had been in bed only a few minutes when they heard the creak of the springs on Danny's cot, as he got out of bed.

"Anything wrong, Danny?" asked Henry.

"A noise outside," replied Danny. "Listen! Sounds like them horses are millin' around. Damn it, I never can find my boots in the dark!"

"What is all the fuss about, if I may ask?" yawned Judge. "Lie down, Henry; you've uncovered me completely."

Then came the thudding report of a revolver shot. Danny swore as he yanked on his pants. Henry said:

"What is it, Danny?"

"Horse-thieves! They've shot the padlock."

4

MUH-MUH-MURDER

HENRY AND JUDGE almost upset the bed, pawing around in the dark for their clothes. They could hear the thud of running hoofs, as the herd circled the house on the hard-packed ground, and the whooping and yelling as the rustlers stampeded the heard toward the main gate.

Henry and Judge did not wait for clothes. Clad in only their full length underwear they headed for the doorway. Danny was outside, and they heard the reports of his six-shooter as he blazed away in the dark.

"I have the shotgun!" yelled Judge. "I'll fix them!"

"And everyone else!" yelped Henry. "Be-e-e-e careful, Judge!"

They jammed in the doorway together, but tore loose. Out of that haze of moonlit dust came two running horses, straight for the porch. Almost obscured behind them came the buckboard, bouncing like a rubber ball. Other loose horses had turned and were coming back with the team and buckboard.

An instant later the team swung aside just in time for the two wheels on the left side of the buckboard to crash into the porch. For a moment the air was full of broken wheels and other parts of the equipage, along with porch-posts and splintered boards.

Something hooked under Henry's chin, throwing him backwards into the house, and he dimly heard the crash as Judge fired both barrels of the shotgun through the porch roof before being knocked off the porch.

There was a following crash, as the runaway buckboard team failed to avoid the corral. Then there was comparative silence for a few moments, broken by Judge's complaining voice:

"Do not ask me, sir. I have no idea what happened. Certainly, I was there, but just at present I must be excused from trying to make any coherent statement."

From inside the house came a husky voice, saying:

"Who in de ha'al vars to blame? Not me! Ay am yust as innocent as—oh, hallo, Hanry!"

"I give you good evening, sir," replied Henry. "Caesar's ghost, I believe I was kicked by an elephant! Is that you, Oscar?"

"Yah, su-ure. Ay t'ought Ay hord Yudge's voice."

"Judge? Oh, of course. He had escaped my mind entirely. Queer how one forgets. I hope he is all right. My goodness, I remember that shotgun! Judge! Oh, Judge!"

Danny came stumbling over the wrecked porch in time to hear Henry calling Judge.

"Are you all right, Henry?" he asked quickly.

"I feel rather silly, with my head under a chair, but I suppose it is a normal position under the circumstances."

Danny lighted the lamp, just as Judge came staggering in. The staggering was due to the fact that his union suit had been torn loose from each shoulder, and was now hunched around his bony knees. Beyond some sanded spots on his anatomy, he seemed all right.

Danny removed the chair from over Henry's head. Oscar was sitting upright against the wall, about six feet of lines still gripped in his right hand.

"Ay don't vant to be personal," stated Oscar, "but Ay feel that somet'ing vent wrong. Ve are coming back from town and oll to vonce, right by de gate, ve are run into by a herd of hurses. Den somebody shot a gon right by my team, and ha'al bruk loose."

"Aptly stated," nodded Henry.

"Oscar saved the herd," said Danny. "He blocked the gate long enough to turn that herd, and most of 'em went east. I'll bet there wasn't five of 'em that made the gate."

"Ay am smort faller," declared Oscar.

"I admire the decoration on the sofa," said Henry. "I always did feel that a buckboard wheel, with half the spokes missing, would be very, very ornamental."

"But what," asked Judge wearily, "became of Thunder and Lightning, Oscar?"

"Yudas Priest! Ay forgot de two! Dey ver in de back of de bockboard, along vit sacks flour, oatmeal and butter. Oh, my!"

TWO QUEER-LOOKING FIGURES came in over the broken porch. They were Thunder and Lightning, dusted white with flour and smeared with butter. The three men stared at them in the lamplight.

"*Buenas noches, amigos,*" said Lightning. "How am I, you hope? These ees my leetle brodder."

"You both look terrible," said Henry soberly.

"Sure," agreed Lightning. "Everytheeng ees bad those day."

Frijole managed to awaken, and came stumbling through the kitchen into the main room, where he stood and looked them over, a queer little figure, in sagging, red underwear, a misfit sombrero on his head.

"I dreamed about runnin' horses and folks shootin'—and look what it turned into!" he said. "My gawsh, Judge! Shoulder-pads and hopples! And at yore age. Ain't yuh got no shame?"

"How are you filling, I hope?" asked Lightning. Frijole considered the flour-covered Mexicans and rubbed his stubbled chin.

"Gawsh, you two must have been awful drunk to git like that," he said huskily. "Where-at's my flour?"

Lightning gestured wearily, sending a shower of flour dust from his sleeves.

"You—you incompetent, unreliable, nut-headed, scrambled-brains!" wailed Frijole. "Yuh can't even go to town after—"

"Hush, Frijole," interrupted Henry. "This is no time for recriminations. Bring out the jug again, if you please. In times of great disaster, we must remain calm and collected."

"Disaster, huh? So that's what it was. All right. I'll wake up after while and I'll laugh like hell. I allus make up my mind that I'll tell all about my dream next mornin', but I never can remember what happened. Do you have that trouble, Henry?"

"Ordinarily—yes. But I think we will all remember this one next morning. Just bring the jug, and do not worry about the dream."

THEY WERE UP fairly early next morning, looking over the damage. The buckboard was smashed beyond repair, and the front porch looked as if it had been struck by a cyclone.

Both Judge and Henry were stiff and sore, but the rest of them were all right. Lightning and Thunder still had flour paste in their hair.

The rustlers had smashed the padlock with a bullet. It apparently had resisted their efforts to break the chain or lock with a small steel bar. But Danny was sure that their efforts had been in vain, as far as stealing the herd was concerned. Lightning threw a little light on the subject, when he said:

"My onkle, wheech ees Juan Fernandez, on Agua Frio, he ees tell me last night that the *Mejicano soldados* look for horse for the army. The man who ees buy from these army ees een Agua Frio. My onkle he ees saying that eef I can still cople horses and breeng them to heem, I can get pretty damn reech—I hope."

"So that's it!" snorted Danny. "Rustlin' horses for the Mexican buyers. Well, they didn't show much profit last night. Who's that down the road, raisin' all that dust?"

The fast-traveling rider proved to be Tommy Roper, manager of the livery stable at Tonto City. A very likable, well-intentioned young man; but about his speech he could do nothing.

He made a fast dismount from his saddle, took a deep breath and said, "Sh-Sh-Sh-Sh—"

"Sheriff," prompted Henry calmly. "Take it easy, Tommy, my lad."

Tommy drew another big breath, bobbed his head and said:

"Zeh—Zeh—Zeh—Zell Huh-Huh-Hork was sh-sh—he's dud-dead."

"Zell Hork was shot and he is dead," translated Henry.

"Where was he shot?" asked Judge anxiously.

"I—I—dud-dud-didn't see the huh-huh-hole."

"Where was the body found?" asked Henry.

"Well"—Tommy drew another deep breath—"it was bub-back of the Tut-Tut-Tonto, bub-by the old cuc-cuc-cuc—"

"By the old corral," nodded Henry. "When?"

"Hours ago," replied Tommy. "I gug-gug-got that out all rur-right."

"You show some improvement, Tommy," said Henry. "The body of Zell Hork was found this morning behind the Tonto Saloon, and near that old corral. Quite dead, of course. I wonder if anyone heard the shots fired?"

"Yuh-yuh-yes."

"Judge, we may as well go to Tonto and see about this. Tommy, have you had breakfast?"

Tommy shook his head. Frijole said, "If yuh promise to not try and thank me, I'll cook yuh a breakfast, Tommy. Jist nod, if it's satisfactory."

Tommy nodded and grinned widely.

5

KNOW SHANGHAI CHARLEY?

THE BODY OF Zell Hork had been moved down to Doctor Knowles' office, when Henry and Judge reached Tonto. Danny Regan rode in with them. Hork had been shot in the left side—shot from behind—and had bled to death.

Henry soon gathered all the particulars.

About one o'clock in the morning two shots had been heard. No one paid much attention. Early in the morning the blacksmith saw a saddled horse, tied to the corral fence, and went over to the animal. Just beyond the animal, and inside the corral, was the body.

Hork's gun was in the corral beside him, and it had been fired once. Henry, Judge and the doctor went to examine the spot where the body had been found. The horse was still there.

"Word has been sent to Steve Malloy," said the doctor.

Danny examined the horse and saddle, and when they went back to the office he said to Henry:

"That's the same horse that Zell rode yesterday, Henry; but that saddle belongs to Nick Balleau."

Henry nodded and thanked Danny, who added, "Nick will prob'ly explain how that happened."

"I believe," said Henry quietly, "that we will not question Mr. Balleau. That is, we will not ask for an explanation now."

"Suits me all right," said Danny. "Yuh see, Zell's saddle had a lot of silver on it. Cost three, four times as much as this one."

"Well," sighed Judge, "we have had three killings in this town, only a short time apart. One, of course, was justified."

"A killing," said Henry, "is always justified—by the killer."

Steve Malloy and Nick Balleau came to town. They looked at the body of Zell Hork, swore that they did not know of any enemy that Zell might have had, and led the horse back with them. Neither of them mentioned the exchange of saddles. Danny said to Henry:

"Neither Malloy nor Balleau rode Zell Hork's saddle. Balleau rode an old hull that never cost over twenty-five dollars, when it was new."

Henry nodded thoughtfully. "Danny," he said, "in riding around with Hork and Balleau, did you learn anything about them?"

"Very little," replied Danny. "They're a tight-lipped pair. In fact, Malloy never talks much either. I've been down at the Quarter Circle M, but I never felt welcome. Never since Malloy bought the old Willard place and registered his own brand has he been a bit neighborly. Maybe it's just his way—I dunno. He stocked his spread with Mexican calves, and they've got a few broncs. I've heard that they buy most of their drinks at Agua Frio."

A young woman, well dressed, walked past them, nodded pleasantly and entered the bank. She was Marion Hale, daughter of the new banker.

"Very pretty," murmured Henry.

"Doggone good-lookin'," admitted Danny. "I'll bet half the cowpunchers in the valley will start washin' their necks."

"Yes, Danny—and so will you."

"Not me. A little too young and a little too pretty."

"Anyway," said Henry, "Banker Hale said she is studying design in San Francisco, and will only be here occasionally. He said she might come over once a month to see her old dad."

"What's design, Henry?"

"Oh, I suppose it means the designing of something— possibly hats or gowns."

"She wouldn't get very rich at that job in Wild Horse Valley," said Danny. "Well, I'll be driftin' along. I'm goin' to try and pick up a bunch of those horses."

THE TRIPLE INQUEST brought little result. No one seemed to know anything about the two strangers.

Jim Morton, chief of the Border Patrol for that district, was at the inquest. Morton was middle-aged, grizzled, and hard-faced. A job on the desert Border Patrol is decidedly not a beauty treatment.

He came to the sheriff's office after the inquest, where they discussed the attack on Vickers and Bennett.

"Things are gettin' worse down here," declared Morton. "We've only had to contend with petty smuggling for a year or more, but it looks like bigger things were going on. Sheriff, did you ever hear of Shanghai Charley?"

"No," replied Henry, "but he sounds interesting, sir."

"Shanghai Charley," said the officer, "was the finest judge of jewels, especially diamonds, in the world. He became invaluable to those buying contraband jewels. His appraisal was honest. We knew him for what he was, but it is not illegal to appraise jewels. But when Shanghai Charley showed up, we were on our guard, because he did not mess around with any petty deals."

"Interesting to say the least," murmured Henry. "Worked on a commission?"

"That's right. Only a few days ago one of my men spotted Shanghai Charley in Scorpion Bend."

"Well, my goodness!" exclaimed Henry.

"Then he disappeared," continued the officer. "We watched closely for him, but he eluded us. I found him today, Sheriff."

"You found him? Where, if I may ask?"

"He was the stranger who was shot out by the King's Castle hitching-post."

"No!"

"Absolutely. We heard about the shooting, but were led to believe that a cowboy was killed."

"But there was not a single thing on his person," said Henry. "Not even a match."

"That's kinda queer, Sheriff."

"Exactly. But it proves that Shanghai Charley was stripped of everything before he was shot. He was brought there and dropped. The shots we heard were merely to cause an investigation, and cause us to believe that the man was shot at that spot."

Jim Morton smiled slowly. "I believe you're right, Sheriff. We will be interested to know who killed him."

"Yes," replied Henry dryly, "and if anyone comes and demands the right to confess the murder, I shall notify you at once, sir."

Henry told Judge about the identity of Shanghai Charley, and also recited what Jim Morton had told about Shanghai Charley's profession. Judge was impressed.

"Then," he said, "the man killed in the bank—Thomas Mitchell, alias Tom Miller, alias Tom Marsh—may have been an accomplice of Shanghai Charley. You remember, he asked about Mr. Jones, who turns out to be Shanghai Charley, but Mr. Jones was already cooling off in the morgue. What do you make of it, Henry?"

"Judge," replied Henry soberly, "I am really surprised at myself, because I am unable to make anything of it. For instance, Shanghai Charley, unknown, as far as we know, in this country, is shot down at the King's Castle hitch-rack. Then a man, who evidently knew this Shanghai Charley, came to town and attempted to rob the bank, but was put in cold-storage with Shanghai Charley.

"Then a common or garden variety of cowboy died with a bullet in his back in a corral behind the King's Castle Saloon. He is said to have started for Agua Frio, and is said to have had no enemies. Three dead men in a space of a few hours—and not a clue to the death of two."

"I am anxiously awaiting the next issue of the Scorpion Bend *Clarion*," said Judge.

6

WIRED TO MILLIONS

FREDERICK HALE INVITED Henry and Judge to supper that evening, and the invitation was eagerly accepted. The banker lived in a modest cottage at the outskirts of Tonto City, with his daughter, Lawrence Eddy, the cashier, and a Chinese cook named Sing.

Hale's liquor was of the best, and Sing's reputation as a cook was known all over Wild Horse Valley.

Marion Hale was a gracious hostess. She confided in Henry her ambitions as a designer, but admitted that she was not extremely enthusiastic about Tonto City.

"I have hardly slept since Daddy shot that robber," she declared.

"Your father," said Judge, "is a very brave man."

"Nonsense!" exclaimed Hale. "I was desperately afraid."

"Mr. Conroy," said Lawrence Eddy, "I understand that you have had some thrilling experiences as sheriff of this county. What was your most thrilling experience?"

"I believe my most thrilling experience," replied Henry, "was in the Middle West, years ago. My act followed the Cherry Sisters. As I stepped onto the stage, a belated and slightly ancient egg struck me in the right eye. Someone mistook me for an encore, I believe."

"I meant thrilling experiences as a sheriff," said Eddy, laughing.

"My boy," said Henry soberly, "in the performance of duty there are no thrills."

"But," said Marion, "there must be a thrill in working out a solution in a murder or robbery."

"I am unable to answer that one, my dear."

"You are too modest, Sheriff," said Hale. "For instance, you have the murder at the hitch-rack, and the murder at the corral."

"That is what I mean," said Marion. "How would anyone go about getting a solution to either of them?"

"Rather puzzling," admitted Henry. "The man at the hitch-rack had nothing in his pockets, nothing on him to serve as a clue to identification. When he arrived at the hotel he had a valise. This valise disappeared. Someone stole the valise from the room, before the shooting.

"This man paid in advance for his room at the hotel, and yet his pockets were empty when we searched his clothes. The man was shot twice, and yet there was no blood on the ground where the body lay. This proves beyond a doubt that the man was murdered, brought to the hitch-rack, where he was placed on the ground. Then two shots were fired in the air."

"That is remarkable!" exclaimed Frederick Hale. "No mention was made at the inquest, Sheriff."

"No one asked me a question," said Henry.

"And no one seems to know who the man was," said Eddy. "Possibly just a drifter."

Henry shook his head. "No, I am afraid that the man does not measure up to that standard, Mr. Eddy. This

Through the rain of shots Henry might get back to
the ranch—if he and the mustang held out.

man paid his fare on the stage, and paid his room-rent in advance. The man came here for a purpose."

Frederick Hale smiled. "You have built up quite a theory, Sheriff, but—well, the poor devil is dead and buried."

"True," said Henry, "but the old saying still lives: murder will out, Mr. Hale."

"Yes, the saying persists; but it is not always true."

"I feel," stated Judge ponderously, "that the man who attempted to rob the bank was connected in some way with this first man. At the hotel, he inquired about this man who had registered under the name of Jones, only to find that Mr. Jones was dead."

"Perhaps," suggested Hale, "this Mr. Jones and Mr. Marsh had planned to meet here and rob the bank together. When Mr. Jones was killed, Mr. Marsh decided to make it a single-handed job."

"That sounds like a plausible theory," said Eddy.

"Possibly," said Henry, "but Jones was not murdered and left at the hitch-rack to prevent him and Marsh from robbing the bank."

"I think we should talk about something more pleasant," said Marion.

"I second that motion," said Henry. "When do you go back to San Francisco, Miss Hale?"

"I am not sure yet," she replied. "Possibly within a week. After all the years you spent in traveling from city to city, meeting famous people, living in big hotels, it is strange that you should be satisfied to live in Tonto City, Mr. Conroy."

"Miss Hale," said Henry, "the cowboys have a saying that just fits the case: You never can tell which way a dill pickle will squirt. All of us are more or less of the dill pickle variety. Your father and Mr. Eddy are not Wild Horse Valley types, and still they are here, running a bank. Ask them if they are satisfied."

"I believe in the future of Tonto City and this valley," said Frederick Hale soberly.

"And I," said Henry, "believe that we will always have crime; so I suppose I shall be content to stay here, and, in my own puny way, try to keep the peace."

"Well said," Judge applauded. "And now suppose we go home and let these good folks go to bed."

DOWN AT THE Border, close to where the two Border Patrolmen had been shot by smugglers, there is an old unused road which runs parallel to the border for a mile, and then angles north through the mesquite, intersecting with the road from Tonto City to the JHC.

It is not a good road. In fact, disuse has allowed the desert to reclaim much of it.

Along the wire fence of the Border came Thunder and Lightning Mendoza in a makeshift buckboard. Totally lacking in mechanical ability, these two had taken the wreck of the JHC buckboard, and patched it up, in order to haul mesquite-root for fuel. A huge wooden box, roped and wired to the rear and resting on the rear axle, was nearly full of the twisted roots; and they were making their way carefully home.

The vehicle creaked and groaned, threatening at any time to collapse.

"She ees damn good boggy," declared Lightning. "I'm theenk Henry be teckled."

"Look out for the rock!" exclaimed Thunder.

Spang. A front wheel struck a boulder, and the iron tire fell in against the body of the buckboard.

"You yall too damn late," mourned Lightning. "This ees a hell of a feex you are in. We can't go now. One more turn and that damn wheel ees no use."

"Sure," agreed Thunder. He leaned back in the seat, put his feet over the crumpled dashboard and proceeded to roll a cigaret. Lightning yawned, relaxed and looked thoughtful.

"Eef we have blacksmeeth shop here, we feex heem," he said.

"Sure," agreed Thunder. "Feex heem easy. I know how."

"How?" queried Lightning.

"Oh, jus' feex heem. I see somebody ees coming."

It was Jim Morton and one of his men, patrolling the border. They stopped and looked over the two Mexicans.

"They work for Henry Conroy at the JHC," said Morton.

"We have wrack," stated Lightning.

"Lost a tire, eh?" remarked the chief.

"No lose—jus' come off," yawned Lightning.

The officers grinned and rode on.

"Good theeng we are honest men," observed Thunder.

"Sure. I'm jus' been theenk, my leetle brodder. Eef we can fin' piece wire, we can feex the tire."

"*Por Dios,* that ees ver' smort. We steal piece wire from the fence."

"When they mak' fools they make you, too," declared Lightning. "Eef you cut piece wire from those fence, you go to jail for the res' of my life. I tak' look."

Lightning sighed heavily, dismounted and strolled over to the fence. There was always a chance that the builders might have discarded a piece of wire. After searching at four or five posts, he saw the end of a piece of rusted bailing wire sticking out of the grass, just inside the fence.

With a piece of crooked stick he was able to draw the wire to his side of the fence, where he began hauling it through. There was about six feet of the old wire, and attached to that was a smaller wire. He pulled the bailing wire through the fence, examined the fastening of the lighter wire, and gave it a pull. There was a weight on the other end.

Curiosity prompted him to keep pulling, until he saw an object, fastened to the wire, which he was drawing through the weeds and low brush. He pulled it to the fence, reached through and picked up the object, which was about the size of a small cigar box, wrapped in oiled silk, which showed no sign of having been out in the weather.

COILING UP THE wire he went back to where Thunder dozed on the buckboard seat. His curiosity was great, but he tossed the box in among the mesquite roots and began trying to work the tire back on the wheel.

Thunder came awake enough to assist him, and they were wiring the tire back into place when Steve Malloy and Nick Balleau came riding down the old road.

The two cowboys stopped to watch them fix the tire.

"That's shore a hay-wire outfit," declared Steve Malloy.

"She ees damn good for haul," declared Lightning.

The two cowboys laughed and rode on. With the tire in place, Lightning chirped to the horses, and they headed for the JHC. About two miles from the Border, Lightning drew up, handed the lines to Thunder and retrieved the package from the mesquite-box.

"W'at ees those?" queried Thunder. "I never see heem biffore."

"He was fasten' to end of the wire," replied Lightning.

He unwrapped the oiled silk, disclosing a wooden box. With the aid of a pocket-knife he drew out the small nails, and opened the box. Inside was a closely-packed mass of cotton, and inside the cotton were three black, woolen sacks, with red draw-strings.

Lightning opened one sack and drew out the tissue-wrapped contents.

"*Madre de Dios!*" gasped Thunder. "*Diamantes!*"

It was a necklace of diamonds, sparkling in the sunlight. Lightning blinked foolishly, spread the necklace on the knee of his dirty overalls, took a deep breath and declared:

"I cross your heart!"

Thunder, recovering from his shock, grabbed another

of the black bags and yanked away the draw-string. More diamonds, unset, each wrapped in tissue. Thunder stuffed them quickly into the bag. Lightning put the necklace back into the bag and they quickly fastened the box.

"How you fill—being reech, my leetle brodder?" queried Lightning hoarsely. "We got meelion dollar wort' diamonds. Don' you leesten to me? Wake up! "

"Stop shak' these wagon!" snorted Thunder. "You wan' nodder wheel from falling off? I'm filling all right, you hope and pray."

"*Madre de Dios!*" gasped Lightning. "On the end of a wire! W'at you theenk?"

"You wan' go back and find nodder wire?"

"*Idiota!* You theenk every wire got diamond on end. W'at we do now?"

Thunder scowled thoughtfully. "I theenk we better go like hell. If somebody fin' those diamond we get keeled or go to jail. I'm theenk we better hide heem and keep your mouth shut."

"Not to telling anybody?"

"You wan' keep diamond and not go to jail?"

"Sure."

"*Buena!* Keep mouth shut. We feeger out sometheeng *mañana.*"

They managed to get back to the ranch, unloaded their fuel supply and hid the diamonds under the bunk-house floor.

7

BANG GOES THE NIGHT

ABOUT SIX O'CLOCK that evening, Danny Regan, foreman of Conroy's JHC, came into the sheriff's office, where Henry and Judge were discussing civilization. Danny said:

"Can yuh imagine this? A few minutes ago I met Mr. Hale, the banker, and his daughter, and they've invited me over to their house for supper."

"Right neighborly, Danny, my lad," said Henry. "You accepted?"

"What else could I do? I've got to go buy a clean shirt and a tie."

"I wish I could lend you one of mine," said Henry, "but I'm just a bit bigger around the neck, and shorter in the arms. You know that Judge and I partook of their hospitality last night?"

"No, I didn't, Henry. What kind of folks are they, anyway?"

"Very charming, Danny, just be yourself."

"I reckon I better find that shirt. *Hasta luego, amigos.*"

"That," declared Judge, after Danny left the office, "would make a fine match. She would search a long time to find a better husband."

Henry frowned thoughtfully, and Judge gave him a sharp glance.

"What ails you, Henry?" he asked.

"Nothing at all, my dear sir—nothing at all. Just wondering."

Things were quiet around Tonto City that evening, and Henry and Judge went to bed early.

"Tomorrow the Scorpion Bend *Clarion* will be out," said Judge.

"And day after tomorrow," added Henry, "the Board of Commissioners will drop in to ask what is being done about the crime situation. I am afraid they believe everything they read in an editorial."

"And you," remarked Judge, his voice muffled in the folds of his shirt, "will be obliged to admit that you are baffled."

"I? Baffled? Why, my dear Judge, you pain me."

"If you are not baffled, what are you, sir?"

"My dear Judge," replied Henry soberly, "I may be puzzled, but never baffled. There is a distinction. In time, I may not even be puzzled. It is my nature to move slowly but surely, picking up a thread here and a thread there, which I will weave into a net that will most surely encompass the guilty."

"But as yet," said Judge, "you haven't found a damn thread."

"Why, I—er—perhaps you are right, Judge. You understand—"

"What in the devil!" exclaimed Judge.

SOMEONE HAD COME up the stairs and was coming down the hallway, clumping heavily and swiftly on the uncarpeted floor. A heavy fist banged on the door, shaking the panels.

"Yuh—you go!" urged Judge. "You've got your pants on, Henry."

"Yes, yes!" called Henry. "Who is it?"

"It's me—Frijole! Lemme in!"

Henry unlocked the door and Frijole stumbled in. The little cook's left eye was swollen shut, and his nose puffed all out of shape. He was hatless, his shirt torn, and he was shaking with rage.

"By the mud of the mighty Mississippi!" he shrilled. "Look at me! Ain't I a sight? Ain't I?"

"Yes," nodded Henry soberly, "if you must have an answer to that question, Frijole, you really are a sight. What happened?"

"Masked men! Gawsh, there must have been a million of 'em! I ain't exaggeratin', Henry. They busted in on me and Thunder and Lightnin' in the bunk-house. I says, 'Git out of here, before I squirsh yuh.'

"Thunder and Lightnin' tried to crawl under a bunk, but they yanked 'em out. Well, I seen that it's me agin all of 'em; so I turned loose, bare-handed. I dunno how many of 'em I sunk, but I had a pile higher than yore head."

"You and Bill Shakespeare!" snorted Judge. "Tell the truth."

Frijole drew a deep breath, glared at Judge with his one good eye, and turned back to Henry.

"Well, they finally got me," he said meekly. "Force of numbers."

"But why, Frijole?" asked Henry. "Why would masked

men beat you up? Are you—Frijole, have you been drinking prune whisky?"

"Honest to gawsh, I'm sober, Henry. Ain't had a drink today. They got me cold. I dunno how long I was knocked out, and I dunno what became of Thunder and Lightnin'. When I got back on m' feet they're gone."

"It doesn't make sense," declared Judge.

"Sit down, Frijole," ordered Henry. "Let us get to the bottom of this thing. How many masked men were in the gang?"

Frijole caressed his swollen eye, flinched when he touched his nose, and finally said:

"I seen four, Henry. Mebbe there was more—I dunno."

"Four. What did they say to you?"

"Nothin'. They jist moved in, socked hell out of me, and was gone."

"Thunder and Lightning very likely are still running," said Judge.

"I dunno," sighed Frijole. "The last thing I seen, one of them men had a strangle-holt on Lightnin', and was tryin' to pet him over the head with a six-gun."

"Did Thunder and Lightning put up a defense?"

"I dunno, Henry. I was too busy with my personal affairs."

"Frijole, you better go down and have Doc Knowles look at that nose and eye before he gets to bed."

"Well, all right, but ain't yuh goin' to do anythin' about it?"

"You run along, Frijole," said Judge. "After you have gone, Henry and I will pass a resolution condemning such practices. That is our usual procedure toward crime."

"Yeah, all right. I'll see yuh later."

"Your sarcasm was wasted on Frijole, Judge," said Henry soberly, after the little cook had closed the door. "Resolution indeed!"

"Just what do you think of Frijole's story?" queried Judge.

"Until I find out just what deviltry Thunder and Lightning have been into, Judge, I reserve comment."

"I do not see why you keep them, Henry. They are not worth their salt, and they—"

"We have been through that a hundred times, Judge. It pleases me to have them around, in spite of their ignorance."

"Just because they murder the King's English," muttered Judge.

"Perhaps. I surely hope that the poor fellows are not in trouble."

"Men, armed and masked, desperate enough to enter private property and beat up the inhabitants, must have a grievance, Henry."

"Or a terribly distorted sense of humor, Judge. I suppose we may as well go to bed—unless you feel that we should saddle the horses and go hunting for criminals in the dark."

"Heaven forbid!" snorted Judge. "Lock the door before you get into bed; we may be next on their list."

FRIJOLE MET OSCAR JOHNSON, Conroy's jailer, in front of the hotel, where Oscar looked him over critically. "Yudas Priest, vat happen to you, Free-holey?" he asked.

"Right now," replied Frijole, "you're lookin' at the man who put up a fight that'll go down in histree. I whipped 'em until my arm give out. Oscar, I had 'em piled six feet high, but when they called in their reinforcements, I was outnumbered."

"Good!" exclaimed the giant Swede. "But Ay vant to know who hit you, Free-holey. Ay vill tie him in hord knot."

"I'm goin' to buy a drink," declared Frijole. "After I've had a few, I'm goin' to have Doc Knowles fix me up."

They went over to the nearly-empty King's Castle, where Frijole had to tell his troubles all over again to the bartender.

"There ain't a million men in this valley," declared the bartender.

"Ain't now," agreed Frijole, " 'cause I ran half of 'em out. Have a drink, and let me git m' wind."

After each of them had imbibed six drinks, Frijole's story grew. It assumed the proportions of a Custer Battle. The little cook with the bobcat whiskers, one eye swollen shut and his nose the size of an egg, nearly became unmanageable. He wanted to declare war, and he did not care whom he fought, except that he wanted the odds against him.

"I'll take 'em like Grant took—what did Grant take?"

"Ay don't know him," replied Oscar. "Ay vill take visky."

"Yuh say they captured Thunder and Lightnin'?" asked the bartender.

"Them two!" snorted Frijole. "They didn't last a minute. After I'd knocked down about a dozen of them big fellers, I says to Lightnin', 'Watch me, see how I'm doin' it.' But yuh can't hammer sense into one of them Mexicans. Ain't got no fightin' instinct. Nice fellers in time of peace, but a total loss in war. Fill 'm up, barten'er."

"Ay vould like to know," said Oscar, "yust why you didn't shoot."

"I'll tell yuh why," explained Frijole loftily. "When I start fightin', I can't be bothered with cockin' a gun."

They had a couple more drinks. Frijole wanted Oscar to ride with him and rescue Thunder and Lightning, but Oscar demurred.

"Ve don't know where to look, Free-holey."

"Yuh might find a lot of cripples," suggested the bartender.

"Prob'ly all died by this time," said Frijole sadly.

"Ay t'ink," proclaimed Oscar, "ve better go over to office and go to bed. You vant sleep mit me, Free-holey?"

"Shore. I'll sleep with yuh. I ain't proud."

Arm in arm they left the King's Castle and headed across the street; hit the high sidewalk with their knees, got to their feet and continued to the office.

The street was dark. At that time of night the only illumination came from the windows of the King's Castle Saloon.

They bumped into the front of the little office, and were groping for the door knob, when a voice rasped;

"Git away from there, you drunken, damn fools!"

"Who's drunk?" demanded Frijole. "Who said that, Oscar?"

"Some smort alex, Ay suppose," replied Oscar.

Just then Oscar found the knob and yanked on the door, which came open very suddenly. In fact, it came open so suddenly and with such force that it carried both Oscar and Frijole across the pavement and into the street.

The office window also came out, and some of the clapboard siding of the office decided to let loose along with the window and the door.

THE EXPLOSION AWOKE Tonto City. Judge and Henry sat up in the bed, listening to excited voices in the street, and wondering what had happened.

Oscar got to his feet and lifted the door off Frijole. Henry went to an open front window of their room and leaned out. Oscar was yelling an answer to someone's question.

"How in de ha'al do Ay know? Ay yanked on de door, and it yust busted."

"Something busted," said Henry. "Oscar yanked on it."

"What wouldn't bust if he yanked on it?" complained Judge. "Of all the nights! Light the lamp, Henry—if we must dress again."

Henry and Judge found quite a crowd around the wrecked front of the sheriff's office. Henry's desk was upside down against the wall, its contents scattered. Most of the small safe had gone through the roof, while the rest of it had gone through the floor, through which a four-foot-wide hole had been blasted.

There was no reasonable explanation for the explosion. Oscar and Frijole remembered that someone had yelled at them, telling them to get away from the door.

"Yeah," added Frijole, "and they called us drunken damn fools."

"Possibly someone who knew you both well," said Henry dryly.

"Aw, we wasn't so awful drunk," said Frijole meekly.

"It is a wonder you were not both killed," said Judge.

They secured a lamp and managed to pick up most of the scattered papers and legal documents which had been in the desk. Henry and Judge took them back to the hotel, rather than leave them in the wrecked office.

"Ay vill go to de ranch vit Free-holey," said Oscar.

Back in their hotel room, Henry and Judge tried to puzzle out the reason for the explosion. The voiced warning to Oscar and Frijole proved that someone had planned it. But just why anyone should want to blow up the sheriff's office was more than they could understand.

They rarely kept anything in the safe. It was an ancient affair, with a combination which worked about once out of three tries.

"More baffling than ever," sighed Judge. "An unreasonable act."

"True, my dear Judge, true. An attack in force on the JHC, and then an attack on the office. Well, we may as well go to sleep and wait for the next unreasonable move."

They were nearly asleep, when Judge said, "Henry, except for a pair of broken handcuffs and a half-can of paint, was there anything else in that safe?"

"Yes, Judge," replied Henry quietly, "there was. Danny wanted some dynamite to try and open up an old water hole; so I bought twelve sticks for him, and put them away in the safe."

"Ah-ha-a-a! Spontaneous combustion!"

"Very likely," said Henry dryly. "And the voice outside, which said, 'Get away from there, you drunken damn fools,' was their guardian angel."

"I forgot about him. Good night."

"That," said Henry, "is not my conception of the night at all."

8

WON'T YOU SIT DOWN?

THE MORNING STAGE brought copies of the Scorpion Bend *Clarion*. Judge secured his copy and perused it at the breakfast table, while Josephine Swensen, Oscar's sweetheart, waited on him and Henry.

"Ay read the paper olready," she told them, smirking a little.

"Indeed?" said Henry. "Interesting and instructive, I suppose."

"Yah. Ay have to laugh—sometimes."

"That is rather hard to believe, Josephine. Did you know that Oscar nearly got killed last night?"

Josephine sniffed. "Ay have new faller."

"Is that so? I heard Oscar say that he was through with women. Perhaps he has another girl."

"Listen to this, Henry," interrupted Judge. "The editorial has the heading, 'Premature Praise,' referring to the recent editorial in which he gave us some left-handed compliments. It reads:

" 'In a recent editorial we went out of our way to say a good word for Henry Harrison Conroy and his misfit organization. For the moment we had the mistaken idea that the Shame of Arizona had at last begun to realize the necessity of intelligent action.

" 'Since that editorial was published much has happened at Tonto City. An unidentified stranger was shot down on the main street, a stranger attempted a clever bank robbery, but was foiled and killed by Frederick Hale, the new banker, while within a few hours, Zell Hork, a Quarter Circle M cowboy, was murdered at a corral behind the King's Castle Saloon.

" 'A triple inquest was held at which time Banker Hale was exonerated and congratulated, but the other two murder cases were passed over lightly—killed by a party or parties unknown—and filed with the closed—because-of-lack-of-evidence cases. Nothing has been done to apprehend the killers. As far as we are able to determine, all that the sheriff has done so far is to rub his tomato-like nose and blink knowingly.

" 'The Commissioners of Wild Horse Valley will do well to get rid of the three siesta-loving incumbents of that mismanaged office, and install men who will at least make some visible attempt to protect the lives and property of the tax-payers. Our congratulations to Banker Hale for his prompt action. If Tonto City had a few more like him, it might be possible for the sheriff's office to support an incumbent for comedy purposes alone.' "

"These eggs," remarked Henry, "are not exactly fresh."

Judge sighed and folded up his paper. "You have no comment on that editorial, sir?"

"None," replied Henry. "I expected worse."

"I do not know what could be worse, Henry."

"Wait until he finds out about the attack at the ranch,

and the blowing up of our office. Will we roast! That writer has possibilities, Judge, but he repeats too much. True, I rub my nose. I also blink. But that is of no interest. I had a cowlick, before I lost my hair, and for years I have flinched from a corn on my left little toe. I do wish I could have kept that cowlick, Judge. At times of emotion it used to raise straight up on my head. You do not seem interested, sir."

"Bragging about an extinct cowlick at a time like this!"

"I believe," said Henry, "we should go to the office and estimate the repairs."

THE USUAL CROWD of curious people were inspecting the office when Henry and Judge arrived. Frederick Hale, Marion Hale, and Lawrence Eddy were there, as was Danny Regan.

Danny knew nothing about the trouble at the ranch. He had left the Hale home at about the time that Frijole arrived at Tonto City, and supposed that Frijole, Thunder and Lightning were asleep in the bunk-house. Oscar and Frijole were still asleep when Danny came to town.

"Was the contents of the safe of value to anyone except you?" asked the banker of Henry, who caressed his nose thoughtfully.

"I do not believe it, sir," he replied.

"Then," said the banker, "it must have merely been a malicious act."

"Very, very," agreed Henry heartily. "However, the damage is not great. And we shall endeavor to continue business."

"What about the warning to Oscar Johnson to keep away?" asked Lawrence Eddy, the cashier.

Henry shrugged his shoulders. "Possibly imagination.

However, if anyone had an idea of cracking our safe, they overloaded badly."

"Which proves," remarked Frederick Hale, "that valuables are not at all safe in an out-of-date depository."

"That remark has a commercial aspect, Mr. Hale."

"Yes, I believe it did," laughed Hale. "But it is true."

Oscar and Frijole came in later and reported that Thunder and Lightning had not put in an appearance at the ranch. Henry was worried and puzzled over their disappearance, and queried Danny about the actions of the previous day.

"Well, in the first place," said Danny, "they repaired that busted buckboard, fastened a big dry-goods box on the back, and said they were going after wood. I was at the ranch when they came back, and that vehicle was still runnin'. They dumped out the wood and went to the bunkhouse. Lookin' at it now, it was kinda funny they didn't come and brag about fixin' that buckboard, but they never said a word."

"Where do they gather wood, Danny?"

"They've always got the best mesquite roots down near the Border, and I think that's where they went yesterday."

"Along the Border, eh? Now just what devilment did they get into?"

"We'll ask 'em, when they come back," said Danny.

"Perhaps they will not come back," muttered Judge.

Henry sighed. "It is all very puzzling."

"Well, what are we going to do?" queried Judge.

"Find a carpenter," said Henry, "and ask for an appropriation from the county to fix up the office. We will move the office to our room at the hotel until repairs are made."

IT WAS ABOUT suppertime when Thunder and Lightning came into Tonto City, sore-footed and limping badly. They stopped at the wrecked office and looked it over critically.

"W'at you theenk?" asked Lightning huskily. Thunder hitched up his overalls.

"I'm theenk sometheeng bosted," he said wearily. Oscar strolled out from behind the jail and looked the Mexicans over.

"Where the ha'al have you been?" he asked.

Thunder started to reply, but Lightning said, "Shot up!"

Lightning shrugged his shoulders and said to Oscar, "Veeseting."

"Yah?"

"Sure. I go see your onkle."

"Ay t'ink you better see Hanry. He is in his room at hotel."

"Seek?" asked Lightning. "Een bed—you hope not?"

"He ain't sick. Go ahead."

Wearily they started for the hotel. They had no desire to meet Henry, nor anyone else for that matter.

"You go see heem," said Thunder. "I am too tire. I seet out here."

"I theenk," replied Lightning, "we both seet down. Maybe Henry come pretty queek."

Lightning started to sit down, but changed his mind, as did Thunder.

"My leetle brodder," said Lightning, "I'm having ideas. We have Pancho trus' us for quart tequila, and go home. *Por Dios*, all I am wanting is lay on my face for week and dreenk tequila."

"Sure," agreed Thunder quickly.

They stepped off the sidewalk, and Henry and Judge came from the hotel doorway. Lightning groaned aloud. Henry and Judge looked them over carefully, while the two Mexicans smiled wanly and fidgeted.

"So you came back," remarked Henry. "How interesting."

"How?" queried Lightning. "Nice day."

"For this time of year," agreed Henry. "You boys look tired. Why don't you sit down on the sidewalk and take it easy?"

Lightning shook his head. "Not so tired for seeting."

"All right, all right," said Judge impatiently. "What happened to you two? Where have you been? Beating around the bush!"

"No bush," said Lightning. "We go veeseting. W'at ees all the trobble here?"

"We are asking you," replied Judge severely.

"*Por Dios!*" exclaimed Lightning. "We don' know anytheeng and we are just as guilty as new-born baby—I hope."

"I'm fill like crying," declared Thunder.

"Go ahead," urged Judge. "Cry hard."

"Too damn tired," said Thunder. "Foot sore like a bleester."

"Let me refresh your memory," suggested Henry. "Last night a number of masked men invaded the bunk-house, beat up Frijole, and you two have been missing ever since. Explain, please."

"*Dios mio!*" exclaimed Lightning. "Ees that so? How ees Frijole?"

"Never mind Frijole. What happened to you two?"

"Hm-m-m-m," mumbled Lightning. "Ees that so? W'at time those 'appen?"

Henry shook his head slowly, realizing that Lightning and Thunder were evading any explanation of what happened to them.

"This might interest you two," he said. "Last night somebody blew our safe through the roof of the office, and ruined the front of the place."

"*Si, si,*" said Lightning quickly. "We see heem w'ile ago. W'at happen?"

"And now," said Judge disgustedly, "we are right back at the beginning. What happened! What devilment were you two up to yesterday? What were you doing down on the Border?"

"Haul wood," replied Lightning meekly.

Judge glared.

"What happened down there?"

"Oh-h-h-h-h!" gasped Lightning. "I know what you mean, The tire fall off the wheel. *Por Dios,* I mus' theenk you are ignorant."

Lightning started to sit down on the sidewalk, but straightened up quickly. Henry's brows lifted slightly, as an idea occurred to him.

"So someone kicked you in the seat of your pants, eh?" he said.

"Me neither," said Thunder quickly, and Lightning gave him a malevolent glance, which shut Thunder up quickly.

GO HOME," ORDERED Henry. "Get the liniment bottle from Frijole, and as soon as you recuperate I want to know what happened—and I want you both to tell me the truth. Do you understand me?"

"Sure," agreed Lightning quickly. *"Mañana,* we tell you anytheeng but the truth, I cross your heart, you hope I die."

"That is very satisfactory," sighed Henry.

"Hasta luego, amigo," said Lightning. "Goodnight, Jodge."

"Unmitigated liars," groaned Judge. "They're in trouble of some sort. Can't even sit down. A few extra kicks might bring out the truth."

"You have the soul of a savage pirate, sir," said Henry soberly. "I am very sure we will get at the bottom of this, without resorting to violence."

"I'll swear that they are at the bottom of that dynamiting at the office. Henry, this might be a life-or-death situation—and you smile."

"Merely a grimace, I assure you, sir."

Judge went back to the hotel, while Henry sauntered over to the King's Castle Saloon. Three of the Commissioners were in there, having a drink; but their conversation lagged when Henry came in, and Henry surmised that he had been the topic under discussion.

It was hot in there, and the odors of liquor and tobacco smoke were heavy in the air. Suddenly Henry had a desire to go out to the ranch, where he could sprawl in an easy chair on the porch and think things over without interruption. He might also get a statement from Thunder and Lightning.

It was dark as he crossed the street and went down to the alley beside his office, which led to the small stable. He was glad that Judge was not there to complain about riding a horse. By the light of a dirty lantern he saddled his horse and led it outside.

As he turned to fasten the door, a loop of rope slapped

against the door, came down over his head and around his shoulders.

A sharp yank on the rope threw him off balance, and he sat down heavily, his hat flying off. Before he could make any sound, a heavy body landed on him, and strong fingers at his throat cut off any chance of a cry for help.

9

REVOLUTION BY THUNDER

JUDGE VAN TREECE read until after ten o'clock, but Henry did not come up to the room. Judge finally slipped on his boots and went on a search, which proved futile. He even went down to the Hale home, just in case Henry might have gone down there.

Finally he went to the stable and found that Henry's horse and saddle were not there. Judge decided that Henry had gone out to the ranch, when a ray of light from the lantern picked up Henry's expensive Stetson, crushed and dirty, lying a few feet from the doorway.

A search of the ground near the doorway disclosed a smashed fountain-pen, a pencil and a small notebook, all belonging to Henry.

Judge managed to saddle his horse and headed for the ranch, where he found Danny and Frijole playing cribbage. The two Mexicans, barefooted, were stretched out on a mattress. The air was redolent of horse-liniment.

Without a word of explanation, Judge placed Henry's hat and other belongings on the table.

"By the mighty Mississippi!" exploded Frijole. "Have yuh lost yore voice, Judge?"

Judge soberly shook his head, and replied, "Henry's

gone—somewhere. I found these near the door of the stable. His horse and saddle are gone."

"Gone?" gasped Danny. "Gone where, Judge?"

"Captured, stolen, kidnaped—anything you wish; he has gone!"

"Why?" asked Danny, "Why would anybody—"

Judge whirled on the luckless Mexicans, his voice wrathful.

"You two! Damn you, you are at the bottom of this! They had you; now they've got Henry. You will surely talk and tell the truth, or I will break every bone in your bodies. Do you understand me?"

Lightning looked at Thunder. "You know w'at he ees talking about?"

"Sure," nodded Thunder, "and neither do I."

Judge sat down in a rickety rocking chair and glared at Lightning.

"It's no use, Judge," said Danny. "I argued with 'em for an hour, and all I got out of 'em was that they had promised to tell it to Henry."

"Tell it to Henry? Merciful Heavens, can't they understand that Henry is missing?"

"Meesing?" queried Lightning. "What he ees meesing, Jodge?"

"I give up, I give up!" choked Judge helplessly.

"Jodge geeves up," said Thunder. "W'at you theenk now?"

No one replied. Judge sighed deeply and got to his feet.

"I shall go back to town, Danny," he said. "It—it is just barely possible that Henry is still in Tonto."

"I'll go with yuh, Judge."

"You theenk we need you for going along?" asked Lightning.

"No!" roared Judge. "We don't want you along. We don't even—oh, what's the use?"

Danny and Judge walked out of the house. Frijole gave Lightning a malevolent glance and said, "You ort to both be killed."

"I cross your heart, you hope—"

"I don't *hope*—I wish! Go to bed, you bug-brained idiots!"

Frijole slammed the kitchen door and went into his room.

"Henry ees gone," whispered Lightning. "Maybe they keel heem, biccause he say he don't know w'ere ees diamond. Come on, my leetle brodder. We tak' copple horses and a shotgon."

"I theenk we are too sore for seeting on saddle," said Thunder.

"Forget those hind-end from you," ordered Lightning. "Go easy. We don' want nobody from hearing."

"W'en I'm seet down I'm got bleester and w'en I'm stand up, I'm got more bleester than een the firs' place," wailed Thunder.

Traveling as if they were walking on eggs, the two Mexicans helped themselves to a shotgun and then proceeded down to the stable, where they cautiously saddled two horses and rode away from the JHC.

FOR ONCE IN his life, Henry Harrison Conroy found himself in a position where his sense of humor was of no account. He was roped hand and foot to an old kitchen chair, and forced to accept the abuse of three masked men who seemed delighted in taking turns questioning him and slapping his face.

Henry's nose was larger than normal, and his face was nearly raw.

It was a small room, crudely furnished, with one door but no window. Henry was sure he had been taken to Mexico, because at times he could hear a babel of Mexican voices, and an occasional strain of Mexican music.

After a whispered conversation between the three men, one of them walked over to Henry, who winced visibly.

"For the last time," said the man, "are you goin' to tell us where yuh hid them diamonds?"

"I have told you a hundred times that I know nothing about any diamonds," said Henry wearily. "You accuse me of having diamonds, but I assure you that I have never had any diamonds. Why not explain what this is all about?"

"Those two Mexicans who work for you turned over thirty-five thousand dollars' worth of diamonds to you. They thought yuh put 'em in yore safe, but yuh didn't. What about that, Fat-face?"

"My goodness!" exclaimed Henry. "Thunder and Lightning said—I see a light, gentlemen. They told you that they—Wait just a moment. Where on earth did Thunder and Lightning get the diamonds?"

"Never mind where they got 'em," growled one of the men. "We want to know what became of 'em."

"So do I," replied Henry. "You dynamited my safe to get them, not knowing that the safe contained a dozen sticks of dynamite."

The three men looked at each other.

"So that's what busted it, eh?" chuckled one of the men.

"All right," said one of the men, "you may be tellin' the truth, Conroy. God help yuh, if yo're not. We're goin' back and get them two Mexicans. This time we'll get the truth, or they'll get somethin' worse than havin' their pants kicked across the Border."

"If you do not mind," said Henry, "I hope you will untie my feet and give me a chance at them first."

"All right. We'll lock yuh in and let yuh think things over for a few hours. There'll be a guard at yore door; so don't get any ideas. And yuh can't yell loud enough to get yuh more'n a kick in the ribs; so yuh might as well be a good boy. *Adios.*"

They closed the door and fastened it from the outside. Henry sighed dismally and considered his predicament. Although they had blindfolded him, he knew he was in Agua Frio, upstairs in the biggest cantina in the little town.

At first there had been more than the three masked men. One was a Mexican, and Henry surmised that he was Tony Gonzales, a gambler from Chihuahua, who had taken over the cantina.

Henry had not been told how Thunder and Lightning came into possession of thirty-five thousand dollars' worth of diamonds. It seemed incredible, although a fact.

From what he could learn, these men had kidnaped Thunder and Lightning, who had sworn that they gave the diamonds to Henry, who put them in his safe. That was why they attacked the ranch, beat up Frijole and kidnapped Thunder and Lightning, after which they tried to crack the office safe, only to explode the twelve sticks of dynamite locked there.

Afterward they had turned Thunder and Lightning

loose, given them a few kicks for good measure, and kidnaped Henry, trying to force him to tell where he had hidden the jewels. Evidently his captors were nearly convinced that Henry was telling the truth—but not quite. A further interview with Thunder and Lightning might convince them.

Henry hoped that nothing would prevent them from acquiring this information, because that chair was getting mighty hard, and those ropes were too tight for comfort.

THUNDER AND LIGHTNING cut directly across the hills to the Border—which accounted for the fact that they did not encounter the riders who had gone to get them—and entered Agua Frio without incident. They had no idea of what to do when they got there, except that they must rescue Henry. They had been held captive in an upstairs room of the cantina; so they felt sure that Henry was in the same place.

Lightning carried the twelve-gauge pump shotgun, and had his pockets stuffed with quail loads. Lightning was also the board of strategy. He led the way in a half-circle to a point behind the cantina. The long hitch-rack in front of the cantina was lined with saddle horses, attesting to the fact that business was good.

Leaving Thunder to take care of the two horses, Lightning proceeded to remove one saddle horse from the hitch-rack, and brought it back to Thunder. They tied the three animals to a section of old fence, and then considered their next move.

"We got to be damn smart," declared Lightning, "or I get your head shot off. Leesten, I got you an idea!"

"Good! Maybe we get two head shot off, eh?"

Lightning whispered his instructions to Thunder. They were to cut loose every horse at the hitch-rack. Then Lightning was to go over to cantina doorway; and as soon as the music stopped, Thunder was to start shooting with that big shotgun. During the excitement, Lightning would be able to get up the stairs and try to find Henry.

"They weel think," explained Lightning, "that it ees a revolution!"

"Sure," agreed Thunder. "I'm mak' plenty noise."

Leaving his revolutionist in the shadow of an adobe wall across the street, Lightning made his way over to the lights of the cantina. As he came up to the doorway, two men started out.

Wham! That old shotgun roared, and a spray of quail shot pinged off the windows, stinging Lightning and the two men, who yelled loudly and dived back, with Lightning such a close second that he and another man fell over each other.

Wham! Wham! blasted the shotgun again, and more shot came through the doorway. Lightning leaped to his feet and yelped, "Revolution! Revolution!" and dived for the stairs.

The place was in a panic. One man at the bar drew a revolver and shot a window out, while the rank and file made a break for the back door. Thunder had twenty-five shells, and he was having the time of his life.

The street was full of milling horses, and a man yelled, *"Caballeria! Caballeria!"* mistaking the milling horses for the cavalry of an attacking force.

Lightning reached the top of the stairs. The man who had been on guard at Henry's door ran to the railing, his rifle ready, trying to see what was going on in the street. The railing was only three feet high, and as the man leaned out Lightning grasped him by the bottom of his bell-bottom pants, gave a lift and a heave, and the guard landed on his neck and shoulders square on top of a deserted escarte layout, which crashed under his weight. Lightning got his rifle.

The door to Henry's prison was fastened but not locked. Henry was so surprised at sight of Lightning that he said nothing, while the diminutive Mexican cut his bonds. They could still hear the occasional blast from Thunder's shotgun.

"My goodness!" exclaimed Henry, testing his cramped muscles. "This is extraordinary!"

"Pretty queek we be in hell of a feex," warned Lightning. "Come queek!"

Limping a little, Henry followed Lightning to the end of the hallway, where Lightning smashed out a window with the butt of his rifle.

"Climb out queek," ordered Lightning.

"And break my neck?" queried Henry.

"Not break *mucho*," replied Lightning. "Small shed roof. You slide off."

"That is much better," panted Henry.

HE WRIGGLED OVER the edge, clinging to the frame, lowered his body and let loose. Lightning followed quickly, leaving the rifle in the hallway. There was no shed roof, Lightning landed on his heels, fell over Henry, and got to his feet in a daze.

"Every damn bone in my body is broken," declared

Henry. "My goodness! Where is that shed roof, Lightning?"

"*Quien sabe?*" wheezed Lightning. "I meese heem very much myself, personally. *Madre de Dios,* we fall one damn mile! You break sometheeng?"

"I feel," replied Henry, "as if I broke everything. Strangely enough I am able to stand almost erect. Where next, Lightning?"

Several pistol shots rattled from the front of the cantina, echoed by the whanging boom of Thunder's shotgun.

"Has the revolution really started?" gasped Henry.

"I hope," said Lightning painfully, "he know when to queet. Come—we find those horse—I hope and pray."

The shotgun boomed twice in quick succession, and Thunder's voice shrilled, *"Viva la Enrique! Viva la Enrique!"*

"My goodness!" exclaimed Henry. "Cheering for me?"

"Mus' cheer for somebody—I hope," panted Lightning. "Over theese way, Henry."

They found the horses, and in a few moments Thunder came running. He was out of cartridges and out of breath.

"I keel meelion men!" he panted. "Maybe more—I hope."

"The Frijole Bill complex," sighed Henry, accepting a tie-rope which Lightning thrust into his hands in the darkness.

In some unaccountable way Henry mounted that horse. It was the one which Lightning and Thunder had stolen from the hitch-rack—proved to be a half-broken Mexican mustang.

"My goodness, what am I riding?" gasped Henry.

But there was no time to make a change. Thunder and Lightning spurred away, and the mustang was right at their heels. They nearly ran down a knot of men at the corner, which scattered like a flock of quail.

Henry was clinging to the saddle-horn with both hands, and riding high.

He yelled at Lightning, "We better be careful! Those men went to find you and they might be on their way back."

Lightning reined in closer to Henry and yelled, "We go t'rough hills. Thonder got twizzer to cut the fence!"

He meant wire clippers, of course. The going was rough. Only part of the time was Henry in the saddle, but he never relinquished his grip on that saddle-horn, and he managed to keep both feet in the stirrups.

He nearly fell off when they halted against the fence. He felt that his stomach would never go back to its former level.

That half-broken mustang danced in circles, while Thunder cut the fence.

"Go easy," warned Lightning. "Horse might peek up wire."

As the two Mexicans rode through the gap, Henry's mount lunged in behind them, almost unseating him. Somewhere a voice yelled an order, and a pencil of flame licked out from the darkness of the brush and rocks. The mustang leaped forward, like a thoroughbred from a starting gate, as shots crashed out, and men were yelling.

It was too dark for Henry to have any idea where he was going, but the mustang seemed to have certain ideas on the subject. Henry had no idea what became of Lightning and Thunder, nor did he care—much—as mesquite clawed at his clothes, slashed across his face.

It was a nightmare ride, and Henry prayed that he would awaken before that devil horse killed both of them.

After what seemed like hours of crashing brush, expecting death at any moment, the horse seemed to be galloping free again, and on better footing. Henry managed to get his eyes open, and in the starlight he could see that they were on the old road which—if both he and the mustang lasted long enough—would take them very close to the ranch house of the JHC.

10

WELCOME TO OUR RIOT

AFTER JUDGE AND Danny reached Tonto City that night they found Oscar Johnson and told him something of what had happened. "Henry," said Judge, "is gone."

"Yudas priest!" exclaimed the giant Swede. "Ay vill do somet'ing."

"What'll yuh do?" asked Danny. "Yo're no magician, Oscar."

"Ay vill go seeking the trut'—and Ay vill seccur it."

While Judge and Danny went up to the hotel, hoping against hope that Henry might have returned, Oscar saddled his horse and headed for the JHC ranch.

"Ay vill get de trut', you bat you," he told his horse, "or Ay vill tie dose Mexicans in a hord knot."

Oscar arrived at the ranch and nearly hammered down the front door of the ranch house, before awakening Frijole, who came to the door with a six-shooter in his hand.

"What in hell do you want at this time of night?" demanded Frijole.

"Ay am seeking de trut'," declared Oscar grandly.

"You've shore come to the end of yore trail, brother," declared Frijole. "Ask and thou shalt git."

"Well"—Oscar rubbed his button-like nose—"how 'bout snort of prune yuice forst?"

"Yeah, we can do that, too. Set down and rest yore big feet, while I git the jug and some cups. Any word of Henry?"

"Ay didn't hear any vords."

Frijole brought in the jug and cups, which they filled to the brim and drained. Oscar relaxed and smacked his lips.

"Das is the best Ay have ever tasted," he declared. "Yust a little veak, but inwigorating, Ay vould say."

"Weak!" snorted Frijole. "This stuff is seven hundred proof."

"Ay vill vait to pass yudgment," stated Oscar, as Frijole filled the cups again. Oscar emptied the cup and relaxed more.

"Yah, Ay can see Ay vars wrong. Das is forst-class yuice, Free-holey."

After the fourth cupful, Frijole said, "What kinda truth was you lookin' for, anyway?"

"Trut'? Oh, yah, Ay forgot. Ay came ha'ar to make Lightning tell me de trut' about Henry."

"Yeah? Well, they're out in the bunk-house, pardner. If you can make 'em talk, yo're a wizard. C'mon, seeker for truth."

They took the jug and cups along. Frijole said it might be a long session, and there was no use of going thirsty. They made their way out to the bunk-house, traveling in a decided quarter circle, kicked open the bunk-house door, lighted a lamp and gazed at the empty beds. There was no indication that either of the Mexicans had been in bed that night. They sat down on a bunk and considered the situation.

"I'll tell yuh thish mush," remarked Frijole, "I have found the Mex'can peop'l ver' unreliable."

Oscar sighed dismally. "No Mesicans," he mourned. "Free-holey, Ay vould like to shing a shong."

"Nossir," declared Frijole. "In the firs' place, you've got a voice like a road-runner with the pip, and you don't know the words. How 'bout 'nother snort?"

"Ay vould love it, Free-holey. Das is goot yuice, you bat you."

They drank another cupful apiece. Frijole tried three times to blow out the lamp, missed it very time, and finally extinguished the light by kicking over the table on which the lamp was sitting, and fell on the bed along with the already snoring Oscar.

EVERYTHING WAS VERY quiet and peaceful around the JHC. Even the coyotes, which usually shrill their chorus during the night, were silent. Three dim, masked figures came in past the corral, walking quietly toward the bunkhouse. Near the corner they grouped together to confer on their final plans. One man whispered:

"It's a cinch they're all in town, except the Mexicans; so this will be easy. If yuh have to bat 'em over the head, do it, but not hard enough to kill the meddlin' fools. All right, let's take 'em."

They walked quietly around to the front, discovered that the door was not fastened from the inside, and walked in. Raucous snores indicated the location of their quarry, both on one bed. Then, without any preliminary action,

*Two wheels of the buggy dropped into a ditch; and the lurch
was so great that Marion was thrown completely out.*

the three men fell upon what they thought were Thunder
and Lightning.

For several moments there was only the muffled sound
of struggling men, as Oscar and Frijole were awakened
from their stupor. Then, it seemed that Oscar came to life,
much as a grizzly might, awakened by prowling wolves.
There was a rending sound as Oscar grasped a handful of
clothes; the bed creaked alarmingly, and a choking voice
gasped:

"My gawsh, look out!"

Crash! A body hurtled off the pile and landed half-way
to the door. There was a sound of a solid blow, and Oscar's
muffled voice saying, "You vould, eh?"

Frijole was fighting like a wildcat with both hands and
kicking with both feet as he fought himself loose. Oscar

was up now, both feet on the floor. A bunk-post snapped off, a window crashed out. Then followed a limping rush as the three men managed to fight loose, with Oscar in close pursuit. He and Frijole collided at the door and went rolling.

The attackers were mounting as fast as their racked bones and sore muscles would allow. With a bellow of rage, Oscar got to his feet and headed for them. One man, already mounted, blazed away at the charging Oscar with his six-shooter, but was shooting wild. For a moment or two there was a grand mêlée of whirling horses, yelling men.

Then two horses seemed to crash together, and one went down. The rider rolled almost into Oscar, who fell upon him like a football player falling upon a fumbled ball. With a clatter of hoofs, the rest of the riders dashed for the main gate.

Frijole was yelling, "What in the hell's goin' on, anyway? Oscar, did they get yuh?"

"Ay got von of 'em, by yimminee!" exulted Oscar. "Das von von't get avay, you bat you! Don't yerk, or Ay vill unyoint you at once."

"Take him in the house," ordered Frijole. "The bunkhouse lamp is busted."

Frijole stumbled into the main room and lighted the lamp while Oscar came in, triumphantly carrying his victim, whom he sat in a chair. Panting heavily, Oscar and Frijole stood there and looked at their captive.

Finally Frijole said, "Somebody's crazy, but I don't know who."

"I don't believe," said Henry Harrison Conroy, in a weak voice, "that we need a vote on the matter."

"Ay vill be damned!" gasped Oscar. "Ay yust vill be."

Henry was in rags, hatless, his face scratched. Frijole brought him a glass of water. Henry squinted at Frijole and wheezed, "What does a man have to go through in this country, before he gets something to drink beside water?"

Frijole got the jug from the bunk-house and after a cupful Henry announced that he was going to bed. No one objected. Oscar and Frijole had another drink.

A few minutes later Judge and Danny came to the ranch, fearful of what Oscar might do to Thunder and Lightning in order to force them to talk. Henry was in bed. In answer to Judge's question, he replied, "Please—not tonight, Judge."

"But tell me what happened to you. You are a mess, sir."

"I am," agreed Henry. "Externally and internally. Just try and remember the most harrowing tale you have ever heard or read, and multiply it by ten. Then, sir, you will have a faint glimmering of what happened to me this night. And at my age!"

It was just before daylight when Thunder and Lightning limped in at the ranch, sneaked into the bunk-house and went to bed.

11

OVER A BARREL

NO ONE GOT up early at the JHC next morning. Henry was so stiff and sore he could hardly get around, and his face looked as if it had just recovered from a severe case of smallpox. Thunder and Lightning answered Frijole's breakfast bell, bright and shining, showing no ill effects from their adventure. Henry eyed them curiously, wondering just what had happened to them.

Judge groaned from rheumatism and lack of sleep. Oscar, except for a discolered eye, was in fine fettle, and Frijole looked normal. They sat down for breakfast, and were in the middle of their meal when Frijole said:

"Here comes Jim Morton and two of his Border Patrol, leadin' two unsaddled horses. If you've got any lies to tell, think fast."

Henry swallowed heavily and looked at Lightning. "You *rode* home last night?"

"No," replied Lightning.

"Then keep your mouths shut," advised Henry.

The three officers drew up at the kitchen doorway. Henry went out and called a greeting to them. Morton said, "Sheriff, have you lost any horses lately?"

"Why, I—er—possibly, Morton. In these days—"

"Well, here's two of yore JHC horses."

"My goodness!"

"Where did you find them?" asked Judge from the doorway.

"We took 'em in battle last night," said Morton. "Three smugglers cut the fence last night. We didn't take any chances this time, but cut loose on 'em. I reckon one got away on his horse, but two of 'em dived off in the brush and got away on foot. It was too dark to find 'em."

"On my horses!" exclaimed Henry. "My goodness!"

"We've got the saddles," said Morton, "which we will keep for evidence. Someone might identify them."

Henry was profuse in his thanks to the officers for returning the two horses, and watched them ride away.

"Well, that's that," sighed Danny. "Two perfectly good saddles."

"All right, Danny," said Henry. "Do not worry about the saddles—do your worrying later, when they find out who owned the saddles."

"In the meantime," suggested Judge, "suppose you tell us what happened to you, Henry."

"I feel," replied Henry, "that it is time for a general confession. Lightning, suppose you tell us where you found those diamonds, and what you did with them. There is no use trying to evade the issue. You found thirty-five thousand dollars' worth of diamonds. In some way it was discovered that you and Thunder got them. In order to get away, you both swore that you gave me the diamonds and that I put them in my safe at the office."

"Sure," grimaced Thunder, "and I get my pants keeked so hard you can not seet down for two day."

"What diamonds are you talking about?" asked Judge. "Is this a riddle?"

"Worse," said Henry. "They blew our safe to try and recover the diamonds. Later they kidnaped me and took me to Agua Frio, where they tried to force me to tell what I did with the diamonds. I feel that they were convinced that Thunder and Lightning still had the stones; so they left me tied up and under guard, while they came back to get Thunder and Lightning."

"Yudas Priest!" snorted Oscar. "That is why they yoomp on me and Free-holey last night."

"Exactly," agreed Henry. "But Thunder and Lightning came to Agua Frio, started a shotgun revolution and released me. In order not to meet the men who were searching for Thunder and Lightning, we crossed the border in a secluded place. Well—"

"I see it all!" shouted Judge. "The Border Patrol mistook you three for smugglers."

"THAT, MY DEAR Judge, is elementary. They have our saddles, which may be easily identified, especially by Tommy Roper. Thunder and Lightning cut the fence. That, in itself, is a criminal action. If I may say so, sir, as a peace officer of Wild Horse Valley, I am in a hell of a fix."

"What on earth is to be done?" asked Judge.

"There is only one thing to do," stated Henry. "Thunder and Lightning will give me the diamonds, which, in turn, I shall give to Jim Morton. I shall explain everything in detail, and I believe there will be no action."

"All very well," agreed Judge. "But where in the world did Thunder and Lightning get their hands on thirty-five thousand dollars' worth of diamonds? It is incredible!"

"You see," explained Lightning, "we break a wheel off the tire, and I am peeking een the grass for piece wire to feex heem. On odder side from the fence I am seeing a wire. I pull these wire t'rough the fence and I am finding nodder wire, fasten to heem. On the wire ees these small box."

"And you did not tell anyone, eh?" growled Judge.

Lightning shrugged. "I'm like be reech sometime, Jodge."

"Where are the diamonds now?" asked Henry.

Lightning sighed deeply. "I get heem for you."

The rest of them sat there and looked at each other. Judge glared at Thunder, who was looking very dejected.

"It's a wonder you did not get us all killed," said Judge.

"I guess I'm goin' be poor man all the res' of your life," complained Thunder.

Lightning came back with the little, black bags, which he gave to Henry.

"Open 'em up," urged Danny. "I'd like to see the things."

"No, Danny," said Henry firmly. "We will leave the inspection to Mr. Morton. Frijole, you will please saddle horses for Judge and myself."

"What horse did you ride home last night, Henry?" asked Danny.

"I have no idea who owned the brute, Danny. Like the devil, it had wings and a tail. Possibly sired by a skyrocket, and dammed by a stick of dynamite. I hope and pray that I may never be placed astride another such animal. Danny, in plain words, I am the first man that ever rode his own nightmare."

"But you stayed with the animal, Henry."

"True—until it ran into the escaping marauders, routed by Oscar and Frijole."

Lightning sighed and addressed Henry: "Eef there ees any reward, you hope I get some?" he asked.

"Lightning," replied Henry, "the reward for smuggling diamonds into this country is a mighty long sentence to a Federal prison. According to your own words, you did smuggle them, you know."

"I theenk I mak' damn bad meestake for talking. I theenk I am liar."

"So you want to change your story, eh?" remarked Judge.

"Sure, Jodge. I fin' heem in the road."

"I'll do what I can for you, Lightning," promised Henry. "I may get them to let you off with ten years in prison."

FRIJOLE BROUGHT THE horses, and the two men mounted. Henry grimaced from strained muscles, but said nothing as they rode away from the JHC. Henry had the sacks of jewels stuffed in his coat pocket. Luckily, he had a change of clothes at the ranch house, because the suit he wore out of Mexico was in shreds.

"You were not able to identify any of the masked men, Henry?" asked Judge, as they jogged along toward Tonto City.

"No, Judge. They spoke in husky voices, and there was nothing about their garb to attract my eye. The light was none too good, of course."

"Imagine those Mexicans going boldly down there to rescue you."

"Rough but effective, Judge. I dropped from a second-story window, and nearly killed myself, while Thunder, armed with a shotgun, intimidated the whole town. They thought a revolution had started."

"Well, I hope that the delivery of the gems will clear up things for the Border—*whoa!*"

Two masked men stepped from the brush into the road only a dozen feet in front of them, covering them with six-shooters.

"Wh-what nonsense is this?" demanded Judge.

One of the men laughed huskily. "Get down!" he snapped.

Henry and Judge slid out of their saddles. While one of the men covered Henry and Judge, the other holstered his gun and came in close to them.

"We ain't takin' no chances," he explained. "Keep yore hands up, while I see what yo're packin' in yore pockets. That's fine."

Henry's bulging pockets were quickly emptied. Neither Henry nor Judge was armed.

"We got 'em!" exclaimed the searcher. "All four sacks!"

"Good! Our idea wasn't so bad, eh? Now, you two misfits, get on them broncs and head for town. And next time, keep yore damn red nose out of things that don't concern yuh."

A moment later the two men slid into the brush and disappeared.

"It seems to me," remarked Henry sadly, as they got back into their saddles, "that men should be content with merely robbing, and not add insults by remarking about their victim's personal appearance."

"The allusion to your red nose, I presume, sir."

"Not merely the red nose, Judge—the *damn* red nose."

"And now," sighed Judge, "that we have so successfully disposed of thirty-five thousand dollars' worth of diamonds, what is our next big move? You still have those two saddles to explain away, you know."

"Yes," said Henry, "I am afraid that, in the vernacular of this beautiful valley, they have us over a barrel."

"Us? Not me, sir. I had nothing to do with it."

"My mistake," said Henry quietly.

"Your mistake was in ever employing those misbegotten Mexicans. You should discharge them at once and disclaim any responsibility for their former actions. Let the Federal officers incarcerate them."

"After they risked their lives to rescue me? Why, Judge!"

"All right, all right. It's your funeral, not mine."

"Funeral? My goodness, I hope not."

Tommy Roper met them at their stable, all excited. He said, "Sh-Sh-Sh—"

"Yes, Tommy," said Henry. "What happened?"

"The Bu-Bu-Bu—"

"Border Patrol?"

"Uh-huh. They gug-got your sus-saddles. They asked me who owned them and I sus-sus-sus—"

"Said that I did," prompted Henry. Tommy nodded violently.

"Thank you, Tommy," said Henry. Tommy helped them unsaddle and put their horses in the stable.

THEY MET JOHN CAMPBELL, the prosecutor, in the little hotel lobby, and he went up to their room with them.

"I don't know what it is all about," he told them, "but the Border Patrol have two captured saddles, purported to have been used by two of three smugglers who cut the fence last night and were routed by the officers. I have heard that the horses were wearing the JHC brand, and that the saddles belong to you, Henry. Three of the Commissioners are over in the courthouse, discussing the situation with Jim Morton. I thought you'd like to know."

"This is rather interesting, John," said Henry wearily. "But I am afraid that saddles and horse brands are not evidence as to who was in those saddles and on those horses."

"The horses and saddles were stolen—of course."

"I would rather say—taken without leave, John."

"It would be absurd to accuse you of smuggling, Henry."

"I believe," said Henry, "that a smuggler must be caught with the goods, and as far as I am aware, I have not been apprehended—yet. And, John, I am far from what might be termed a slick article."

"The whole thing is ridiculous!" snorted Judge. "You leave it to me. If Jim Morton or any of those Commissioners gets personal, I'll tell them a few things."

"Good!" exclaimed Henry. "Go right to it, Judge—but do not stick too closely to the truth."

NONE OF THE Commissioners came near the office, but they sent a note to Henry, notifying him that the Commissioners were meeting next morning, and that his presence at that meeting was urgently desired.

"If you will accept my advice," said Judge, "you will go to Jim Morton and tell him the whole story. Knowing that the smugglers have the diamonds, he has something to work on, and you will be exonerated."

"Thank you, Judge. Perhaps your advice is sound, but I prefer to handle the case in my own way."

"In spite of the Commissioners, Henry? You never know what they will do."

"You may depend on their doing the wrong thing, Judge. This is not the first time that the Shame of Arizona has weathered a hard blow. And you must admit that we have always triumphed."

"And you, my dear Henry," said Judge, "must admit that you haven't a single clue to any of the recent crimes. In my opinion, you are too bull-headed to admit defeat."

"Or too smart," added Henry. "I have never been quite able to decide that point myself."

Henry met Frederick Hale at the post-office, and the banker was filled with sympathy.

"I wanted to tell you," he said, "that I have absolute faith in you and the operation of the office. I feel that you are doing everything humanly possible."

"Thank you very much," said Henry. "It is good to know that at least one of our leading citizens has faith in my work."

"I might speak to the Commissioners," suggested Hale.

"Thank you—no," said Henry. "Very decent of you, I'm sure. But this is my own personal battle. Your charming daughter is well, I hope."

"Yes, thank you. I believe she will leave on the stage tomorrow night, unless she changes her plans."

"Our loss will be San Francisco's gain," said Henry. "I wish her all the success in the world. A very, very charming young lady."

"Thank you," said Hale. "She is quite fond of you, Mr. Conroy."

"Well, I am flattered. To even think that such a young and charming girl would even give a thought to an old, flea-bitten trouper like me is remarkable. If I am unable to see her, I hope you will thank her for even remembering me."

"I will do that, Mr. Conroy."

"Thank you, sir—very, very much."

12

FORTY WINKS

THE MEETING OF the Commissioners was set for ten o'clock in the morning at the courthouse. Henry was a few minutes late; he was clad in a pearl gray suit, gray fedora, and white shoes; and he carried a gold-headed cane. His linen was immaculate, his tie the exact shade of his suit.

There were four men in the room. First was Al Cooper, chairman of the Board; then Edward Mitchell and Thomas Handley. The fourth man was rather youngish, tall and slender; nearly bald, and long-nosed. His eyes were squinty behind a pair of huge horn-rimmed glasses.

Henry nodded to the Commissioners, looked questioningly at the stranger, and started to sit down. Cooper said:

"Conroy, I don't believe you've ever met James Wadsworth Longfellow Pelly. Mr. Pelly, this is Henry Conroy, our sheriff."

Henry had started to shake hands with Pelly, when Mitchell said, "Mr. Pelly is the editor of the *Clarion*."

"Oh!" exclaimed Henry quietly. "That!"

Then Henry sat down and fondled the head of his cane. The awkward pause was broken by Pelly himself, who said, "I wanted to get the facts, not rumors."

"You seem to have done very well so far—on rumors," said Henry.

"The *Clarion*," said Pelly, "hews to the line."

"But draws its own line," murmured Henry. "But I am very sure that this august body did not meet to listen to a debate between us, sir. Suppose we proceed with the business at hand."

"That's right," agreed Cooper. "There's no need to tell you that we had had two murders here in Tonto City recently, and there is no need to mention to you that nothing has been done about either of them. And there is the matter of two horses and saddles belonging to you, Conroy, which were taken from smugglers, after a gun battle on the Border. The horses were returned to you, but the saddles were held for evidence, or identification."

"If them horses and saddles were stolen from you, that's different," supplemented Mitchell.

"Different than what?" queried Henry.

"Well—uh—different than if you'd used 'em, of course."

"Of course," nodded Henry. "Much different. Thank you, Mr, Mitchell."

"Perhaps you can explain this note," said Pelly, handing a folded piece of paper to Henry. It was written in pencil and read:

Ask the Sheriff of Tonto City what he paid for the diamonds he smuggled out of Agua Frio, and what he did with them.

It was signed *A Constant Reader.*

Henry smiled as he handed back the note. "A constant reader. It is really remarkable what will happen to a man

who reads a paper like that constantly. It must gradu-
ally wear one down to a point where one might imagine
anything."

Pelly flushed, adjusted his glasses and looked appeal-
ingly at Cooper.

"That," said Cooper, "is the first time I knew anything
about any diamonds bein' mixed up in the deal."

"Constant Reader did," said Henry. "Perhaps, Mr.
Cooper, you do not read the *Clarion* constantly. However,
that is beside the point. Smuggling of diamonds is a
Federal charge, if you will permit me to point this out to
you. I will admit that the two horses and saddles belonged
to me. I will neither admit nor deny that the horses and
saddles were stolen. Neither will I admit nor deny that I
knew who rode those horses.

"But I do deny having bought, smuggled, or disposed of
any illegal gems. The charge, or assertion, is an untruth. In
words more understandable, it is a damned lie, gentlemen!"

"There still remain the two unsolved murders," said
Mitchell.

"Unsolved as yet," corrected Henry.

"Tell me of one thing you have done," demanded Pelly.

"Failed to read the *Clarion* for one thing, Mr. Pelly."

"THIS AIN'T GETTIN' us any place," declared Cooper.
"We want action, Conroy. Oh, I'll admit that you fooled us
several times, when we had no idea that you were workin'
on a case. But you can't always be lucky."

Henry winced, but smiled. "Would you like to be fooled
again?" he asked.

"Gladly!" exclaimed Mitchell.

"I shall do my very best," promised Henry.

"How soon?" queried Pelly.

"Well," said Henry, "if I were you, Mr. Pelly, I would not hold the presses—unless you wish to do the readers a favor. When do you return?"

"I have to go back on the evening stage, Mr. Conroy."

"Well, if anything happens, I suppose you will hear about it sooner or later. My middle name is Harrison, and if convenient, I wish you would leave out all reference to the Shame of Arizona."

Mr. Pelly looked bleak, but did not reply. Cooper said, "That seems to be about all, gentlemen."

"Wait a moment," said Pelly quickly. "This meeting doesn't bear out what you told me a while ago. You said that you were going to give the sheriff a very short time to clear up this situation, or resign. You have let him talk—"

"Just a moment!" snapped Cooper. "This happens to be county business, and is none of your affairs, Mr. Pelly."

"I know, but I came all the way down here to—"

"To see me humiliated," said Henry, smiling. "I believe we can get long without you, Mr. Pelly. Go home and write your feelings—if anyone is interested in reading them, which I am not."

"Oh, I shall write them," promised Pelly defiantly. "At least this meeting has proved to me that the Commissioners of this county are as lax as the sheriff. Gentlemen, I bid you good-day."

"Why not," asked Henry, "borrow a soap-box and find a vacant corner. I'm sure Tonto City needs educating."

"I bow to your superior knowledge of local conditions!" snapped the editor.

Henry went back to his room and changed his clothes.

At least the Commissioners had done nothing drastic. But it did not alter the fact that they wanted something done at once. Henry sighed as he sat on the edge of the bed, clad in his underclothes. In his mind was a glimmering of an idea; but just how to prove anything he did not know.

Suddenly he straightened up, his eyes half closed, his brow wrinkled.

"No, Henry," he said half aloud. "No, you can not do that. The idea is too far-fetched, in the first place. Too many elements. And yet—"

Slowly he drew on his clothes, scowling thoughtfully.

"If I could trust Oscar and Tommy and—Judge. Danny would do it, I am sure. By goodness, it might work. But if it doesn't work we will truly be the Shame of Arizona—in every respect."

JUDGE WAS WAITING for Henry, as he watched the carpenter putting the finishing touches on the work at the office; but Henry was on his way to the livery stable. There he found Tommy Roper, the stuttering cowboy, washing harness. Henry squatted beside Tommy and spoke quietly and at length, while Tommy merely nodded and grinned.

"Do not ask me why I want you to do this, Tommy," said Henry. "It is an order from the sheriff; and one must obey orders."

Tommy nodded and went back to the washing his harness.

Judge had gone to the hotel when Henry got back to the office. Oscar was there. Henry drew him aside. Oscar listened in amazement to what Henry proposed, but was agreeable. Henry gave him some money, and waited until Judge came back.

"We are going to ride out to the ranch and have a talk with Danny," Henry told him. Judge groaned and protested that it would only require one of them.

"I ask you what the Commissioners said to you," complained Judge, "and you order me to ride a horse."

"We must see Danny together, Judge," explained Henry. "I have a scheme which needs cooperation from both of you and Danny."

"Have we ever failed to cooperate?" asked Judge. "Can not my cooperation be confirmed, without me riding clear out to that ranch?"

"I prefer to talk with both of you at the same time, sir."

"We could send Oscar out to summon Danny," suggested Judge.

"This scheme," said Henry, "concerns our immediate future, Judge. If it fails in its purpose, my resignation as sheriff goes to the Commissioners tomorrow morning. In fact, they will demand it. They may also demand my arrest."

"I feel," said Judge, "that we had better saddle immediately."

"On second thought," said Henry, "I believe we will hire a horse and buggy. This may be my last day as a public defender of the peace, and it may well be spent in comfort."

BY EIGHT O'CLOCK that evening, Slim McFee was too drunk to drive the stage to Scorpion Bend; so Tommy Roper was drafted for the job. Oscar Johnson and Slim had spent a blissful afternoon at the King's Castle Saloon; and the world, while a bit dim and shadowy, was decidedly of a rosy hue.

James Wadsworth Longfellow Pelly spent his time absorbing conversation, possibly with the intention of writing a constructive article on Tonto City. He ventured into the King's Castle, where he was obliged to pass the close scrutiny of Oscar and Slim.

"Ay am not sure," remarked Oscar, "but Ay t'ink it is somet'ing that got loose."

Slim roared. Mr. Pelly had been his passenger, and had pumped Slim dry regarding Henry Harrison Conroy.

"He's kinda got it in for Henry," he told Oscar.

"Ya-a-ah!" snorted Oscar. "C'mere, faller!"

Mr. Pelly tried to evade Oscar, but a huge right fist was fastened around his necktie, making him rather submissive.

"Ay am Oscar Yohnson, de yailer," he explained to Mr. Pelly, with his nose almost buried in Mr. Pelly's face. "Who in de ha'al are you?"

"I am James Wadsworth Longfellow Pelly," gasped the victim.

"You vill be Yim—or not'ing," declared Oscar. "Have drink."

"Sorry, but I—I—oh, I may take something soft."

"Soft!" exclaimed Slim. "My gawsh!"

"Soft!" parroted Oscar. "By yee, Ay have yust de t'ing. Come on."

They crossed the street and entered the sheriff's office, which was being rebuilt, and went back to the jail, where Oscar had a jug of Frijole's prune whisky.

"If you don't vant hord liquor, dis fills de bill," declared Oscar. "It yust inwigorates."

Oscar filled three cups and they drank solemnly. Mr. Pelly smacked his lips.

"By jove, that is good!" he exclaimed. "What is it?"

"Prune yuice," grinned Oscar.

"Prunes? Well, that *is* a novelty. I never knew a prune to taste so good. I must get the recipe."

Oscar filled the cups again, and a lowered eyelid warned Slim. But Slim was too drunk to heed any warning; so they absorbed that cupful right away.

"What's yore business, Misser Pelly?" asked Slim owlishly.

"My job?" Pelly's question was followed by a giggling laugh. "Why, I am the editor of the Scorpion Bend *Clarion*. You see, I came down here to—now wha's the difference what I came for, anyway?"

Pelly rubbed the palm of his right hand all over his face, as if to brush away the cobwebs. Oscar filled the cups again. Slim said:

"Frien' of my youth, I need thee every hour."

Pelly said, "Honeshtly, I never felt like thish before. I wonner wha's matter 'ith me."

"Yo're drunk, par'ner," declared Slim.

"Oh, tha's imposshible," argued the editor. "Why, it's only prunes."

"Can you shing?" asked Oscar.

"Shing? Really! I used to shing in a church; don't you know that?"

"Only one church in town and tha's closed except on Sunday, for which we may be gra'ful. I'd hate to hear you shing, Jim. Better pour that down, before you spill it, par'ner."

James Wadsworth Longfellow Pelly drank it down. A few moments later he made an ineffectual grab at a bar of the cell door, missed it by a foot, and sat down heavily on the floor, where he began snoring.

Oscar spent about five minutes trying to recork that jug, and in the meantime Slim lay down with Pelly, pillowed his head on Pelly's bosom and joined in the snores. Oscar went back to the office. The carpenter had quit for the day. Oscar found the office alarm clock, and spent another five minutes setting the alarm for eight o'clock.

"Ay don't vant that yigger to miss the stage," he told himself. "Ay vill catch for me forty vinks."

13

LADY IN A DITCH

AT EIGHT-FIFTEEN THAT evening Tommy Roper swung the four stage horses around in front of the stage depot. Oscar and James Wadsworth Longfellow Pelly were there sitting on a bench in front of the depot. The editor of the *Clarion* had been quite a burden to Oscar, but the big Swede had vowed to put him on that stage.

Marion Hale was there, clad in a gray traveling suit, accompanied by her father and Lawrence Eddy, the bank's cashier. Marion carried a hand bag, and Eddy carried her large Gladstone. Quite a number of local cowboys were at the depot—just casually, of course.

Oscar succeeded in helping the *Clarion* editor to a seat with Tommy Roper, instead of letting him occupy the stage with Marion. Her bag was placed inside the stage, instead of being tied to the top; goodbyes were said, and the stage started its monotonous night journey to Scorpion Bend.

Tommy Roper was no conversationalist, and James Wadsworth Longfellow Pelly was in no mood to talk. He was inclined to be a bit weak about the stomach, and that lurching stage did not help him in the least.

There was a full moon. They made good time on the

valley floor, but soon struck the heavier going of the upgrade along the canyon.

"You-you-you huh-hang on, or I'll have to tut-tut-tie yuh to the sus-seat, pup-pardner," said Tommy. "That ch-ch-ch-chuck-hole almost gug-got you."

"Oh, Lord," groaned Pelly, "what do I care?"

"Sus-sick?"

"Slowly dying," gasped Pelly.

"Sus-stick with it. I've been dyin' like th-that myself."

"I drank something they called prune juice. Oscar had it."

Tommy roared. He had sampled the stuff himself and knew its potency.

"That stuff's dud-dynamite," he declared.

Tommy was an expert with four horses, and his long whip crackled inches above the backs of the leaders as they ground along the grades above the canyon. As the leaders swung wide on a hairpin turn, the stage lurched to a stop, swung full into the moonlight around a rock.

Two masked men, armed with Winchesters, had halted the leaders. One of the men stepped in close to the driver, while the other came swiftly to the door of the stage and yanked it open.

"Git out of there and line up!" he snarled.

Marion Hale stepped out, stumbling on the uneven roadway. The man said, "Woman, eh? Anybody else in there?"

"I—I am alone," faltered the girl. "I haven't anything."

"No?" The man yanked the hand bag from her grasp. Then he motioned her to move over and face the rocky wall at the inner side of the grade.

James Wadsworth Longfellow Pelly was too miserable to care what they did to him, and Tommy discreetly kept his mouth shut. Both bandits had moved in toward the door of the stage, examining the interior.

"Keep lookin' ahead and mind yore own business," warned one of them.

Gravel crunched under the boots, and suddenly they were gone, stepping around the corner of the wall, back toward Tonto.

No one spoke for a long time. Finally Marion said weakly, "They—they took my hand bag!"

"Sus-son-of-a-gug-gun!" gasped Tommy. He handed the lines to the unresisting Pelly, and climbed down. He lighted a match and looked into the stage, with Marion at his shoulder.

"My bag!" she exclaimed. "It's gone!"

"Your valise?" queried Tommy.

"Yes!"

"I'll be a dud-dirty name!"

THEY HEARD THE rattle of wheels on the rocky grade, and Tommy ran around in front of his team. It was a horse and buggy, coming from the opposite direction, with barely enough room to squeeze past the stage. The driver worked his vehicle carefully to where he could draw up beside the stage.

The driver was Henry Harrison Conroy. He asked, "Is something wrong, Slim?"

"Th-this ain't Sus-Slim," replied Tommy Roper.

Henry got out and recognized Tommy in the moonlight. Then he saw Marion. "What happened, Miss Hale?" he asked anxiously.

"We were held up by two masked men, and they took my valise," she replied bitterly.

"My goodness! Which way did they go?"

"Back toward Tonto City. They have only been gone a few minutes."

"This," declared Henry, "is insufferable. You get back on the stage, Miss Hale, and I shall do my best to—"

"But I can't go now," interrupted Marion. "My tickets are gone—and all my clothes. I must go back home."

"Yes, I suppose that is true, Well, you may ride back with me. Tommy, if you will pull ahead a few feet, we can make it easily."

Tommy climbed back on the seat, swore feelingly about something, and the stage lurched ahead, leaving Henry plenty of room to proceed. Marion started to climb into the buggy, when a voice said:

"If you do not mind, I shall ride back with you, too. I find that I am in no condition to ride on that stage."

It was James Wadsworth Longfellow Pelly, climbing in beside Marion without leave from anyone. The seat was not built for three people, but three of them were in it. Apparently Pelly had not recognized Henry, because he said:

"I have suffered a lot of discomforts in this trip to Tonto City, but I feel I have gathered enough material to enable my paper to be of great benefit to the tax-payers of Wild Horse Valley."

"In what way?" asked Henry quietly.

"In awakening them to the fact that the present peace officers in their county are the most incompetent in the world. The county is a hotbed of crime, encouraged by negligence and incompetency."

"You are Mr. Pelly, the famous editor?" queried Henry.

"I am," replied Pelly stoutly. "And you?"

"My name is Henry Harrison Conroy."

"Oh!" choked Pelly. "I—I did not realize—"

Henry wasn't sure whether Marion was laughing or crying, because the moon was at their backs, and the top of the buggy cut off any illumination. He said to Marion, "I'm sorry you were molested tonight. We shall make every effort to find and return your baggage, Miss Hale."

"That is—is quite all right," she said quietly.

They descended the grades to the floor of the valley, where they were able to make much better time. They were badly crowded in the seat, and Pelly finally said, "If you could stop for a moment, I'm sure we can arrange things much better, Mr. Conroy."

Henry drew up; and as Pelly started to get out, he pitched forward flat on his face. Marion had neatly booted him. Before Henry realized her intentions, she grabbed the whip and slashed it across the rump of the horse, which reared and broke into a run.

THE NEXT MOMENT a blunt instrument was shoved into Henry's ribs, and the girl snapped, "Keep your hands where they are and keep driving, or I'll pull the trigger, sheriff! And I'm not fooling!"

"My goodness, Miss Hale!" gasped Henry, trying to control the horse.

"Never mind that. You drive and I'll watch for the turn-off."

"The turn-off?" queried Henry.

"The road to Agua Frio, my fat friend. We are not going to Tonto City."

"You—you rather amaze me!" panted Henry. "What is the—"

"Drop it!" she snapped. "You haven't fooled me. Fred and Larry thought you were dumb, but I never subscribed to that idea."

"Amazing, my dear! But why to Agua Frio?"

"At least I shall save my own skin."

"I see—just another skin game, Miss Hale."

"You can drop that Miss Hale idea, too. Slow down and turn here."

"Gladly, my dear, gladly, But you will never get to Agua Frio, because I attended to that detail. I was afraid there might be an exodus, in case anything went wrong in Tonto City."

"Bluffer," said Marion. "I'm going to call it, Conroy."

"As you wish; I am merely your obedient servant."

"Yes, and you better be obedient. A bullet through the belly is not a nice reminder that you took a long chance."

"Messy. And I would also add—unnecessary. You know, my dear, it was a shock to discover that a sweet-faced, innocent little maid should turn out to be a—well, not such a nice person, after all."

"Ditch it! I figured that you were getting wise, but I never thought you'd have my hand bag and valise stolen."

"You pain me, my dear. I deducted that the evidence would be in those containers. Had we forced them from you in Tonto, it might have been embarrassing, in case they were not what I imagined. While we are being brutally frank about things in general, why did you folks murder poor old Shanghai Charley? Was it because you doublecrossed him on a big deal, and he came to get his pay?"

"You knew who he was?" asked the girl quickly.

"Oh, certainly. And the alleged bank robber, whom your dear old daddy murdered and who caused you much loss of sleep. I believe he was also crossed and was following Charley's trail, trying to be in on the kill."

"You seem to know a lot," said the girl huskily. "Too much. How did you know all this?"

"Observation and deduction. For instance, you would not leave town until those diamonds were recovered. You invited Danny Regan to supper, in order to have him away from my ranch, when your men were going to capture my two Mexicans. You invited me to your house, in order to try and discover what I was doing about the murders.

"You see, I even know that Zell Hork was shot by Danny Regan, while trying to stampede horses off my ranch. They took him to Tonto, placed his body in that old corral and fired two shots—to indicate, I believe, that he was shot at that spot. The same tactics were used on Shanghai Charley. But you overlooked the fact that men bleed where they die."

The girl laughed harshly. "You are wasting your talents in Tonto City. I mean, you have wasted them. When this ride is over, so are you."

"You forget the men at the Border," said Henry.

"They would let you pass."

"I do not see—"

"You *will* see. You will either pass them, or you'll never tell them what happened."

And just at that moment Henry found the place he had been looking for. With the horse at a trot, he swung off the road and dropped two wheels into a deep ditch.

14

MONUMENT FOR HENRY

THE LURCH WAS so sudden that Marion was thrown completely out of the buggy. Henry managed to keep his seat and swung the horse around. Drawing up quickly he climbed out. The girl's gray suit was plainly visible, as she tried to stand up but sank back.

Her gun was gone. Henry grasped her by the arm and she cried out that her ankle was twisted. Henry grasped her two hands, found that they were empty, and picked her up bodily.

"The tables are turned, my dear," he told her. "Now we go back to Tonto City. Without the gun, you are just a foolish little girl who must sit and take what is given to her."

"I believe my leg is broken," she whimpered.

"Very likely. You promised me a bullet in the belly, my dear. Rather a crude expression, but effective."

They drove into Tonto City and stopped at the front of the office, where they found Judge, Danny, Oscar, Thunder, Lightning, Jim Morton and one of his officers.

"Put the young lady on a cot and send for Doc Knowles," ordered Henry. "Is everything all right?"

"You bet it's all right!" exclaimed Morton. "The diamonds were in the hand bag and the other bag was full of drugs. I would estimate the whole works to be worth at least fifty thousand dollars. What a haul!"

"It took you a long time to get here, Henry," said Judge.

"We thought for a while that we were going to Agua Frio," replied Henry, "but I drove into a washout and the young lady lost her gun."

"It wasn't a gun," groaned Marion; "it was an ivory cigarette holder."

"My goodness!" gasped Henry. "You should be ashamed to fool an old man."

They carried her into the office, and Morton drew Henry aside. "You've got the goods on Hale and Eddy?" he asked anxiously.

"Entirely circumstantial," replied Henry wearily. "I am going down there now. I want you and Danny in close, in case of trouble. Leave Judge with the doctor and the young lady. I believe I can handle it alone."

THE HALE HOME was dark, when Henry knocked loudly on the door. After a few moments he heard Frederick Hale's voice saying, "Who is there?"

"This is Conroy, Mr. Hale," replied Henry.

"Just a moment, Mr. Conroy."

It was quite a while before Frederick Hale came to the door; and he barely opened it. Henry said, "The stage was held up tonight, Mr. Hale, and your daughter lost her hand bag and valise. She sent word to you that she was going on."

"What was it?" queried Lawrence Eddy from further back in the house.

Hale turned and told him what Henry had said. Eddy lighted a lamp and invited Henry in. Foolishly Henry stepped in, Hale closed the door, and Henry found himself looking into the muzzle of Eddy's gun.

The young man was wild-eyed and determined. Hale started to say something to Eddy, but the young man interrupted. "So they got her bags, eh?"

"Why, yes," replied Henry. "But I do not see any use of pointing that gun at me, Mr. Eddy."

"Sit down there!"

Henry slumped in a chair. Eddy quickly removed a gun from Henry's coat pocket and handed it to Hale.

"I—I do not understand," said Henry nervously. "I only said—"

"We know what you said. You can't fool me any longer, Conroy."

"But, Larry—" protested Hale, his eyes showing fright.

"He thinks he's got us," said Eddy. "They got those valises. Marion's message. Fred, we've got to move fast. Steve and Nick were at the King's Castle a while ago. You keep this fat-nosed coyote here, while I get 'em. We can get to Mexico, but we've got to move fast. Watch him, Fred, and I'll be right back."

Lawrence Eddy slipped quietly out of the house, and was gone. Hale's eyes narrowed as he looked at Henry.

"Sorry about Malloy and Balleau," said Henry. "He will not find them at the saloon."

"Why won't he?" asked Hale quickly.

"Because they are in jail," replied Henry, "charged with smuggling and murder."

"You lie! You can't prove—"

"Malloy," said Henry, "was yellow. He says that you killed Shanghai Charley—you and Eddy. I didn't believe—"

"He lies!" rasped Hale. "Malloy fired both shots and— Damn you, Conroy, I'll get you if it's the last act of my life!"

He shoved the six-shooter within inches of Henry's midriff and pulled the trigger.

THREE TIMES HE squeezed the trigger, but there was only the sharp click of a falling hammer.

"I never carry it loaded," said Henry. "They've got Eddy by this time; so you may as well surrender. I arrest you for murder, Frederick Hale."

In his panic Hale whirled toward the door, but changed his mind and made a dash for the stairs. He dropped Henry's gun, and Henry picked it up, took some cartridges from his pocket and quickly loaded it.

Someone banged against the door, and it flew open. Lawrence Eddy stumbled into the room, looking wildly back, as footsteps sounded outside. Ignoring Henry, he swung up his gun, pointing toward the doorway, as Henry fired from his lap.

The heavy bullet knocked him sideways into the table, where he upset the lamp and crashed down to the floor. Danny yelled from the doorway, "Are you all right, Henry?"

"I am a bit in the dark," replied Henry calmly. "Be a little careful, Danny; Eddy may be still able to bite."

"Where's Hale?" asked Danny.

From upstairs came the dull thud of a muffled shot. Henry said, "I do not believe there is any forwarding address, Danny."

They found another lamp, and in a few minutes the room was filled with men. They brought Hale down from upstairs. His aim had been very good. Eddy was still alive, but refused to talk.

When John Campbell told Marion she would have to stand trial for murder, she was willing to talk. She accused Malloy and Balleau of killing Shanghai Charley in Hale's house, and admitted that Hale had killed the man in the bank, when that man demanded an accounting and a percentage in their new deal. They killed Shanghai Charley and later stole his bag.

"You are not—were not Hale's daughter?" asked Judge.

"No. Hale was the brains of the gang. He bought out this cow-town bank, intending to use it to cover smuggling. Malloy and his gang moved in here to do their part. It looked good, you must admit. Eddy was a first-class peter man, but—"

"Safe cracker?" asked Henry.

"He thought so, until he blew your safe through the roof."

"How on earth did you ever get mixed up in that gang?" asked Henry.

"Larry Eddy was my husband," she replied.

James Wadsworth Longfellow Pelly came limping in, dusty and tired. "Who shoved me out of that buggy?" he demanded. "Of all the unkind things I have ever had happen to me! You did it!" he snapped, pointing at Henry. "You wanted to be alone with this lady. When I get back to Scorpion Bend—"

Judge Van Treece put the palm of his bony right hand against Pelly's nose and banged his head back against the rough wall.

"Put that in your scurrilous rag!" he snorted. "And for your information, you scum, two men are dead, two are in jail and this lady has a twisted ankle. The sheriff of Tonto

City has more than justified his position in clearing up both murders; in fact, there isn't a single mystery left, unless it is why do they let you live."

Pelly was speechless.

"Prune yuice, Yimmy," chuckled Oscar. "He vanted somet'ing soft."

THEY TURNED MARION over to the Federal officers and went up to bed. Danny, Oscar and Pelly went over to the King's Castle to get a drink, and there were only Thunder and Lightning alone on the street, standing on the edge of the sidewalk. Lightning said:

"I don' know w'at you theenk, my leetle brodder. The banker ees keeled and the mos' beautiful *señorita* ees got tweested leg. Two d'ad mans and two *vaquero* een jail. The diamonds are gone. *Madre de Dios,* I drim from getting reech, and look at you."

"I'm fill seek about the diamond," agreed Thunder.

"Sure. I don't know who got heem. Everybody talk fast and I leesten and leesten, but I can' get tail from those heads. Judge poosh those man een your face and call heem a scom, and the man just take paper and write like hell. Those beautiful *señorita* 'ave 'osban', too, I am hearing."

"Too bad," sighed Thunder.

"W'at ees too bad?"

"Everytheeng."

"*Por Dios*—no! Henry say everytheeng ees all right again."

"*Buena!* Come on, we fin' out queek."

"Fin' out w'at, my leetle brodder?"

"Fin' out eef Pancho trus' us for bottle tequila."

And they went hurrying down to Pancho's cantina,

anxious to prove if Henry's word was true. Up in their room, Henry and Judge adjusted themselves in bed. The town was quiet and everything seemed peaceful. Henry sighed deeply and waved for Judge to extinguish the lamp.

"I hope the Commissioners will be satisfied," said Judge.

"I saw my duty and I done it," said Henry soberly.

"In the most intricate and roundabout way I have ever known. You had more cogs in your scheme than that alarm clock on the table. However, each cog worked to perfection. They should build a monument to you."

"My goodness! That is an idea, Judge."

"Yes, indeed. An upset buggy, with a pretty girl digging you in the ribs with a cigarette holder."

"One of the most ticklish situations I have ever been in, Judge. Goodnight. The Shame of Arizona is not ashamed."

THREE GUNS FOR TONTO

Where's the sheriff? Is he campaigning?
Is he furiously pursuing the bandits who
have looted Wild Horse Valley's wealth?
No, Sheriff Henry is snoozing in his office,
dreaming that his name is Sherlock Holmes.
But gunfire always wakes him up

1

SHERIFF GOING OUT

OSCAR JOHNSON, THE giant Swede jailer of Tonto City, stood in the middle of the JHC bunkhouse, clad in full-length red underwear, and glowered around at Frijole Bill Cullison, the ranch cook, and Thunder and Lightning Mendoza, horse-wranglers, cowpunchers, post-hole diggers, or anything that needed doing.

Frijole Bill was past sixty, small, wiry, with a fuzzy mustache and a fuzzier disposition. Frijole had often declared that he was "bullhide warp with whalebone fillin'." Thunder and Lightning, diminutive brothers, more Yaqui than Mexican, were gambling on the respective abilities of two jumping beans to roll outside a six-inch circle.

Frijole was reading a copy of the Scorpion Bend *Clarion*, an old pair of spectacles far out on the end of his long nose.

"Ay yust vant to know who in de ha'al stole my rad short?" roared Oscar.

"I heard yuh," grunted Frijole. "I'll betcha they heard yuh in Tonto City. Man, you shore beller like a bogged-down bull."

"Ay am commencing to get sore," declared Oscar. "Every time Ay vant to go to a dance, Ay find out somebody took

117

The golden-haired kid said, "Howdy"; and
Henry exclaimed, "The angel speaks!"

my Sunday suit out of my var-sack. Now Ay find my rad short gone."

"Oh, yes," said Frijole. "I remember now. Judge and I got into an argument as to whether a bull knows red from yaller. All we had for a flag was that old red shirt; so we—"

"You shook my short in front of a bull, Frijole?"

"Yea-a-h."

"Where is de short?"

"Some'ers back in Smoke Tree Canyon. At least, she was still wavin' from that bull's horns the last we seen of it. If yuh want to put on a lot of dog, why not wear my polky-dot shirt? That's a dinger."

"Your polky-dot short vould not make a sleeve for me."

"Anyway," said Frijole, "you won't know if Josephine will go with yuh, until Slim gets back with the note from her. Lemme read some of this here newspaper to yuh. Man, this shore takes one awful slam at you and Henry and Judge. The editor says yo're a squarehead and that yuh ain't got brains enough to pour sand out of a boot."

"Ay know dat liar," growled Oscar. "His name is Yames Wadsfellow Longworth Pellet; and some day Ay am going to tie his two legs in a hord knot around his neck."

"His name," said Frijole, "is James Wadsworth Long-fellow Pelly."

"My onkle," stated Lightning, "ees tell me that Henry ees going for get beat so bad you won't know wheech end I am standing on—I hope."

"My onkle, too," added Thunder. "I theenk he ees my seester's cousin, or not, as these cases might be, but he ees damn smart."

"Your uncle is a damn horse-thief and he can't even vote," said Frijole. "What does he know about politics and elections?"

"I don' know—he ees talk about it pretty good."

"Talk, yeah! Oscar, why don'tcha put on some pants?"

"Ay vant my rad short."

"Oh, yeah. Well, you'll prob'ly git it if yuh stand there long enough. Figurin' the law of averages, you stand there a few years and somebody is bound to come along with a red shirt. Why don'tcha go to Tonto City and buy a shirt?"

"Somebody ees come," announced Lightning. A horse drew up near the bunkhouse, the door was kicked violently open, and Slim Pickins strode it.

SLIM WAS RIGHTLY nicknamed. He was six feet tall and so thin that if he ate an olive it would make a bump on him. Slim's left eye was discolored and a cut lip had trick-led blood down over his unshaven chin.

"Yeah!" he growled, sailing his sombrero into a corner and turning to Frijole. "You write a note to Josephine Swansen, sign Oscar's name to it and ask me to deliver it to her. Well, I done it! Damn yuh, don't ask me what happened—jist look at me!"

"She don't answer?" queried Oscar anxiously.

Oscar looked Slim over, and turned to Frijole. "What in de ha'al did you say in de note, Free-holey?"

"Say?" queried Frijole, slightly aggrieved. "I said jist what you told me to say. I told her that if she felt like associatin' with a gentleman you'd take her to the dance at Scorpion Bend."

"What else?" asked Oscar.

"Well, I told her jist what yuh said, Oscar. You said if she didn't want to go with you, she could go plumb to hell."

"Yudas Priest!" exploded Oscar. "You write that to her?"

"That's exactly what yuh said."

"Yeeminy gosh! Now Ay have lost her!"

"Feller," said Slim wearily, "all you've lost is the heavy-weight champion of the world."

Josephine Swensen, Oscar's light o' love, was a huge, raw-boned, two-fisted woman who worked as a waitress and maid at the Tonto Hotel, and asked odds from no one in a fight.

"Ay am a hord-luck yigger," complained Oscar. "First, Ay lose my rad short, and then Ay lose my girl—and Free-holey is to blame for both."

"Don't blame me," said Frijole. "The shirt was lost in the interests of science. Slim, didja see Henry or Judge in town?"

"They've done gone to Scorpion Bend," replied Slim.

"To the dance, I wonder?"

"I dunno," replied Slim.

"Ay vonder if Yosephine is going to the dance," said Oscar.

"I think," said Slim, "she's goin' with Eric Olson, that little Norwegian from over at the Shoshone Chief mine."

"Yah? By Yimminy, Ay am about to go to de dance myself."

"Wait a minute!" exclaimed Frijole. "How about all of us goin'? We shore need some recreation. Slim can ride a horse, and the rest of us can ride in the buckboard."

"*Viva* Frijole!" cheered Lightning.

"Yah," agreed Oscar, "Ay believe that would be goot job. How 'bout little drink of prune juice?"

"Jist right," agreed Frijole. "I jist drawed off a new batch this mornin', and she ages in fifteen, twenty minutes."

When he was not cooking food at the JHC, Frijole Bill spent most of his time distilling prunes into whiskey that had the potency of a depth-bomb. While Thunder and Lightning preferred their native tequila, they were not adverse to prune whiskey.

"Ay vill show Eric something," declared Oscar, as they drank from tin cups. "Ay vill also show Yosephine."

"You do the showin', brother," said Slim, "I've done been showed."

ALONG THE HIGH grades above Piñon Canyon a horse and buggy followed the rocky road. In the buggy were Henry Harrison Conroy, sheriff of Wild Horse Valley, and "Judge" Van Treece, his deputy.

They were a queer pair, these two. Henry was short and fat, with a moon-like face and the biggest and reddest nose ever to exist in Arizona. Just now he was wearing a dove-gray suit, white shirt, baby-blue tie, patent-leather shoes and a pearl-gray derby hat. Resting between his well-tailored knees was a gold-headed cane.

Judge Van Treece, six feet four inches in height, bony, angular, and with the face of a tragedian, was clad in a rusty-black frock coat, striped trousers, high-heel boots and a shapeless old black sombrero. Judge was driving, one booted foot hanging over the side of the buggy and almost touching the ground.

For many years Henry Harrison Conroy had been a featured player in vaudeville. In fact, until vaudeville waned and his contract was cancelled, Henry knew less than nothing about the cattle country. But his uncle, owner of the JHC spread in Wild Horse Valley, died and left the ranch to Henry, who came bewilderedly to claim his inheritance.

Clad in rather extreme tailored clothes, even to spats and a cane, Henry was a decided novelty in Wild Horse Valley; and that bright red nose, large and shapeless, highly entertained the cowboys and cattlemen. Henry had only been a resident of that country a few months when a county election came along.

Some of the voters, strictly as a joke, passed the word that they would write Henry's name on the ballot, instead of voting for a regularly nominated candidate for sheriff. The joke spread. In fact, Henry was elected. Henry knew it was a joke; so in a similar spirit, he chose for his deputy sheriff Judge Van Treece, who had been a successful criminal lawyer until liquor drove him out of the profession. In addition, Henry appointed Oscar Johnson as jailer.

The three of them made up what the *Clarion* called,

"The Shame of Arizona". Unlike the popular conception of Arizona lawmen, they did not dash across the hills on their horses, swinging six-shooters in both hands and followed by a hard-jawed posse. In fact, they did not dash at all. Both of them disliked horseback riding and neither of them was a good revolver shot. They loved quiet contemplation, good food and good liquor.

While the paper ridiculed them and citizens swore at them, they had proved themselves efficient. Henry had his own ways of catching criminals, and even his bitterest critics were obliged to admit that Henry had done his job in a competent if unorthodox fashion.

"YOU WERE SPEAKING of Big Jim Harris," reminded Judge, shifting his cramped leg to a more comfortable position. They did not build buggies with enough leg-room for Judge.

"Ah, yes," murmured Henry. "Big Jim Harris, a very estimable gentleman, indeed."

"Estimable!"

"Well, it is all in the point of view, Judge. He is backing Cash Silverton for the sheriff's office, and in a case of that kind one must be lenient. He did say that if he had had his way all three of us would have been out of that office a year ago. Presumably the other commissioners refused to vote with him."

"He mentioned your nose, I presume," remarked Judge.

"Oh, yes. Yes, indeed. Said it was laughable."

"Did he—er—mention me, by any chance, sir?"

"Oh, yes. He said you were a broken-down lawyer who had drunk himself out of the profession."

"I resent that!" snapped Judge.

"I told him you would."

"After the things he told you about yourself—and me, sir—I am surprised that you did not smite him hip and thigh."

"What with?" asked Henry quietly.

"Why—er—indignation, I suppose, Henry."

"The truth never made me indignant, Judge."

"Truth! Broken-down lawyer—"

"Well, Judge, you are not exactly a—Watch that turn! My goodness, you almost drove into the canyon!"

"This country needs better roads," growled Judge.

"Or better drivers," added Henry.

"All right. Henry, I have been thinking about Wild Horse Valley lately, and Tonto City in particular. Did you ever realize that Big Jim Harris is getting rather powerful? He furnished the money for the reopening of the Tonto Bank, owns the King's Castle Saloon, and they say he owns the stage line. Now he is trying to dictate the politics of this county."

"I am wondering how that bank will fare," remarked Henry. "Since it went broke, everyone banks in Scorpion Bend. I am afraid Big Jim will find it difficult to lure the money back to Tonto City. The Bank of Scorpion Bend is a solid institution, and Charles H. Baker, the banker, is above reproach."

"Yes, I believe that is true, Henry. I hope the Tonto Bank will be a success, because it will save us from making these trips."

"True. But I do not mind it. The money for the Shoshone Chief mine payroll must come through. I do not blame them for being afraid of a stage robbery. All we have to do is get the payroll from the banker at about ten o'clock this evening at his home, place it here in the buggy and drive home to Tonto City. No one will be the wiser."

"I hope it will be that simple, Henry. I hope no one will suspect the reason for our visit to Scorpion Bend."

"Of course, they won't, Judge. There is a dance tonight. Half of Tonto City will be there. We will appear, of course, mingling with the good folk. At ten we disappear—to be seen no more at the dance, because we will be wending our way home, bearing between eighteen and twenty thousand of coin of the realm."

"I hope so," sighed Judge.

"Getting back to Mr. Harris and Mr. Silverton," said Henry. "It is evident that Harris is backing Cash Silverton for office, not because Mr. Silverton is such a paragon of virtue but because we are so absolutely unbearable, incompetent, immaterial and—er—"

"Thirsty?" suggested Judge.

"Thank you very much, sir. Thirsty is the word I was groping for. Perhaps you do drink a bit too much. Try and taper off a little, at least until after election, Judge."

"I?" gasped Judge. "You ask *me* to taper off?"

"As long as Mr. Silverton is running on the temperance ticket, we must not add fuel to their flames, Judge. Surely you can see—"

"But Henry! Damn it, man, you are the candidate—not me!"

"Ah, yes, yes. True, Judge. I see your angle. Well, it might be a novelty at that. I wonder just what stand the *Clarion* will take?"

"Will take? My God, did you not read the last issue, Henry?"

"I believe Frijole carried it out to the ranch."

"The editor advises you to resign or be boiled in oil."

"Ah, yes," sighed Henry. "To resign. As the immortal bard might have said, 'To be or not to be: that is the question'. Whether it is nobler in the mind to suffer the slings and arrows of the—er—*Clarion*—"

"Or like a doughnut—crisp and brown," added Judge.

"You paint a beautiful future," sighed Henry.

"Future?" queried Judge. "Henry, do you realize what will happen to us if Cash Silverton is elected?"

"Ah, yes, Judge. We will retire to the simple life. We will sit all the day in the shade of the porch at the JHC, drinking prune whiskey, full of reminiscence and home-made alcohol. Just a pair of grand old philosophers taking life easy. What more may a man ask?"

"Still optimistic," sighed Judge. "With no income, you must perforce fire Frijole Bill, Oscar Johnson, Slim Pickins, Thunder and Lightning. That will mean that you and I will have to punch the cows, if any are left, fix fences, cook mulligan—not a bright outlook, sir."

"You are excessively gloomy, Judge."

"I look facts squarely in the face, sir."

"Do you," said Henry, after a long period of silence, "have any idea that Cash Silverton can defeat me in the election?"

"I do."

"Sounds like a marriage ceremony," said Henry dryly.

"The voters," said Judge, "might not be in a joking frame of mind this time, Henry."

2

PELLY OF THE POISON PEN

JAMES WADSWORTH LONGFELLOW PELLY, editor of the Scorpion Bend *Clarion,* finished his weekly editorial, leaned back in his old, cowhide-covered chair, removed his glasses and squinted into space. This editorial had to do with the coming county election, and it was a masterly, scathing denunciation of Henry Conroy and his associates.

The editor was a youngish man, skinny, nearly bald, and entirely vitriolic in his writings, especially when they concerned the sheriff's office, which he had dubbed "The Shame of Arizona."

Flies buzzed up and down the dusty windows of the editorial sanctum, which was partitioned off from the press room by a six-foot pile of old *Clarions,* some boilerplate boxes and other dusty debris.

The *Clarion* was strongly behind the candidacy of Cash Silverton. The editor had no doubt that Henry Harrison Conroy would be defeated, for Pelly was confident that the *Clarion* moulded the opinions of Wild Horse Valley. The election of Silverton would be a triumph for the *Clarion,* and Pelly had already written an editorial for the front page of his first issue after election day.

The front door opened and closed quietly. Pelly sighed

wearily and turned around in his chair, facing the counter near the door.

"A very, very good afternoon to you, sir." Henry Harrison Conroy beamed, bowing courteously.

"Oh!" gasped Pelly. "You!"

Henry's eyes scanned the dingy interior of the room for several moments. He flicked some imaginary dust from coat lapel, and said:

"Even with the scarcity of water in Arizona, you should be very much ashamed, my dear Pelly."

"Ashamed of what?" asked Pelly.

"And still," continued Henry, ignoring the question, "I suppose it is all in keeping. Dusty words, filthy innuendo, and over it all cobwebs of imagination."

Pelly flushed hotly. "You came here to insult me?" he asked.

"Have you been insulted, sir?" asked Henry anxiously.

"I certainly have! If you—"

"Good, good!" Henry beamed. "Will you give me a written statement to that effect, Mr. Pelly?"

"Damn you, why should I?"

"Merely to settle a bet, my dear fellow. You see, I wagered ten dollars with Judge, who contended that you are so hidebound and egotistical that you would not recognize an insult were it flung into what few teeth you have left. I really must have a written and signed testimonial from you to the effect that I did insult you."

"My God!" gasped Pelly in amazement.

"Ghastly, isn't it?" said Henry calmly.

"You've got a damn lot of nerve, Conroy!"

"Yes? But in a recent editorial you said I did not have the nerve of a cotton-tail rabbit."

James Wadsworth Longfellow Pelly got to his feet and came over to the counter. He was really mad.

"The *Clarion* is solidly behind Cash Silverton," he said huskily, "and we will go to almost any lengths to defeat you, Conroy."

"I appreciate the word 'almost'," said Henry. "It means, I suppose, that you will not resort to physical harm. By the way, Oscar Johnson said he wanted to come here some day and see how you published your paper."

"You keep him away from here!" blurted Pelly. "I don't want you or any of your gang in here. Do you understand that?"

"I can only speak for myself, sir," replied Henry soberly. "As far as Judge is concerned, I do not think he will come here—but I make no promises about Oscar. He has a play-ful disregard for orders. By the way, Judge asked me to give you his best regards."

"You can tell Judge Van Treece that I do not want his regards."

"Well," said Henry, "I shall leave them here with you, sir, if you do not mind. In a few days they will be so dust-cov-ered that you will not know what they are. Mayhap some day when you are badly in need of some best regards, you will accidently brush some dust off them and recognize that for once you have something of true worth in your dingy print shop. Good afternoon, sir."

CHUCKLING TO HIMSELF, Henry went up the street. In front of a general store an old rawhider was loading supplies into the back of a buckboard. He recognized Henry, and smiled widely.

"I ain't goin' t' vote for you because yo're any hell of a sheriff, but because I don't think Cash Silverton knows sic 'em. I dunno why this here valley can't git a decent candidate for the office."

"Ah, yes," said Henry. "I wonder that myself, sir."

"Shore funny. Didja ever try puttin' flax-seed poultices on that nose?"

"No, I never have," confessed Henry.

"They shore do wonders. My oldest boy got a swelled-up nose like that, and it shore looked turrible. I thought it might stay that way and ruin his looks entirely, but the old woman fixed up a flax-seed poultice and drawed her to a head over night. Yuh can git flax-seed here at the general store."

"Thank you very much," said Henry soberly.

"Yo're welcome. It's jist plain flax-seed. I think she softened it up in hot water. Just daub her on and she's shore do wonders."

"I shall remember—and thank you very much."

"Flax-seed!" exclaimed Henry to himself as he went on. "I am very glad Judge did not hear that one."

He found Judge and they went down the street to a restaurant where they had planned to eat supper. But before they reached the restaurant they saw the ranch buckboard enter town, with Oscar and Frijole on the seat and the two Mexicans in the back.

"Completely petrified," said Judge, as the vehicle passed them.

"You mean to say that they are inebriated, Judge?"

"Absolutely. Did you note that Frijole and Oscar had a line apiece? The two worst drivers in Wild Horse Valley, splitting the chore between them."

"I believe," sighed Henry, "that Frijole was to bring off another batch of prune whiskey this morning. Ah, well, they are contented. Let us eat, Judge. No use glaring after them—they cannot detect a glare. Or are you jealous?"

"Envious, perhaps. But we must refrain from the flowing bowl tonight."

"You saw the banker?"

"Yes. We will got to his home at ten o'clock, when he will turn the payroll money over to us."

"And no one will be the wiser," added Henry.

3

PARTY AT THE BANK

A DANCE AT Scorpion Bend was always an occasion. They came from far and wide, in wagons, buggies and on horseback; and the dance lasted from early evening to late morning. Henry and Judge appeared at the hall, where dozens of couples clattered to the two-step, scraped to the waltz and banged to the square dances. There was much liquor, raucous laughter and not a few fist fights.

Oscar was there, followed by Frijole Bill, Slim Pickins and the two Mexicans. Josephine Swensen was there, squired by Eric Olson, a half-pint Norwegian, red-headed and freckled. Danny Regan brought Nellie Adams, the Tonto City schoolteacher, and was quite the envy of all the cowboys.

Oscar wanted to fight, but he could not find a suitable opponent. This Eric Olson was too small. Someone told Oscar that Eric had a gun. Anyway, Eric seemed content to stay in the dance hall, and Oscar was too much of a gentleman to start trouble up there—at least until he got real drunk.

"I'm tired of follerin' yuh around, Oscar," declared Slim. "I'm goin' t' set right down here and git m' fill of watchin' the bull-fiddler. All m' life I've wanted to saw one of them them over-growed violins. I jist natcherally love 'em."

"Huh!" snorted Frijole. "Allus sounds t' me like a Injun with wooden teeth, down in a well and singin' a war-chant."

"Ay don't like music," declared Oscar. "Ay am hortsick, Ay ta'al you. Pretty qvick Ay have to fight somebody."

"You keep away from Eric," warned Frijole. "That little varmint has got a gun."

"Ay am not 'fraid from a gun."

"Let him go," advised Slim. "If he wants to corpse himself, it's all right with me. Eric's behaving himself, far as I can see with the one eye that Josephine didn't land on. Believe me, I'd rather be heartsick than in Eric's boots, if she thinks he's done wrong. Hell, he won't make a decent rug, after she's tanned him. Go git yourself a long slug of liquor and be glad yuh can swaller."

"Ay vill take de gun away from him," declared Oscar.

"Now I know I'm stayin' here," said Slim. "I don't want to see the operation. But I'll come to the funeral. That's the least yuh can do for a feller."

Eric left the hall, mopping his perspiring face. Oscar signaled to Frijole, and they went out, with Thunder and Lightning behind them.

There was no question in Oscar's mind that Eric had gone to the saloon across the street. It was ten o'clock, and the dance was just getting into full swing. Oscar went over to the saloon, but Frijole, Thunder and Lightning stopped to have a drink from Frijole's jug, which he had left in the buckboard.

"Dawgone, we should have put that team in the stable," complained Frijole. "Standin' out here all night, with nothin' to eat. It ain't right. Lightnin', you go over to the livery stable and buy a half-sack of oats. Me and Thunder will set here and wait for yuh."

Lightning came back with less than a half-sack, and they were about to remove the bridles from the two horses when there was a commotion in the saloon. A shot was fired, and men seemed to be rushing about. A man came from the saloon, running like a rabbit toward the three men grouped around the buckboard, and behind him came another man, yelling and whooping. The first man cleared the sidewalk in a bound and ducked into a dark alley between the general store and the bank.

The pursuer skidded across the wooden sidewalk, and also vanished into the alley.

"Oscar Johnson!" yelped Frijole. "Come on, boys!"

FRIJOLE, LIGHTNING AND Thunder had barely dashed into the alley, when a shot was fired behind the bank. Frijole was carrying the oat-sack, and suddenly a running man crashed into him and knocked him sprawling. Some-one kicked him in the ear, but he scrambled to his feet, grabbed his sack and kept on going. In a few moments the alley seemed full of men.

Someone was claiming that Oscar Johnson had shot Eric Olson. Eric had been shot through the leg, and they were taking him over to the saloon. Frijole stumbled back to the buckboard and threw the oat-sack in the back.

He wanted to find Oscar and see if Oscar had really shot the little, red-headed Norwegian. He found Thunder and Lightning in front of the saloon, where they were watch-ing the crowd.

"I'm theenk they goin' to leench Oscar," said Lightning.

"Eric ain't dead yet, is he?" asked Frijole.

"Pretty queek, I'm theenk," replied Lightning. "He yall like hell."

"You ain't dead, when yuh can yell. Where's Oscar?"

"We never see heem," replied Thunder.

"Sa-a-ay!" grunted Frijole. "What happened to you fellers when we ran down that alley? You was ahead of me."

"Somebody," said Lightning, "shoot and we go eento house."

"What house?"

"*Quien sabe?* A door ees open, so we go een."

Frijole digested that statement. "Yo're loco," he declared. "There ain't no door, except the back door of the bank."

"Sure," agreed Thunder heartily. "That door ees open."

"Huh? The back door of the bank—wait a minute! C'mon."

They went across the street, down the alley and to the back door of the bank. It was wide open.

"I'll be a nephew of a sidewinder!" grunted Frijole. "Yuh don't leave bank doors open at night."

"We didn't leave heem open, he was open biffore," said Lightning.

"Huh!" grunted Frijole. "All right, we'll investigate."

They moved in slowly, groping in the darkness, until they were about halfway down the room. They could see the saloon lights across the street. Frijole said, "We've got to have a light, that's a cinch."

So each one of them lighted matches. Frijole stepped over to the railing and held his match high. The flickering light revealed Charles Baker, the banker, stretched out on the floor, his arms and legs roped, his eyes blinking at the match. His mouth was stuffed with cloth.

From outside the bank came a yelp of warning. Someone had seen the flickering matches, and a voice bellowed:

"Robbers in the bank! Robbers in the bank!"

"Lovely dove!" blurted Frijole. "C'mon—fast!"

The three of them made a dive for the rear doorway. There was no illumination from that side, and all three of them crashed into the wall, but they managed to stagger outside into the alley. Then they rushed off in different directions. Frijole tried to go straight ahead, past some sheds, but a huge body fell upon him, and strong arms wound around him tightly.

"Ay told you Ay vould feex you," growled a voice in his ear. "You can't get avay from me, you little son of a sea-cook!"

"Oscar!" gasped Frijole. "Yo're chokin' me, you square-head!"

"Free-holey?" whispered Oscar. "Ay t'ought—"

"Sh-h-h-h!" hissed Frijole. "Keep still!"

Men were running into the alley. Someone shouted for a lantern. They heard Bill Sims, the marshal, saying:

"Go easy, boys—we'll get 'em! They're still in there. We've got 'em blocked! All right!" Sims raised his voice, "Come out of there, or we'll come in. Yuh can't git away; so yuh may as well surrender."

Naturally there was no reply. Someone brought the lantern. The men held the lantern into the doorway, expecting to draw a shot, but nothing happened. Finally they went into the bank, guns ready. There was a commotion when they found the banker.

"What in hell happened to you?" asked Frijole in a whisper.

"Ay must have been hit," replied Oscar. "Ay have lomp like an egg on my head. Ay vill fix that damn Eric, you bat you."

"They say you shot Eric and they're fixin' to lynch yuh."

"Ay never shot anybody," declared Oscar. "Eric vars going to shoot me in de saloon, but de gun go off accidental, and Ay take it avay from him. Ay tell him Ay am going to shove it down his neck, and he run like ha'al; so I run after him. But Ay never shoot de gun."

"Where's the gun now?"

"Ay don't know. Somebody hit me so hard Ay lose it. You say Eric is dead?"

"Dyin'," amended Frijole. "They said they was goin' to lynch yuh."

"Yudas priest, Ay don't vant that to happen."

"Sh-h-h-h!" hissed Frijole. "They're comin' out."

The men came out, bringing the banker, who was saying:

"We must hurry, men. Henry and Judge are tied up in my home."

FRIJOLE AND OSCAR cautiously followed the crowd up to the Baker home. There Henry and Judge were roped to chairs in the main room, unable even to wiggle a finger. The crowd cut them loose, and the banker told them that the vault of the bank had been cleaned out.

"My goodness!" exclaimed Henry. "The payroll of the Shoshone Chief mine—and all the rest of the bank money. Mr. Baker, how much did they get?"

"I don't know," groaned the banker. "Everything is gone. Until we make a complete check—"

"After they tied us up here, they took you to the bank?" asked Judge.

"Yes. They threatened to kill me unless I gave them the combination. Oh, they were desperate enough. And after they took everything away, they came back again, lighting matches. Perhaps they overlooked something vital to their getaway."

"Them's the matches I seen," declared a voice triumphantly. "I sure woke up the town."

"Was it the same men?" asked Judge.

"Absolutely," declared the banker. "I only saw one of them this time, but he was a big man, masked, with a gun in his hand. I thought for a moment he was going to kill me. It was terrible!"

Frijole scratched his stubbled chin thoughtfully. Henry said:

"Identification is impossible, gentlemen. The three of us were here in this room, talking business, when two masked men stepped in. They covered us, roped Judge and myself to chairs, and went out, taking Mr. Baker with them. We had no chance to resist."

"You spoke about the payroll of the Shoshone Chief, sheriff," said one of the men. "What about it?"

"Judge and I came to Scorpion Bend to take it back to the mine, sir. Mr. Baker had it here, all ready to hand over to us."

"They got that, too?"

"As a matter of fact," replied Henry calmly, "they got that first."

Frijole led Oscar outside and they headed back for the street.

"We better find them two Mexicans and head for home," said Frijole. "Yo're wanted for murder, and I'm a big man, masked and with a gun in my hand. This town shore has a queer effect on a feller."

"Yah, su-ure," agreed Oscar meekly. "Maybe it is de prune yuice."

They were standing nearly in front of the *Clarion* office when two men started across the street toward them. Frijole and Oscar stepped into the deeper shadows. The men were Big Jim Harris and James Wadsworth Longfellow Pelly, the editor. They stopped near the doorway.

"I've certainly got something to blast Conroy with now," declared Pelly. "Guardians of the Shoshone Chief payroll! And that square-headed Swede jailer, shooting a little man in an alley. You watch that next edition, Mr. Harris. I am going to work all night on it. When I get through with him, Conroy won't have a vote in this country."

"Go to it, Pelly," said Big Jim. "Make it strong. I'll see yuh later."

Pelly went into the office, and Big Jim went back across the street. In a few moments a lamp glowed on James Wadsworth Longfellow Pelly's desk.

"Sqvarehead, eh?" muttered Oscar.

"Ain't you done enough tonight?" asked Frijole wearily.

"Ay ain't done not'ing, except have hord luck," declared Oscar. "You find Lightning and Thunder and have dem in de bockboard. Ay vill be vit you soon, Free-holey."

"Well," sighed Frijole, "I don't reckon they can hang yuh more'n once."

Ten minutes later an extraordinary figure staggered into the saloon across the street, where Henry and Judge were discussing the robbery with the crowd. This figure was an almost solid gob of black sticky stuff, oozing and dripping on the floor in oily globules. Everyone drew away, awed.

Then the apparation spoke in husky tones: "Whole edition… pied… and my ink's… all gone…."

Then he sank in a swoon in the middle of the saloon floor.

4

THOSE MONEY

IT WAS NEARLY noon next day when Judge and Henry came down to the office. Big Jim Harris and Nick Borden, owner of the Shoshone Chief, were there to meet them. They both liked Nick Borden, and knew that the loss of that payroll would cripple him badly. Harris said:

"I was right. Nick said that maybe you were out lookin' for the men who got his payroll, but I said you were both asleep."

"All of which," remarked Henry blandly, "earmarks you a seer, Mr. Harris."

"I wasn't criticizin' yuh, Henry," said Borden. "It wasn't your fault."

"Thank you, Nick," said Henry. "I regret it more than I can tell you."

"You saw the men," said Big Jim testily. "Why can't you even give us a description? We might find them for you."

"That," said Henry, "is my business, Mr. Harris."

Nick Borden looked keenly at Henry. "You have an idea, Henry?" he asked.

"I am never without one, sir," replied Henry.

"What about Oscar Johnson?" asked. Big Jim. "He shot

that red-headed Eric last night. Is nothin' to be done about that?"

"The fatal shooting of Eric Olson," said Henry, "amounted to a superficial flesh-wound in his leg. Eric was shot from in front, and he contends that Oscar could only have shot him from the rear. Ergo, Eric must have been shot by one of the men who came from the bank after robbing the vault. Eric was able to drive a horse from the dance and return Miss Josephine Swensen to Tonto City."

"All right," growled Big Jim, "but what about James Wadsworth Longfellow Pelly?"

"I suffer no qualms, sir," replied Henry.

"But Pelly insists that Oscar Johnson done it to him."

"That lovable Swede," murmured Judge.

"Pelly," stated Big Jim, "will sue him for that."

"Quite likely," agreed Henry. "But is that any reason for you to stand there, a picture of outraged dignity, and chide me for what Oscar Johnson may or may not have done? I am not Oscar Johnson's keeper, and if he made an ink-spot out of your pet, for once the *Clarion* ink has been used to good advantage."

"Maybe it was your suggestion," said Big Jim angrily.

"Mental suggestion perhaps, Mr. Harris. Will you join us in the office, Nick?"

Big Jim went away, grumbling and threatening, and the three men entered the office. They were not happy.

"The loss of that payroll hits me pretty hard," said Borden. "You see, Henry, I had other money banked in Scorpion Bend, and I wonder if that bank can make the grade. If it can't I'm sunk, along with a lot of other people."

Henry nodded sadly. "I'm afraid, Nick, they cleaned out

the vault. The question is this: Who, beside the banker, Judge, you and I, knew that we went up there to get the payroll?"

"I don't know," replied Borden miserably. "How anyone found out, I have no idea. Evidently they knew."

"Well, they came to Baker's house to get that payroll."

"I am afraid," said Judge, "it means the failure of the Scorpion Bank. I do not believe that Baker has any considerable fortune, even if he wanted to make good with the depositors. The Cattlemen's Bank is due to open here in the near future, but I'm just a bit afraid people will not want to put their money in it. It has been busted twice. But I really had a lot of faith in the bank at Scorpion Bend."

"I'm afraid this will mean the closing of the mines," said Borden. "I can't meet that payroll, and the others will find themselves in the same fix."

"Unless we find the money," added Henry quietly.

"That," said Judge, "would be a feather in our caps, Henry."

"Feather!" exclaimed Henry. "That would be a whole war-bonnet!"

IT WAS NEARLY noon when Frijole awoke, snorted, yawned audibly and licked his dry lips. It had been a hard night on the boys of the JHC. Thunder and Lightning were occupying a single bunk. Oscar had a double bunk, while Slim Pickins was sprawled on the floor with a blanket over his feet.

Oscar snorted and awoke. Then he threw both his boots, one of which hit Lightning on the head. The other boot clipped Slim on the knee-cap.

"Vaking a man up in de middle of de night!" he growled.

"Middle of the night!" snorted Frijole. "Take a look at that alarm clock, will yuh? Dang near noon."

Slim Pickins groaned and kicked the blanket aside. "What find of a mad-house is this?" he demanded. "Feller might as well try to sleep in the middle of a corral full of locoed broncs. Has anybody got a sample of the hair of the dog that bit me? I'm shore a wreck."

"Must be a quart in that jug on the table," said Frijole.

Slim shuddered and drew on his boots.

"Somebody," suggested Frijole, "ort to feed and water the horses."

No one volunteered to do it. Frijole and Slim dressed silently, none too happy. Frijole said:

"How'd yuh like a nice oystew stew, Slim?"

Slim shuddered. Oscar lifted his heavy head and glared at Frijole. Slim and Frijole went outside and yawned widely.

"I don't even remember takin' the harness off the team," said Slim.

"You didn't," reminded Frijole. "You was in bed when we got here."

"Oh, that's right. Sa-ay! I just remember, Frijole. I threwed my saddle into the corral and tried to hang my bronc on a peg. Didja ever try to hang a horse on a peg? It's shore a novelty."

"Yeah, I reckon so. Well, we might as well take care of the horses before cookin' breakfast, Slim."

They went down past the corral, where they left the buckboard with one front hub driven tightly into the fence. Frijole stopped, went back and picked a grain sack from the back of the vehicle.

"Jist remembered buyin' these oats and never—" Frijole's

voice faded. He blinked thoughtfully, hefted the bag and then scratched his stubbled chin with his free hand.

"I told yuh that prune whiskey will give yuh the jim-jams," remarked Slim. "Do yuh see spots before yore eyes?"

"Git into the stable, will yuh?" whispered Frijole.

"All right, but don't git violent, feller. If yo're goin' to start seein' things you see 'em alone."

He kept an eye on Frijole, who came in behind him, closing the door. Frijole carefully upended the grain sack and out tumbled packages of currency, rolls of coin, papers. Frijole quickly scooped them back into the sack, panting audibly.

Slim was shaking his head violently and rubbing the back of his neck.

"Let's git real calm-like," suggested Slim. "No use goin' off half-cocked, Frijole. We both seen somethin', but we ain't exactly sure. Ain't no question in my mind about it bein' the effect of whiskey; so we've jist got to have patience."

"Whiskey—hell!" exploded Frijole huskily. "This is money!"

"Aw, take it easy!" said Slim. "There ain't that much money in—huh? You saw money, too? Frijole, we must both be loco."

"We ain't," declared Frijole. "That bank money must have—I've got it, Slim! I've got it!"

"I dunno, but I think yo're worse than I am, Frijole. Yo're yellin'! That's a bad sign. I had a uncle oncet which got snakes. He was all right until he got to yellin'. As long as yore voice—"

"Listen, Slim! When I went into that alley last night

I had part of a sack of oats. Somebody fell all over me, tromped me from end to end, yuh understand. Well, I got my oat sack and took it back to the buckboard. Damn it, Slim, the robbers got the oats and I got the money."

"Yuh mean you traded sacks?"

"I hope t' die. I must have been so drunk that I didn't notice the difference. This weighs more than that much oats."

Slim drew a deep breath and said: "Frijole, we're rich!"

"Hm-m-m-m!" Frijole scratched his fuzzy mustache. "Rich, eh? Yuh know," Frijole leaned against the stable wall his thumbs inside his stringy vest, "I've allus wanted te be rich, Slim."

"Well," said Slim, "we've made it."

"Jist like a dream, ain't it?" asked Frijole.

"Right out of a clear sky."

"No, I wouldn't go that far, Slim. It was a damn dark alley. But how can we git away with it? We've got to cache this stuff until we can make plans. If they find it on us, we're stuck."

"That's right. Let's bury it. We'll take a shovel and dig a hole."

"Take that shovel, Slim. We'll sink it before them other hooligans get up. C'mon."

OSCAR WAS STILL snoring. Lightning managed to get out of his bunk and put on his boots. He went over to the window just in time to see Frijole and Slim, acting very furtive, leave the stable, carrying a shovel. They sneaked around a corner of the corral and entered the willows along the dry-wash.

Oscar managed to awaken sufficiently to dress, grunting and groaning in the process.

"How am I, you hope and trust?" queried Lightning brilliantly.

"Ay feel like ha'al," replied Oscar. "Do you remember if Ay killed Eric last night?"

"That ees w'at I hear," said Lightning. "You keel heem pretty dead, eef w'at I hear ees true, I hope not."

"Yah, su-ure. But, of course, at de same time, Eric is a liar if he say Ay killed him. Ay never shoot dat gon vonce. Ay am chasing Eric behind the bank and something hit me. Jeerusalem! Ay vars hit hord. Somet'ing smalls funny around ha'ar."

"That ees those black stuffs you got on your knees and on your boots. W'at ees it?"

Oscar grunted and got to his feet. He kicked the door open and went over to the back of the house, where he poured water into a deep basin and proceeded with his morning ablutions. Lightning shook Thunder violently, and the latter looked up at him with bloodshot eyes.

"Sometheeng ees happen," he told Thunder. "Sleem and Frijole snick out and go down to the estable. Pretty queek they snick out from those estable weeth a shovvel. Then they go eento the brosh. You know w'at I theek?"

"Sure," Thunder nodded. "W'at you theenk?"

"I theenk they keel somebody—and go for bury heem."

"*Madre de Dios!*" gasped Thunder. "You theenk we better tell Henry?"

"No, no! *Idiota!* We look firs'. Maybe he ees somebody we don't like, too."

"Buena! My leetle brodder, you sure got a head on my shoulder. I put on boot ver' queek."

"Mucho tiempo! We not look now. W'en nobody ees look, we see heem. We don't want scare from somebody."

Frijole and Slim made their way cautiously back to the stable, from where they came boldly to the house. There was not much conversation at breakfast. Frijole managed to drop some eggs on the floor, spilled the coffee, and otherwise seemed in a nervous state.

However, no one paid any attention. Oscar ate gloomily.

"You worryin' about that Norwegian yuh shot last night?" asked Slim.

"Ay didn't shoot him," denied Oscar.

"Maybe he ees dying from scare," suggested Lightning.

"How do you know he died?" asked Slim.

"I hear heem yall like hell. Somebody say he ees dying hard."

"They don't die that hard," said Frijole. "I heard him, too."

"Ay vonder," said Oscar, "vat Yosephine thought."

Slim shuddered and felt of his eye, which was still purple. "Don't ask me to inquire," he said. "I've had my lesson."

Oscar moved into the main room, but came back quickly. "Ha'ar comes Hanry and Yudge," he informed them.

"Comin' to arrest yuh for murder, I reckon," said Slim soberly.

OSCAR DISAPPEARED THROUGH the kitchen doorway as Judge and Henry rode up to the front porch. "Come in and have a pancake," invited Frijole, as they came into the main room.

"Fine time to be having breakfast!" snorted Judge, but

sat down at the table. Henry leaned against the doorway, looking them over.

"Where is Oscar?" he asked. Frijole and Slim glanced at each other.

"Oscar?" queried Slim. "Oh yeah—Oscar. I'd plumb forgot about him."

"How is your memory, Frijole?" queried Judge.

"I have some trouble in rememberin' things," admitted Frijole.

"If you see him," said Henry, "you can tell him that Eric was not hurt much, and brought Josephine back to Tonto City. In fact, he exonerated Oscar."

"He—what?" asked Slim anxiously.

"He said that Oscar did not shoot him."

"Oh," said Slim. "That word had me worried. Then yuh don't want Oscar for any crime, eh?"

"Merely for questioning, Slim."

"Huh?"

"For instance," said Henry, "where were you when the bank was robbed, Slim?"

"Up in the dance hall, listenin' to the bull-fiddle."

"Where were you, Frijole?"

"Well, I'll tell yuh, Henry," said Frijole. "I was at the buckboard, when Oscar chased Eric down that alley. Me and Lightnin' and Thunder took out after 'em. Dark as hell in that alley, and all to once somebody met me, head-on. Man, I went as flat as a shirt bosom. Then somebody else walked the whole length of me, and I got sore and got out of that alley."

"What about you, Lightning?"

"Me and my leetle brodder go 'long," said Lightning.

"I theenk we are first. Somebody shoot gon in the dark, sometheeng heet me and I'm fall eento house, weeth my brodder."

"You fell into a house?" queried Henry. "What house?"

"Those bank door. He ees open."

"You and Thunder found the back door of the bank open, eh?"

"Sure."

"Could it be that you and Thunder lighted matches in there? No, that was later, I believe. Anyway, Mr. Baker identified one of the men as the leader of the bandits. What did you do, Lightning?"

"Go out pretty queek," said Lightning.

"How much did they get, Henry?" asked Frijole.

"We have not heard yet. Mr. Baker said it would require several hours to check up the loss. However, it was practically all the money in the bank, plus the Shoshone Chief payroll. Frijole, what do you know about what happened last night at the *Clarion* office?"

"*Clarion* office?" queried Frijole innocently.

"The editor, Mr. James Wadsworth Longfellow Pelly, was soaked in his own ink, and claims that his printing forms were so smashed up that he cannot publish this week. He thinks Oscar Johnson did it."

"He *thinks* so?" queried Slim.

"He said that the man wore a handkerchief over his face, but was a big man."

"Oscar," declared Frijole, "wouldn't be that smart, Henry. They'll have to hunt further."

"Unless somebody told him," suggested Judge.

"We didn't tell him," assured Slim. "Mebbe he ain't so dumb."

"Set down," invited Frijole, "and eat these cakes while they're nice and hot."

Lightning and Thunder made their exit and went down to the stable. Putting up an appearance of working, they met in the willows along the dry-wash. Lightning had a good idea where Frijole and Slim had gone, and found their footprints in the sand off a cattle trail. From there it was a simple matter to find where they had dug into the sand.

"Pretty damn leetle man they bury here," observed Lightning.

With their hands they managed to unearth the grain sack. Sitting on their haunches, they made an examination of the contents. The find was so immense that they were speechless. Finally Lightning said:

"Madre de Dios! Sleem and Frijole rob those banks!"

"I theenk so all the time," declared Thunder.

Lightning looked helplessly around. "What ees to do?" he whispered. "Eef they catch Sleem and Frijole, they lock heem up for those?"

"Leesten!" hissed Thunder. "That ees more money than you ever see een my life. That ees not sometheeng for sell— that ees for spend. We hide those money."

"We keep heem, eh? *Dios Mio,* we are reech. Maybe we go back to *Mejico* and be reech man. You wan' be reech man, my leetle brodder?"

"Sure, I'm like try leetle beet, myself, personally. Hm-m-m-m. We mus' hide damn good and keep your mouth shut. Come, we find good place for hide those sack."

A few moments later the two little Mexicans were making their way through the willows, searching for the place to hide their great wealth.

5

THE LAW IS LACKADAISICAL

HENRY HARRISON CONROY stood in the office doorway and gazed moodily up the main street of Tonto City. Judge Van Treece had his favorite chair tilted back against the office wall, and was deeply engrossed in a dog-eared copy of Shakespeare.

"Storm coming up, Judge," observed Henry. Judge lifted his eyes and quickly saved his glasses from falling off his nose.

"Eh? Storm, you say? At this time of year?"

"Yes. I just saw Big Jim Harris, John Calvert and Albert Rose together. I believe they went into the King's Castle for a drink."

Judge groaned. "When three good fellows get together. Well, I suppose it concerns the fact that we have not cleared up the bank robbery at Scorpion Bend."

"Unfortunately, yes," murmured Henry. "I wonder who the well dressed stranger is, who has been most of the day with Mr. Jim Harris."

"I saw him this morning," said Judge. "Possibly a traveling salesman, Henry."

"Bank supplies, I suppose," agreed Henry. "However,

our question may be answered, as the gentleman seems to be coming our way."

The man came directly to the office and Henry welcomed him with a smile.

"You are the sheriff, I believe," the man said pleasantly. "I am Charles Cleary, state bank examiner. My card, sir."

"You are most welcome, Mr. Cleary," said Henry. "Sit down, please. By the way, this is Mr. Van Treece, my deputy, Mr. Cleary."

"A pleasure, indeed," said Mr. Cleary, and sat down in the proffered chair.

"My visit is not at all official," stated Cleary. "I merely ran down here to see what progress had been made in the new bank. That robbery at Scorpion Bend was most unfortunate."

"Most," agreed Henry quietly. "You—er—came to examine the bank, but found that an examination was unnecessary, I presume."

"That is very true. I was a day late. It seems that the Scorpion Bend Bank must close its doors because the assets of the bank have all vanished. That will affect a lot of people."

"Nearly every person in this county who had enough money to make a deposit," said Henry. "It will make bad business for our new banking organization. By the way, Mr. Cleary, do you bank examiners notify a bank as to the date you will appear for the examination?"

"Rarely," answered the examiner. "My work deals only with banks in small towns. However, it is routine work, and they may expect us at fairly spaced intervals."

"Do you know this Mr. Harris, who is to own the bank here, Mr. Cleary?"

"Only by reputation. I met him today for the first time. No doubt he will bring in an experienced man to take charge. It seems that banks in this part of the country have had rather hard times, due mostly to robberies. I advised Mr. Harris to install time-lock vaults, but he said he could not afford such an expense. But as long as they depend on old-fashioned combination locks, I suppose they must take a chance that someone will force them. It does not give the public much protection."

HENRY WAS ABOUT to say something when in walked Big Jim Harris, John Calvert and Albert Rose, the commissioners. Mr. Cleary excused himself and left the office.

"Sit down, gentlemen," invited Henry.

"Was the bank examiner lookin' yuh over?" asked Big Jim.

"Yes," admitted Henry. "He remarked that if our cells were not any more effective than our bank vaults—"

"All right," growled Big Jim. "Of course you realize that the whole country is aroused over the robbery of the Scorpion Bend bank."

"It will financially embarrass many people," agreed Henry.

"Yeah! And here you sit, polishing your nose! Why in hell don't yuh get out and try to find the robbers? Do yuh expect them to come here, confess, and return the loot?"

"Why, the idea is very good, Mr. Harris. I never thought of that."

"What's good about it?"

"It would save everyone a lot of trouble."

"Wait a minute," interrupted Calvert. "Henry, you have solved some pretty tough cases while you have been sheriff.

I just told Jim and Al that we ought to let you go ahead. Jim says you are not going ahead. You must admit that you have done no visible work toward helping the bank get back their money."

"Gentlemen," said Henry quietly, "if you were waiting at a rathole, expecting to kill or capture said rodent, would you proceed quietly and carefully, or would you hire a band to serenade you and the rat while you waited for its appearance?"

"I can see your point," said Calvert quickly.

"Well, I can't," declared Big Jim. "There's no rat-hole for you to watch, and no rat to be captured."

"That is merely your opinion, my dear sir," Henry smiled. "I believe it was the work of a rat or a number of first-class rats—and that they have a rat-hole."

"And," queried Rose, "do you have any idea who the rats are?"

"When you play draw poker, Mr. Rose, you only show your cards after all bets are made. My cards are face-down, if you do not mind."

"I believe I was right," said Calvert.

"How do yuh mean?" asked Big Jim.

"When I said we should let Henry work things out for himself."

"Aw, he's pullin' the wool over yore eyes, John. He don't know a damn bit more about it than we do. I tell yuh, we've got to have another sheriff in this office. If we can elect—"

"Tck, tck, tck!" clucked Henry. "Enter the politician. My advice to you would be to hire a hall, Mr. Harris." Big Jim got to his feet and walked to the doorway, where he turned.

"You two came down here with me, intending to demand

immediate action, or resignation, and what do you do? Listen to a cock-and-bull story and agree with him. Yo're a hell of a lot of good to this county. All right, string along with him. I'll be damned if I do. I'm goin' to let the people of Wild Horse Valley know that I'm workin' for their interests. When I get through, Henry Conroy will be lucky to poll even his own vote."

Big Jim stomped off down the wooden sidewalk.

"As a matter of fact," said Henry quietly, "I have never yet voted for myself."

"Do you think you can beat Cash Silverton?" asked Rose.

"I doubt it," replied Henry calmly.

"I believe you're wrong," said Calvert. "Cash Silverton is not well known, and the people feel that he is strictly Big Jim's candidate."

Henry shrugged his shoulders. "I am no politician, gentlemen. I have never asked a man to vote for me, and I shall not do so this time."

"Henry," said Rose, "if you can clear up this robbery case, you'll be elected in spite of anything you can do."

"I should hate to have anyone feel that the cleaning up of that case was done for political purposes."

"Good!" exclaimed Calvert. "Well, we may as well go, Al. Big Jim will probably hate both of us."

AFTER THEY HAD gone, Henry sat there, his eyes squinted in deep thought. Judge's pouched eyes regarded Henry with jaundiced disgust.

"Little Henry at the rat-hole," he murmured.

"Eh?" grunted Henry. "Oh, yes—ghastly, wasn't it, Judge?"

"Ghastly? It was damnable, sir. Misleading them in that manner."

"For the moment," said Henry quietly, "I was Sherlock Holmes. Had they questioned me further, I might have risen to great heights."

"But, sir, your cards were face-down, you remember."

"Luckily, sir; the back of a deuce is the same as the back of an ace. Unless, of course, they are marked."

"I feel," said Judge, "that you merely staved off the inevitable."

"And," added Henry, "in the long run I shall be unmasked, disclosing only a grinning, red-nosed ex-thespian, who thought he knew something about crime and criminals. Ah, well—it is life, I suppose."

Judge craned his neck and looked toward the doorway. Henry turned and saw a little boy, not over five years of age, barefooted, bareheaded, clad in a misfit shirt and weathered overalls. The child's curly hair was a startling golden blond.

He looked at Henry, his big, blue eyes wide, and said:

"Howdy."

"The angel speaks!" whispered Henry. "Come in, my boy."

The little boy drew a deep breath and shook his curly head.

"Gotta go now," he said, and went pattering up the sidewalk.

Henry rubbed his eyes and looked at Judge, who was staring at the empty doorway over the tops of his glasses.

"Just like a patch of sunshine," said Henry. Poetic figures of speech came easily to him.

"By gad, it was!" exclaimed Judge. "I have never seen that child before. He spoke to you, sir?"

"He said 'howdy'."

Henry got to his feet and walked to the doorway. Further up the street a man was lifting the child to the seat of a one-horse covered wagon. He climbed in and the sad-looking equipage moved up the street. Henry came back.

"If we could clear up that robbery," said Judge, "the voters of Wild Horse Valley would build a monument in your honor, Henry."

"Ghastly things, monuments, Judge; especially if one is still alive. Imagine me, in the full flush of manhood, looking upon a replica of my face and form."

"Full flush of—what?" queried Judge.

"There is no use going into that," Henry said.

OSCAR JOHNSON, LIGHTNING and Thunder went to Tonto City that evening, leaving Slim Pickins and Frijole at the ranch. As soon as the three men were gone, Slim said:

"I'd shore like to feast upon the flesh-pots, as they say, Frijole. All m' life I've wanted to go t' town and have money to spend. Every danged payday I owe more'n I've got comin'."

"Meanin' which?" queried Frijole.

"Me and you," explained Slim quietly, "are rich. Aw, we wouldn't have to take enough to make it look suspicious. Mebbe forty, fifty dollars per each. That wouldn't hurt anybody, would it? Yuh know what I mean, don'tcha?"

"Now that yuh speak of it," said Frijole, "I kinda get m'self a hanker. I'd like to play a few hands of poker and feel that I wasn't causin' m'self a lot of depravity if I lost a dollar and six-bits. We'll jist extract a small amount, eh?"

"That's it. We'll dig her loose before it gits dark, and then we can change clothes afterwards. C'mon."

"I feel jist like I'm goin' to a bank," said Slim, as they climbed through the corral fence.

"I never had any in a bank," said Frijole. "Never had enough. Do yuh know, Slim, we control a fortune? We've got all the money of Wild Horse Valley. But it don't make me swell-headed. Naw, I'm jist as common as I allus has been. Here's where we turn off."

They found the spot, and Frijole began digging in the loose sand while Slim stood over him, eyes searching the hole. Finally Frijole stepped around and looked closely.

"Hell, it was right there!" he whispered. "You know that, Slim."

"Yeah," nodded Slim blankly. "Yeah, that's the exact place."

"And," added Frijole, "nobody knowed it but us."

"I was thinkin' that same thing," said Slim. "Just me and you—and I didn't touch it."

"You think I did, you long-legged gallinipper?"

"I didn't—and she's gone, Frijole. I wouldn't touch it—not unless you was along."

"Yeah?" queried Frijole. "Well, she's gone, and I didn't—" Frijole reached down and picked up an object from the sand. It was a half-smoked Mexican cigarette. Slim leaned in close. Thunder and Lightning were the only ones around the JHC who smoked Mexican cigarettes.

"It was in the bottom of a boot-print," said Frijole. "If I had any idea that them two—"

"They both smoke 'em," said Slim. "They smell like hell."

"I'll tell yuh," said Frijole, "I'll betcha one of them Mexicans was watchin' from the winder that mornin', Slim. They saw us go away with the shovel."

"All right," said Slim savagely, "let's go to town. I aim to get me a couple Mexicans."

"Wait a minute, Slim. We've got to go easy in this. We can't come right out and accuse 'em of takin' that money, yuh know. One word from them little devils, and we'd all be in jail. Nope, we've got to go careful."

"But they've done beat us out of our fortunes, Frijole."

"It's an awful come-down, I'll admit that, but let us go easy. We'll ease it out of 'em, or my name ain't Frijole Cullison. You let me do all the talkin'. It may take time, but we'll git 'em. We'll go to town, jist like nothin' had happened."

"All right," agreed Slim grudgingly. "But I don't know why Henry keeps them two crooked, little devils. They'd steal yuh blind. I've always said that a honest man hadn't ort to associate with fellers like that."

JAMES WADSWORTH LONGFELLOW PELLY glanced cautiously around the office before accepting the chair beside Henry's desk. Judge was tilted against the wall in his favorite chair, while Oscar Johnson, who had recently arrived from the ranch, sat on the edge of the office cot and helped himself to a pinch of Copenhagen snuff. The room was not too well lighted by a single oil lamp.

"You wished to see me, sir?" queried Henry blandly.

"Yes, I came down here to—to protest," replied Pelly. "Unless some restitution is made, I am afraid I shall appeal to the law."

"My goodness!" exclaimed Henry. "Is it that serious, Mr. Pelly?"

"My whole edition ruined," said Pelly. "At least fifty pounds of ink gone. Of all the damnable attacks I ever saw, that was the very worst. I was manhandled, I tell you! My forms all pied."

"But what have I to do about it, Mr. Pelly?" queried Henry.

"You know as well as I do who did it!" snapped the editor indignantly.

"My dear man, you were there—I was not. How on earth—"

"You are not accusing *us,* are you?" queried Judge warningly.

Pelly squirmed and looked at Oscar, who was looking at him, an expression of cold amusement on his big face.

"It—it was a big man," said Pelly huskily. Henry nodded.

"No doubt the same man who robbed the bank, sir. Mr. Baker said he was a very big man, you remember."

"But why should that man do all this to me?" asked Pelly.

"Perhaps he knew you," suggested Judge. "Perhaps he has been the subject of one of your scintillating editorials."

"I do not believe it, sir," declared Pelly. "Mr. Conroy, you said that Oscar Johnson promised to come and see me some time."

"T'ank you werry much," said Oscar blandly. "Ay vill be glad to."

"No, I did not mean that. You see, I—"

"Ay don't like to have anybody kid vit me," warned Oscar.

"Oh, I am not kidding."

"Good! Ay vill come."

"You spoke of the law," reminded Henry.

"It was assault," declared Pelly. "I was nearly killed. Isn't that something for the law? My forms were destroyed, my ink spilled, and my whole office was in terrible shape. I miss one whole week. Surely you can see the justice—"

James W.L. Pelly ceased speaking as a man came into the office. He was a stranger in Tonto City, tall, emaciated, bearded, poorly dressed.

"Are you the sheriff?" he asked huskily.

"I am, sir," replied Henry. "The sheriff, and at your service."

Slowly the man's eyes swept the room. He glanced through the window behind Henry's chair, drew a deep breath and began:

"Sheriff, I've got a job for you. Four years ago I came out of a northern prison. A man framed me into that stretch. He was my brother-in-law—later. My kid sister had money, jewels, a fine home, until that snake came into her life. He robbed her, mistreated her, and she died a short while after her baby was born.

"But he got away with every dollar. I don't know where he went, but I took that kid and started on his trail. I've got tuberculosis, Sheriff. Maybe you can see that. Anyway, my trail ended here—today, when I saw my man. For four years I've only had one goal—and that was to kill him. But"—he steadied himself against the desk, and a queer smile moved his bearded lips—"I—I can't do it. After all these years of hell, I can't kill him, Sheriff."

"I believe I understand," said Henry quietly.

"It looked easy," said the man. "I'm a good shot. The penalty of the law don't bother me. Probably never live to be punished. But I've never committed a crime. I come from a good family, and I—I'd like to have them realize I was innocent. If I kill him, I never can prove it. Don't you see?"

"Of course, I can see it," Henry nodded. "You are right, Mr.—"

"Langley. Fred Langley."

"Thank you, Mr. Langley. What is this man's name?"

"His name is Frank Elkins."

"Elkins? I do not believe I have ever heard of a Frank Elkins."

"A name doesn't mean anything, Sheriff."

"True. Well, my dear sir, if you will just point out this man to me, I will surely make the arrest no matter what his name."

But as Henry surged out of his chair, the window pane behind him disappeared in a shower of glass, and Fred Langley spun around on his heels, buckled at the knees, and almost fell over Pelly. From out in the dark street came the rattling report of a rifle shot.

6

BOY NAMED BUCKSHOT

OSCAR JOHNSON LEAPED to his feet and dived toward the doorway, only to meet two running men. One of them bounced off Oscar, collided with Pelly, and they went to the floor together.

Oscar stumbled and fell sprawling out across the sidewalk, while Judge, trying to tilt forward, skidded the rear legs of his chair and went down against the wall, both feet waving in the air. The second of the two men who met Oscar had landed in a corner, and he sat there mouth wide open, trying to pump air into his agonized lungs.

Henry said calmly, "If this is a game, gentlemen, please deal me out. It is too rough."

"Who hit me?" demanded Pelly, still dazed. "I never was so mortified in my life."

"Somebody kicked my chair loose," complained Judge. "Look at it! The back is broken and—"

"Oscar!" called Henry. "Get Doctor Knowles—quickly!"

"That man!" panted Pelly. "He's hurt?"

"That man," replied Henry, "is dead."

"Dead? My God! Right in the sheriff's office!"

"Something good to write about," Henry told him.

It seemed as though the whole town of Tonto City came

to find out the reason for that one shot. Judge refused to let the crowd in until the doctor had made his examination and report. The two men who had collided with Oscar were Thunder and Lightning.

"Lightning," said Henry, "where did you come from?"

"*Mejico,*" replied Lightning meekly.

"How am I, you hope and trus'?" queried Thunder. "I damn near broke your arm pretty damn close from my elbow."

"I am not asking your nationality, Lightning," said Henry. "Where did you come from, immediately following that shot?"

"Ees that so?" queried Lightning in amazement. "I am ver' much surprise' at theenking about anytheeng—I hope."

Thunder piously crossed himself. "Dead?" he asked.

"Did you see the man with the gun?" thundered Judge.

"Sure, I don' theenk so—much," replied Thunder. "We never have one dreenk. Both of us behave yourself. *Por Dios,* we theenk those man shoot at us; so we come queek. I don't bilieve you, eh?"

The doctor shoved his way through the crowd at the doorway and began his examination.

One man volunteered the information that he had seen this man, together with a little red-headed boy, earlier in the day, and that their one-horse covered wagon was tied at the upper end of the main street.

The dead man was taken to Doctor Knowles' place, and Henry and Judge went up the street to find the little boy asleep in the old wagon. He was too frightened to answer questions, but he clung to Henry. They took him down to the office, where Henry attempted to question him.

Somehow Henry hung on, and they went madly
careening around the perilous curves.

"Where's Uncle Fred?" he asked.

"I suppose we may as well explain," said Henry. "Uncle Fred was shot a little while ago."

"Dead?" asked the little boy. Henry nodded. "But you do not need to worry, my boy. What is your name?"

"Buckshot," replied the boy.

"Buckshot? Have you no other name?"

"Nope—just Buckshot. The horse is named Pancho."

"Do you know how old you are, Buckshot?"

"Nope."

"Did you travel around the country all the time with Uncle Fred?"

"Sure."

"What a life for a baby!" exclaimed Judge.

"Who's a baby?" demanded Buckshot.

"My mistake," said Judge soberly.

"Did you have any supper?" asked Henry.

"Nope. We had some beans for breakfast—cola ones. Uncle Fred said we was broke."

"My goodness!" exclaimed Henry. "Cold beans for breakfast and nothing since. My boy, how would you like a big supper, with milk and perhaps a piece of pie?"

"Where can you get it?" asked the youngster.

Henry held out his arms, and the youngster fairly leaped.

"He certainly takes to you," remarked Judge.

"This boy shows good judgment. While I take him to the restaurant, you go to the hotel and tell them to move an extra bed into our room. For probably the first time in his life, Buckshot is not going to sleep with his clothes on, wrapped in a blanket and on the hard bottom of a wagon. No clothes, not enough food and—how long since you had a bath, Buckshot?"

"I don't remember," replied the boy. "What is your name?"

"Just call me Uncle Henry," the sheriff told him.

"Sure." Buckshot smiled. "I like you."

"Son," said Henry soberly, "I feel blessed above all men. Hang on and we'll soon have you confronting a big meal. Judge, you see about the extra bed."

HENRY CARRIED BUCKSHOT down to a restaurant, where he proceeded to order a meal that would have satisfied a working man. Buckshot looked at it in amazement, but he dug right in, while Henry beamed. Frijole Bill, trailed by Thunder and Lightning, came down there, and Buckshot was more than mildly interested in Frijole's mustache, which twitched nervously.

"What do you think of him?" asked Henry proudly.

"I'm tryin' to classify him," replied Frijole. "Looks fine."

"Pretty swell keed, eh?" said Lightning. "I'm look like heem, w'en I am leetle feller—I hope."

"Red hair and blue eyes, I suppose," said Henry.

"Sure. I'm change leetle beet, I'm theenk, if possible."

Oscar came in, beaming widely. "Das ha'ar is a fine looking boy," he declared. "Ay vant to bounce him on my knee. Ay look like him ven Ay vars young. By Yimminy, Ay had hair yust like mostard."

"And some big brute bounced you on his knee, I presume."

"You bat you, Ay vars bounced good."

"You show it," said Henry. "How are you coming, Buckshot?"

"Pretty full, Uncle Henry. Awful good food."

"That is fine. Tomorrow we will see about new clothes. No doubt you would like some new clothes."

"Boots, too?"

"Possibly."

"And a gun, too?"

"My goodness! At your age?"

"Ay have old von he can have," offered Oscar.

"Indeed! A baby with a gun!"

"Who's a baby?" asked Buckshot.

"Stout fellow!" applauded Henry, as he picked up the little fellow. "Go home and let me put this newest buckaroo to bed."

As they started for the door, Big Jim Harris and Charles Baker, the banker from Scorpion Bend, came in. Henry stopped and looked them over.

"Of all the damned actions I ever heard of, this beats 'em

all!" exploded Big Jim. "A man is murdered in your office, and all you do is act nursemaid to a kid. Conroy, it is time that the county threw you out of office. This town could be full of thieves and murderers, and you would not even be interested. Why, damn it, man, you haven't even tried to find out who fired that shot."

Oscar Johnson shoved his way between Henry and Big Jim. "Ay don't like the way you talk, Big Jim," he said coldly.

"Why, you big squarehead!" snapped Big Jim. "I'll knock your head off!"

Big Jim Harris was a powerful man, nearly as big as Oscar, but his right-hand punch to the side of Oscar's jaw failed even to knock the big Swede off balance.

The next moment Oscar's looping right crashed square on Big Jim's nose, and Big Jim went backward against the little cashier's counter, tearing it loose from the floor, and Big Jim sprawled flat on his back, knocked cold. Oscar whirled on the amazed Mr. Baker.

"You vant some of dis?" he asked quickly.

"My God—no!" gasped the banker.

The two frightened Chinese babbled Cantonese at the top of their voices, as they peered out from the kitchen. Henry said:

"Good evening to you, Mr. Baker. Nice to have met you again."

Then he walked out, carrying Buckshot, who did not seem greatly perturbed over the fight.

Charles Baker managed to get Big Jim back on his feet, and took him down to Doctor Knowles. Big Jim was choking with wrath, and he had a badly broken nose. Doctor

Knowles stopped the bleeding, but he was dubious about that nose ever being very good-looking again.

"Every bit of bone is smashed," he told Big Jim. "I will do my best, but I am afraid it will always look rather flat."

"Figs id ub the best you cad, doc," pleaded Big Jim. "I'll ged thad dabed Swede if id's the last thig I ever do."

THUNDER AND LIGHTNING went back to the ranch without Oscar, who stayed at the office. They took a quart of tequila along to help them recover from a strenuous evening.

"W'en we deeg up those *dinero?*" queried Thunder. "I wan' go back to *Mejico* and be reech man. These damn Wil' Horse Valley get too toff for me, I theenk, eef notheeng happens."

"*Mucho tiempo,*" said Lightning. "Eef you queet now, I weel suspec' you. Take plenty time. Some day we weel queet and go to *Mejico* and leeve reech from our old ages. You onnerstand, I hope."

They stabled the buckboard team and went into the house, where they found a hunk of cold roast beef. Pouring the tequila in two large glasses, they sat down to enjoy life.

Tequila is very potent. Distilled from a mash made of maguey, it has all the stealth of a marauding Apache, and the power of the Supreme Court. Long before the quart was finished Thunder and Lightning had mellowed to the point where they were already sharing their wealth with the peon classes.

Suddenly the front door opened and in came two masked men, guns in hand. Thunder and Lightning sat up.

"Don't move," growled one of the men.

"No move—I hope," agreed Lightning owlishly.

"All right. If yuh lie to us, I'll shave yore ears off. Where'd yuh hide the money yuh stole from that bank?"

"Madre de Dios!" gasped Lightning. "We never still money from banks."

"You stole the money and hid it," declared the masked man. "You show us where yuh hid that money, or you'll die right here. Or do yuh want a bullet in yore darned gizzard?"

"No bullet een the geezard," declined Lightning. "How you know we hide those money? How you prove those theengs, *amigo?*"

"We seen yuh!" snapped the other masked man.

"Por Dios!" gasped Thunder. "They seen you hide heem."

"Now," growled one of the men, "we're gettin' to it. You hid it."

"Ees that so?" queried Lightning. "You know w'ere we hide heem?"

"Yo're damn right we do."

"Eef you know the place, w'y don' you go get heem?"

That was unanswerable. The two masked men debated silently. Lightning blinked thoughtfully. Finally he said to one of them:

"W'ere you get Frijole's shirt? You keel heem maybe—I hope not."

"Keel two," declared Thunder. "Those man got Sleem's belt!"

"Shut up!" snapped one of the men. "You've talked too much. Tell us where yuh hid that money, or we'll—"

"Madre de Dios!" gasped Lightning. "More!"

The front door opened silently and three more masked men stepped into the room, covering the four men.

"Drop them guns!" snapped a voice, and two guns thudded to the floor.

"What the hell!" snorted one of the newcomers. Another said:

"What's the idea of the masks? Step back and let us get those guns."

One of the men secured the guns. Lightning said:

"W'at ees the masquerade for, I hope?"

"All right, you two," growled one of them. "Take off the masks."

Very sheepishly Frijole and Slim Pickins removed their masks.

"Looks like joke, eh?" remarked Thunder.

"Keep thinkin' that, and you'll git yourself a tombstone," growled one of the men. "What did these two masked jaspers want?"

"Money," replied Lightning. "They theenk we rob banks—but I hope not."

"Oh, so they think you robbed the bank, eh? Well, didja?"

"I cross hees heart, I hope you die," swore Lightning.

"I'll be damned! If you didn't, who did? Who got that money? Don't lie about it. We came to get that money, and we're goin' to git it, if we have to kill all four of you and turn this ranch upside down. All right—start talkin'."

"You fellers have got the wrong idea," said Slim. "Me and Frijole was havin' some fun with these two Mexicans. We ain't got no money. We didn't rob no bank, and you know it."

"We ort to," chuckled one of the men. "We robbed it ourselves."

"There yuh are," sighed Frijole. "They got it. We can't stop yuh from robbin' us, but yuh won't git over six-bits."

"Listen, feller. One of yuh swapped sacks with us, and we want the right sack. If you think we're goin' to let such fellers as you beat us out of a fortune, yo're all wrong. Yo're layin' yourselves open to a good pistol whippin', so start talkin'. We ain't got all the time there is—and we want that money."

"Swapped sacks?" queried Frijole innocently. "H-m-m-m. Did any of you fellers swap sacks with anybody?"

"Sounds loco to me," declared Slim. "Who'd swap sacks?"

"Enough of this talkin'!" snapped one of the men. "We came here to get that money. If you don't—"

At that moment one of the horses at the porch evidently decided to shake itself violently, and the heavy romal on the end of the reins slapped against the porch. Frijole, facing the doorway, yelled:

"Look out, Oscar! Git back!"

The three masked men sprang aside, out of line with the doorway, trying to look outside and also keep their eyes on the other four men.

"That damn Swede!" exclaimed one of them. "He *would* come!"

"Uh-huh." Frijole nodded calmly. "And as soon as he gits that sawed-off shotgun from the bunkhouse, you'll wish for better weather. That Swede's bad medicine, if yuh ask me."

The three masked men took him at his word. Swiftly they backed to the doorway, slammed the door behind them and dived for their horses. A moment later and three sets of hoofs thundered back down the road toward the front gate. Frijole barred the door, his mustache twitching with mirth.

"Where-at is Oscar?" queried Slim.

"Prob'ly sleepin' in the office," replied Frijole. "Man, we shore scared them masqueraders. Wait a minute and I'll fetch out a fresh jug of prune juice."

7

TAKE AIM AT THE MOON

DOCTOR KNOWLES, IN searching the clothing of Fred Langley, found a remnant of a letter to Langley from an inmate of the prison from which Langley had been released. It bore the prison stamp. Henry sent the following telegrams to that prison:

> FRED LANGLEY EX-INMATE YOUR INSTITU-TION KILLED HERE PRESUMABLY BY BROTHER-IN-LAW NAMED ELKINS BUT UNDER ASSUMED NAME. HAVE YOU ANY INFORMATION REGARD-ING ELKINS OR ANY DESCRIPTION BY WHICH HE MIGHT BE IDENTIFIED? ANY INFORMATION WOULD BE APPRECIATED.

"Shooting at the moon," remarked Judge.

Buckshot, clad in new clothes, bathed and well fed, sat on the edge of Henry's desk. "Gotta have a dog," he stated.

"I suppose that is true," agreed Henry.

"Named Epidermis," said Buckshot happily.

"Epidermis?" queried Judge. "What a name for a dog!"

"We had one," Buckshot informed him. "Uncle Fred said he ran away with a lady coyote." He looked solemn.

"Was he a good dog?" chuckled Henry.

"Sure. Uncle Fred said you couldn't blame him for pullin' out. Uncle Fred said he was just like a man—always lookin' for love and food."

"My goodness!" exclaimed Henry. Judge shook his head.

"Imagine that from the mouth of a babe!" he said.

Doctor Knowles came down to the office. Arrangements had been made for the inquest. The doctor had just come from the King's Castle Saloon, where he had made an adjustment on Big Jim's nose.

"I imagine his olifactory nerves are rather muddled," said Henry.

"Muddled! I don't believe any are left, Henry. I am afraid that Mr. Harris, depending on his sense of smell, will never know an onion from a rose. A kicking horse couldn't have done a better job."

Nearly every one in Tonto City was interested in the inquest and in the little red-headed boy; so the courtroom was crowded. No one knew the deceased, and only Thunder and Lightning had had any chance to see the killer. Henry warned the doctor that Thunder and Lightning would be of no use as witnesses, but the doctor, acting as the county coroner, insisted. Lightning was solemnly sworn and faced the six-man jury.

"Lightning," said Doctor Knowles, "it seems that you and your brother were outside the sheriff's office when the fatal shot was fired. I want you to tell the jury your story."

"My story?" queried Lightning.

"That's right—tell them your story."

"Sure," smiled Lightning. "Frijole tell me one good story.

You like from hearing those story of the drommer and the former's daughter—I hope not?"

"Hold it!" snorted Judge. "Not that one. It is no use, doc. You may as well forget their testimony."

"But these two men saw the shot fired, Judge. Perhaps Thunder can tell it better than Lightning. Swear Thunder. Yes, you are excused, Lightning." Thunder was duly sworn.

"My leetle brodder," explained Thunder expansively, "ees no good for the telling. Always he ees getting the cart behin' the horses, I'm theenk, probably. W'at you want for hearing, doctor?"

"Did you see the shot fired?"

"Sure. My brodder yalls, *'Cuidado!'* jus' like those."

"We don't care what he yelled. Did you see the man who fired the shot?"

"Sure, I see heem."

"You did? Thunder, who—"

"Just a moment!" interrupted Henry. He placed Buckshot on the chair and came over to the coroner. "If Thunder saw this man, doctor, this is no place to disclose his identity or description. That is something for my office alone."

"Yes, you are right," agreed the coroner. "Gentlemen," he turned to the jury, "there is no further evidence; so you need not leave your seats to bring in the usual verdict."

"You word it for us, doc," said the tall lanky foreman.

"What is to be done with the child?" asked one of the men.

"I will take care of the boy," said Henry firmly.

"But he needs a woman's care."

"Who does?" asked Buckshot, and the crowd roared.

"You'll have plenty time to nurse him after election,"

called a voice from the back of the room, which brought another laugh.

"I believe," stated Judge ponderously, "that the intelligent voters of Wild Horse Valley will speak with ballots and not through the vapid vocal cords of an ignorant heckler, who is ashamed to show his face."

"Yeah, and you'll go back to brushin' flies off a bar," said the voice again.

THE CORONER READ the verdict and people began filing out toward the stairway. Suddenly there was a commotion, a few strangled bursts of profanity, followed by a dull crash. Oscar Johnson shoved his way through the crowd and came back to Henry.

"What happened out there?" asked Henry.

"Oh, Ay yust t'rowed some wapid vocal cords downstairs," said Oscar, grinning.

"My goodness! Who was it, Oscar?"

"It vars Cash Silverton."

"Was he the one who made those remarks?" asked Judge.

"Yah, su-ure. Ay vars right behind him, Yudge."

"Was he hurt?" asked Henry anxiously.

"Ay don't t'ink so, Hanry; he bounced vonce before he hit bottom."

"For once," said Judge soberly, "I have no fault to find with the Vikings."

They took Buckshot back to the office, and on the way they saw Doctor Knowles hurrying over to the King's Castle.

"It appears," remarked Henry, "that Oscar may have been a trifle rough with Mr. Silverton."

"Big brute," said Buckshot casually.

"Exactly!" snorted Judge. "An amazing observation for his years."

Charles Baker, the Scorpion Bend banker without a bank, came down to the office. He was greatly depressed over the situation, and anxious for something to be done about recovering the lost money.

"We are doing everything possible," assured Henry. "It has been a severe blow to everyone, Mr. Baker. I am afraid it will make it doubly difficult for Mr. Harris to launch his new bank here. People will be afraid of banks."

"I realize that," agreed the banker. "In fact, Mr. Harris has offered me the position of executive in this new bank. Of course, you must realize that the Scorpion Bank is ruined. There is no chance to reopen the institution—and I feel that this is my opportunity."

"By all means," said Henry. "Mr. Harris is a very fine man."

Baker looked curiously at Henry. "It is rather queer to hear *you* say that, Mr. Conroy."

"My dear Mr. Baker, I bear no malice. While Mr. Harris and I may not agree on certain policies, I appreciate his right to differ with me. I may be entirely wrong. Every man has a right to his own opinions."

"Was Cash Silverton badly hurt?" asked Judge.

"Painfully, I believe," replied Baker. "His remarks were ill-advised."

"Perhaps," said Henry, "Mr. Silverton has never studied diplomacy."

"He is merely a hard-jawed, ignorant puncher," declared Judge.

"Mr. Harris' choice," added Henry quietly, as he adjusted

Buckshot's neckerchief. "What do you think of our little buckaroo, Mr. Baker?"

"I know little about children," said Baker stiffly.

"I'm a rootin', tootin' puncher," said Buckshot. "Frijole said I was. He's goin' to make me some cookies and learn me to shoot a gun. Then I can have one of my own, Uncle Henry."

"What is to be done about the boy?" asked Baker.

"That is something to be decided in the future," said Henry. "Just at present, Buckshot and I are getting along fine."

"Quite a responsibility. Well, I must go back to Scorpion Bend. We shall all be greatly interested in your investigation, I'm sure."

After Baker had left the office, Judge said:

"Henry, just why in the devil did he come down here?"

Henry smiled slowly. "I suppose he is anxious for the bank robbery to be solved. Judge, how long did Baker run the Scorpion Bend Bank?"

"About two years, I believe. Why do you ask, sir?"

"Just to make conversation, I suppose, Judge. How about some food, Buckshot? Are you hungry?"

"Sure." Buckshot grinned. "I could eat a raw dog. That's what Uncle Fred used to say."

"Maybe that is what became of Epidermis." Judge laughed.

THUNDER AND LIGHTNING got together at the JHC bunkhouse and discussed current issues. They realized that Slim and Frijole suspected them of digging up their treasure cache, and that Slim and Frijole were watching their every move. It was also very evident that the real bank robbers realized that someone at the JHC had accidentally taken possession of that money.

"I theenk they come back," said Lightning. "Pretty queek they cut your ears off right close to my damn head."

"Damn bad," agreed Thunder. "Maybe we better hide heem in place we can' remember."

"Money ees no good w'en you are dead," said Lightning sagely.

They wandered out by the corral where they stood around. Finally, feeling that they were not being watched, they slipped through the fence and made their way to the spot where they had hidden the loot from the Scorpion Bend Bank.

"I'm got queek idea," declared Lightning. "We deeg heem up, hide heem close to the corral. Tonight we tak' horse and go to *Mejico*. We hide those meelion dollar een *Mejico*. Pretty queek, maybe t'ree, four month, we queet those job and go back to *Mejico* to die from old ages, I hope not, weeth all those money. How you like from those?"

"*Buena!*" applauded Thunder. "I'm pretty smart, eh? Come on."

They had marked the spot, and while Thunder kept guard, Lightning proceeded to dig. He dug and dug until Thunder got nervous and came to him, wide-eyed, as Thunder stood staring at the hole in the sand.

"I be a damn liar, and that ees all I hope!" snorted Lightning.

"*Vamoso?*" asked Thunder huskily.

"Not here," whispered Lightning. "This ees the place."

Lightning got to his feet and looked with an evil expression upon his brother. Thunder said: "My leetle brodder, you maybe walk in my sleep?"

"You theenk I—*Madre de Dios*, you come here and deeg—alone?"

They glared at each other like two strange bulldogs, and began circling in the sand, but not getting close enough to grapple. In fact, they kept up that continuous circling, grimacing at each other, until Lightning accidently fell into the hole he had dug in the sand.

"Keeng's Hex!" he shouted, pawing sand out of his ears.

Thunder leaned against a mesquite, observing the scene solemnly. Slowly his brother got to his feet, and they looked each other over thoughtfully.

"W'at you theenk?" asked Thunder.

"I'm theenk we been robbed," declared Lightning. "Every time I get reech, somebody takes heem away from you. I fill for crying."

"You theenk Sleem and Frijole tak' heem?"

Lightning shrugged his shoulders. *"Quien sabe?"*

SOMEONE DOWN AT the ranch was calling Lightning's name; so they went sadly down through the brush and came out near the stable. Henry and Judge were at the ranch house, with Buckshot, who was trying to make a close acquaintance with Bill Shakespeare, the rooster. He stopped to consider Frijole.

"Hyah, cowboy," said the cook, grinning.

"Hyah, pardner," said the little boy soberly. "How's yore folks?"

"Well, I'd tell a man!" gasped Frijole. "I jist would!"

"Tell him what?" asked Buckshot.

"You'd be surprised," Frijole said.

Thunder and Lightning arrived and Buckshot looked them over with considerable interest.

"How am I, you hope?" queried Lightning.

"Beats me," declared Buckshot.

"*Por Dios!*" exclaimed Thunder. "Look at those boots!"

"W'at you theenk from those?" gasped Lightning. "*Chico vaquero.*"

"What are yuh goin' to do with the kid?" asked Frijole.

"Keep him," replied Henry.

"Yuh can't keep somebody else's kid, can yuh?"

"Don't you like him, Frijole?" asked Henry quietly.

"Well, yeah, I—sure, I like him. Buckshot, yuh can call me Uncle Bill."

"Too many uncles," said Buckshot. "I'll call yuh Frijole."

"That shore suits me. Do yuh like cookies?"

"Uh-huh—and mulligan."

"You'll do to take to the wagon," declared Frijole.

Henry and Judge took Thunder and Lightning down by the corral, where Henry said:

"Thunder, at the inquest you said you saw the man who fired the shot that killed the man in my office doorway. Are you able to tell me who that man is?"

"I never seen heem good," replied Thunder. "Pretty dark."

"That is what I suspected," sighed Judge. "Did you see him at all?"

"I don't theenk ver' much."

"Did… you… see… him… at… all?"

"Not all," said Thunder peacefully.

"What did he look like?" asked Henry.

"I theenk he was a man eef you are not meestaken, I hope."

"That should readily identify anyone," remarked Henry. "I felt that your identification would be about that complete, because if there had been any chance of your identification, that man would have killed you long before this."

"Good theeng he don't know heem, eh?" queried Lightning.

"I'm not too sure," said Judge dryly. "Personally, I hoped that the killer might have not been so sure you could not identify him."

8

PASS THE PRUNE JUICE

THE FOLLOWING MORNING Henry received a telegram, not from the warden of the penitentiary, but from the sheriff of an adjoining county. It read:

> STEVE ELKINS STILL WANTED HERE ON CHARGE OF ROBBERY AND SUSPICION OF MURDER. AGE ABOUT FORTY-FIVE HEIGHT ABOUT FIVE FEET ELEVEN INCHES WEIGHT ABOUT ONE HUNDRED AND EIGHTY HAIR DARK MIGHT BE GRAY NOW EYES BROWN. THIS MAN IS WELL EDUCATED AND HAS BEEN AN ACCOUNTANT. DRESSES WELL AND HAS PLEASING PERSONALITY. NO CRIMINAL RECORD BUT HAS USED SEVERAL ALIASES AND IS SAID TO BE DANGEROUS. ONLY IDENTIFYING MARK KNOWN IS A TRIANGLE SCAR ON BACK OF NECK BELOW COLLAR LINE. IF DISCOVERED ARREST AND NOTIFY US AT ONCE.
>
> AL RYAN SHERIFF

"That message simplifies everything," remarked Judge. "All you have to do is go around the country, looking down the back of each man's collar, Henry. The description possibly fitted this man five years ago, and is so meager that it could fit nearly any man, if he had brown eyes. At least, we know he is reputed to be dangerous."

"True," agreed Henry. "But that is superfluous. Any man who shoots his fellow man in the sheriff's office must be rated as dangerous—and nervy."

"You might put an ad in the Scorpion Bend *Clarion*, Henry."

"The *Clarion*, sir," replied Henry dryly, "is giving us plenty of free advertizing. I shudder to think what will be in that next issue, if Mr. Pelly secured another supply of ink. If not, he may open one of his arteries and print it in blood."

"There isn't enough red blood in his body to sign his name, if he only used initials," declared Judge. "But seriously, Henry, have you any inkling as to who might be Elkins?"

"You embarrass me, sir," replied Henry. "Were I to say I do, I would be lying. I am very much like that painting of a dejected-looking lady, trying to coax music from a broken-string harp."

"I believe," said Judge, "the title was 'Hope'."

"Exactly."

"Then you admit that your harp is broken?"

"She evidently did not—why should I? Judge, I feel that Buckshot needs the broadening influence of travel; so, unless something unforeseen happens, I shall take him for a stage ride to Scorpion Bend tomorrow."

"Just for what reason, if I may ask, sir?" demanded Judge.

"Oh just to indulge in my new hobby."

"And that is?"

"Trying to pick up some loose ends, Judge. And while I am gone, you might devote a little time to looking down the collars of a few of our best citizens. At your height, you should find this easily accomplished. Do not make it obvious, of course."

"I, sir," declared Judge, "have never been a collar-peeker."

"No, I suppose not, I presume you know the shape of a triangle, Judge?"

"Why, certainly."

"At least," said Henry dryly, "you could cooperate that much."

"Just what do you mean, sir?" queried Judge quickly.

"Oh, merely that in case I should discover a man with such a mark on the back of his neck, you could agree that it was a triangle mark."

Judge looked thoughtfully at Henry and drew a deep breath. "Did you ever, in your whole life, have a serious moment, Henry?"

"Perhaps—just for a moment, Judge. Just now, for instance, since you ask. You are a serious man. In fact, you have been serious all your life. Has it been a benefit to you? Have you made the people any happier, or made the world any brighter, because you were a serious-minded person?"

"Life itself is serious, Henry."

"Life is what we make it."

"I suppose you are right, Henry. God made you a clown."

"He did not! Don't blame the deity for our faults. He did not make you a lawyer. Take some of the discredit to yourself."

"The law is a dignified profession, sir."

"I believe," said Henry quietly, "we need a drink."

FRIJOLE AND SLIM PICKINS mourned the loss of that money over a jug of prune juice. There was little doubt that it had been unearthed by Thunder and Lightning, but just how to force them to confess and give up the plunder was a problem. But the prune juice solved it. Together they walked into the bunkhouse and pounced upon the siesta-taking Mexicans, who howled loudly.

"All right, you coffee-colored thieves," said Slim, "go ahead and tell us where yuh cached that money, or we'll saw off yore ears."

Frijole already had a long-bladed pocket knife in his hand and was making sawing motions with it. Lightning capitulated.

"*Madre de Dios,* we tell!" he yelped.

"Good!" grunted Slim. "Show us where you hid it."

Frijole took the shovel, and they followed the two Mexicans up through the brush to the spot where they had burrowed into the sand, trying to find it.

"We hide heem there," stated Lightning, pointing at the hole.

"Danged ignorants didn't have sense enough to fill up the hole," declared Frijole. "Lemme at it with the shovel."

Frijole dug and dug, while Slim and the two Mexicans squatted on their heels and watched him sweat. When the hole was about four feet square and four feet deep, Frijole flung his shovel aside and glared at Lightning.

"There ain't nothin' here!" he snorted. "You know dang well there ain't."

"Sure," agreed Lightning blandly. "We try to find heem biffore, but he ees gone."

"Gone?" queried Frijole. "Yuh mean—gone?"

"Went," said Thunder. "Somebody take heem."

"Yuh mean," said Slim, "yuh hid it here and somebody took it?"

"You cross his heart, I hope you die," swore Lightning. "We theenk maybe you get heem, Sleem."

"Listen!" snorted Frijole, thoroughly angered. "You knowed it was gone and yet you let me dig my heart out! I've got a notion—"

"You ask where we hide heem," remarked Lightning.

"Yeah, that's right, Frijole," said Slim. "But who got it? Who saw you hide it, Lightning?"

"Dios," suggested Thunder piously.

"Mebbe the Lord saw yuh hide it, but He never dug it up."

Thunder shrugged his shoulders. He had given his idea on the subject. Frijole sat on the edge of the hole and clawed at his mustache, trying to puzzle out the mystery. Finally he got to his feet and flung the shovel far into the brush.

"Just like a damn dream!" he snorted. "Git rich all to once—and then wake up. Shucks, I'll have to work all my life for a livin'!"

"W'at you theenk," asked Lightning, "Henry will theenk, w'en he know you two rob those bank?"

"We never robbed no bank, you ignorant wrangler!" yelped Frijole.

"I can' help w'at I am theenking," said Lightning.

"Well," said Frijole wearily, "there ain't no use standin' here, cryin' over spilled milk."

"Meelk?" queried Thunder. "Those was money."

"Aw, you danged—"

At that moment a rifle shot blasted along the rocky hills, quickly followed by another. Then came a splattering of revolver shots.

"What the hell!" snorted Slim. "C'mon!"

SLIM'S ORDER WAS entirely wasted because he was bringing up the rear, as all four of them headed for the ranch house, with Frijole in the lead, and gaining more lead at every jump. Several more revolver shots were fired, which only served to spur the runners on. They fairly skidded around a corner of the ranch house and dived through a doorway.

"Close!" panted Slim. "Mighty close."

"Close to what?" asked Frijole, panting for breath.

"My Gawd!" snorted Slim. "There wasn't one of them bullets that missed me more'n an inch. Frijole, I'm scared I'm a marked man."

"Well, you ain't been marked yet, cowboy. Lemme git at that rifle in the corner and I'll shore make 'em hard to find."

"The firin'-pin's busted," panted Slim.

"All right, by doggies, I'll git me an ax. I'm a hard man to attack thataway."

"You theenk somebody ees died?" asked Lightning.

"If they ain't—they will," declared Frijole. "You and Thunder keep back and lemme have m' will with them dry-gulchers."

"What'r yuh waitin' for—the cavalry?" asked Slim.

Thunder had his nose glued against a rear window, and now he yelled: "Here comes Danny, running on hees feet weethout a horse."

"Danny?" queried Frijole. "Must be back from Silver City."

Danny Regan, foreman of the JHC, hurried in through the kitchen and stopped in the entrance to the main room. Danny was limping a little, and one of his hands had been cut.

"Didn't yuh hear the shootin'?" he asked breathlessly.

"Thought I did, but wasn't sure," replied Slim. "What happened?"

"That's what I want to know! I was ridin' down almost to the clearin', when all to once I busted into two masked men on horseback. They both took a shot at me and one of 'em got my horse. It was all done mighty quick and without any conversation. Me and the horse went down together, but I fell free and started workin' on 'em with a six-gun. And more than that, I"—Danny hesitated—"I got one of 'em."

"You killed one?" gasped Frijole. Danny nodded.

"What—what became of the other, Danny?"

"Got away through the brush. I—I took a look at this feller, and he wasn't anybody I knew. Kinda makes yuh feel funny—shootin' a man yuh don't even know."

"Well, sir," said Frijole, "it reminds me of the first man I ever killed. I didn't know him from a side of sole-leather. Yuh see, me and Axhandle Jones was reppin' for the K Bar Seven along the Brazos. We wasn't expectin'—"

"Nobody else was either," interrupted Slim. "I've heard that tale, with variations and gestures for three years, and every time the dead man had a different name. Frijole, yuh danged liar, don'tcha re'lize that Danny's got a dead man out there in the brush?"

"Jist a stranger," said Frijole. "He'll keep."

"Keep!" snorted Danny. "We've got to notify Henry and Doc Knowles as quick as we can. But what on earth were they doin' out there? Why would masked men be watchin' the ranch house, I wonder?"

"Shore queer," admitted Slim. "Suppose we go out there and pack the remains down here?"

"It's agin the law," stated Frijole quickly. "Don't dare move a dead man until the coroner sets onto him."

"We can go look at him, can't we? Let's go do that. I'd shore like to have a look at this supine gent."

"You look kinda white around the gills, Danny," remarked Frijole. "Don't let this git yuh down, feller. I know how yuh feel. First few I killed kinda gave me the creeps, but yuh git over it quick. Shore, I'd like to see him. Want a snack, before yuh go, Danny?"

"No!" snorted Danny.

"Let's go, before he petterfies," said Slim.

FULLY ARMED THEY followed Danny out past where they had dug for the treasure, and back along a bushy trail to a point about two hundred feet from the hole in the sand. Danny stopped and looked around. Pitched headfirst into a tangle of brush was his horse, its hind feet in the air. Danny pushed through a fringe of brush to a small opening, where he stopped short.

"He's gone!" blurted Danny. "He—he was right there!"

Half-concealed under a creosote bush was a battered sombrero, faded and colorless, but with no marks to indicate its owner. Frijole examined the weeds and sand.

"Blood here on the ground," he announced. "Yeah, yuh can see where somebody in high heels lifted hard. See how they dug in deep? Danny, that other feller came back and got the dead man. Or mebbe he was only wounded. Yuh never can tell."

"I dunno," sighed Danny. "Maybe I'm glad he's gone."

"Can't keep notheeng around those places," sighed Lightning.

"What did he mean?" asked Danny curiously.

"Aw, jist a Mexican idea of bein' funny," replied Frijole. "We better take your saddle and bridle back, before some-body steals that, too."

As soon as possible, back at the ranch house, Slim drew Frijole aside.

"It's a good thing we didn't find that money," he told Frijole. "Then two dry-gulchers was watchin' us, dont'cha know it? They would jist about killed all four of us."

"Yeah?" said Frijole. "Not me, pardner. When I got through with them two, they'd wish they'd stayed home."

"Uh-huh. Yeah, I noticed that. F'r a man of yore age, you can shore travel awful fast, when yo're scared."

"Scared? Who was scared? I knowed they was shootin' at you, and I wanted t' lead you out of range as fast as possible. Yeah, they was. You said yourself that none of them bullets missed yuh more'n an inch."

"I guess we're even," sighed Slim. "Let's forgit it."

9

HELL-FOR-LEATHER HENRY

HENRY TOOK BUCKSHOT with him on the stage to Scorpion Bend, and the little fellow rode between Henry and Tony Dunham, the driver. Tony had worked for Big Jim Harris several years; he had only recently taken over the job of driving the stage. He was a garrulous sort, lean and saturnine.

It was a tiresome trip over the dangerous grades and narrow roads, but Buckshot enjoyed it. Henry proudly led the little boy around the town, buying him peanuts and candy and soda-pop until Buckshot fairly waddled. Henry talked with a number of people about the coming election. He saw Cash Silverton, who had a perceptible limp from his encounter with Oscar Johnson.

Later he met Charles Baker on the street. "Campaigning," queried the banker.

"I never campaign, sir," replied Henry. "I could not tell anyone in Wild Horse Valley anything about me that they do not already know. They either vote for me, or they do not."

"Are you going to be with us a few days, Mr. Conroy."

"No, I am going back on the night stage, Mr. Baker. Have you made arrangements to take over the Tonto bank?"

"Next week," replied Baker. "I am finishing up my work here."

Later in the afternoon Henry ran into Tony Dunham, and Tony was drinking. He turned his back on Henry and went into a saloon. By suppertime Tony was nearly to the crying stage. It was the first time Henry had ever seen Tony in that condition.

Henry spoke to the clerk in the stage depot about it, but the man merely shrugged and said, "Aw, he's a good driver; he'll take yuh home safe."

By stage time Tony was quietly drunk, but seemed able to handle his four horses. It was with a certain amount of misgiving that Henry put Buckshot inside the stage and climbed in with him. He had no liking to ride on the driver's seat at night.

Those narrow, winding roads around the Piñon cliffs might very well be disastrous for a drunken driver, but it was a long ways to the grades, and Tony should be sober enough by that time. What Henry did not know was that Tony had a quart of bad liquor in the wrapped-up slicker beside him on the seat.

Within a mile from town Buckshot was sound asleep, in spite of the lurching stage. There was no moon, but the starlight was brilliant. Henry tried to snooze, but he was still apprehensive about Tony Dunham, and dust sifted into the stage, making him very uncomfortable.

They reached the crooked roads which led to the grades above Piñon Canyon, and began the long climb. They reached the top, but the driver did not stop the team for the usual rest there. After they had negotiated several of the sharp turns Henry relaxed, deciding that Tony's condition was all right. Almost at the same moment the stage crashed to a stop against the inside wall.

Henry climbed out when he heard Tony swearing at the team, and found the driver on the ground. At first he thought Tony had been hurt, but he soon discovered that Tony was too drunk to stand up. The left front wheel of the stage had wedged against the wall; otherwise there did not seem to be any damage. The lines had been flung aside, and Henry marveled over the fact that the team did not run away.

He carefully placed the half-awakened Buckshot on the seat, dumped the unconscious Tony into the stage, closed the door and gingerly climbed to the driver's seat, holding the lines. Henry had never driven four horses, and the thought of taking that heavy stage to Tonto City was apalling.

Working carefully, he managed to back the team enough to release that front wheel, and headed down the grades, praying that those four horses knew more about the road than he did. At the first sharp turn he nearly crashed the stage against the inner wall when he turned too short.

But he only needed that one lesson. On the next curve he nearly dropped the right wheels off the grade, swinging too wide. The high rocky cliffs on the left side cut off the light, while on the right side was the mysterious darkness of the deep canyon. Buckshot was asleep, his curly head pillowed on Henry's thigh.

It was a nightmare to Henry. "And men ask for this sort of work!" he marveled aloud. "And do it every day!"

SUDDENLY THE LEADERS swerved in close to the rocky wall. Henry pulled back with all his strength, and at the same time bore down on the brake. Something had frightened the team, but he had no idea what it might be. With the iron-shot wheels skidding sparks from the rocky roadbed, the equipage stopped.

Then the figure of a man stepped past the team, starlight glinting on the barrel of his gun. Henry was not armed. The man said:

"Hold 'em tight!"

The next moment he stepped in beside the stage, flung open the door and barked:

"Get out of there and get out fast!"

Henry tried to twist around to see what was going on, and then there were two heavy shots, spaced very close together, as loud as two claps of thunder. Henry had taken his foot off the brake, and the lines were slack. For a moment there was only the rattling echoes of those two shots, and then the frightened team lurched ahead.

It was a sharp down-grade to the next turn; the lurch had thrown Henry off balance; and his foot was off the brake. Bracing an elbow against Buckshot to keep him on the seat, Henry was helpless for the moment.

He never knew how they made that turn. He felt the stage twist and skid, saw sparks fly from the rocky wall as a hug scraped heavily, and then they were in a straight piece of grade, with all four horses running at top speed.

The next curve was wider, but he heard rocks fly off into space as the wheels skidded again, and he thought for a moment they were all going over the edge. Henry knew enough about driving four horses to know that the leaders must keep the spreaders taut, or the wheelers were in danger of getting their forefeet tangled; so he merely let them run, and gave all his attention to the brake. From here to the bottom of Wild Horse Valley there were few curves, but his brake-blocks were burning long before he reached the bottom. Luckily there was no traffic going toward Scorpion Bend, because except at turn-out places it was a one-team road.

Henry did not stop to make any investigations; drove straight to Tonto City, pulling in at the stage depot at one o'clock. Judge and Oscar were waiting for him, along with several other men who were there to meet the stage.

Henry handed Buckshot to Oscar, and climbed stiffly down. Every bone in his body ached from the strain, and he almost fell off the wheel. His story was quickly told. Tony Dunham was sprawled inside the stage, with two loads of buckshot in him, fired at a distance of possibly five feet. Doctor Knowles was summoned and his examination was brief.

Big Jim Harris was called from the Ring's Castle. It was his stage line and his driver. "Attempted hold-up, eh," he said.

"Presumably," replied Henry, "the idea was to first murder all the passengers."

"I can't imagine who would want to kill Tony."

"And I," said Henry, "cannot imagine who would know that Tony was inside that stage. Someone in this country must have a crystal ball. Come, Judge, we must get Buckshot to bed."

They took the little boy to their room and put him in bed. Danny Regan had been in and told Judge what happened at the ranch. Henry sat down on the edge of his bed and tried to puzzle things out. Why had masked men been watching the ranch—men desperate enough to try and murder Danny Regan?

"Why was Tony Dunham murdered?" queried Judge.

"Because they thought it was I," sighed Henry. "No one, except me, knew that Tony was inside that stage, Judge. I was supposed to get both barrels of that shotgun. That was why Tony got drunk. He did not have the nerve to go through with the scheme; so he took too much liquor, never thinking that he might—oh, well, there is no cause for worry; I am still alive."

Judge cleared his throat raspingly. "I suppose you—er—have all your affairs in order, Henry. With things as they are—you see."

"One never knows, does one?" said Henry. "After all the temperance lectures I have heard, whiskey saved my life."

"You still jest, Henry."

"I am sorry, Judge. I can understand that they might murder me in order to prevent me from—well, cleaning up this mess, or to prevent me from being reëlected; but I cannot figure out why masked men should watch my ranch. What is there at the ranch that men should watch? It doesn't make sense, Judge. I believe we shall go out there tomorrow and talk with the boys—especially Danny. He is very level-headed. If he says he shot a man, I believe him."

"And he says he never saw that man's face before," said Judge.

"Very puzzling indeed, Judge. Please find me the liniment. I feel completely shredded."

THE NEXT MORNING Henry left Buckshot with Judge, secured the ranch mail and rode out to the JHC. There was a letter for Danny Regan, posted at Scorpion Bend. Danny read it quickly, a puzzled expression on his face. He handed the penciled note to Henry. It read: *This is your order to keep away from Laura Adams.*

There was no signature, no explanation—only that one line. Henry handed it back to Danny without any comment.

"Henry, this is a crazy thing," Danny said.

"Tell me about the man you shot, Danny."

Danny told him the same story he had told the four other men at the JHC, and Henry nodded gravely.

"Do you suppose the man was dead, Danny?" he asked.

"I believe he was, Henry. But when we got back, he was gone."

"Because his identity might incriminate men you *do know,* Danny."

"Mebbe that was the reason they took him away. What's new with you?"

Henry sat on the porch and told Danny, Frijole and Slim about the killing of Tony and the wild ride down the grades.

"I'll tell yuh," remarked Frijole, "this country is tougher than a basket of rattlers. Yuh never know what'll happen next."

"But why are masked men watching this ranch?" asked Henry.

Frijole and Slim were a bit uneasy, but no one mentioned a possible reason. Finally Danny and Henry went to the spot where Danny had shot the stranger. There was nothing to be seen. Henry saw the hole in the sand where Frijole had tried to dig up the loot, and asked Danny what the hole was for.

"I've been wonderin' about that myself," said Danny. "Looks like somebody had buried somethin' there."

Henry looked it over thoughtfully, but he did not express any opinion.

"But about this note I got about Laura Adams, the school teacher," said Danny. "I don't understand it, Henry. Why shouldn't I see her?"

"Have you been seeing her often?" asked Henry.

"Oh, once in a while. Not real often."

"Never quarreled with her?"

"Certainly not. She is a fine girl, Henry. That isn't her writin'."

"Danny, what do you know about her?"

Danny was silent for several moments, but finally he said:

"Henry, she is Big Jim Harris' niece. He got her the job."

"Big Jim," said Henry quietly, "seems to have a hand in nearly everything around here. Being his niece is nothing against her."

"Do you suppose he wrote that note?" asked Danny.

"I have never seen his writing, Danny. Suppose you ask Miss Adams for her version of it. She may have an idea on the subject."

"I'll sure do that—today," declared Danny vehemently.

"My goodness! Has it—er—gone that far, Danny?"

"No," replied Danny coldly, "but no man can tell me that I can't see a young lady. That's up to her—not to a third party."

"Miss Adams," said Henry, "is a very beautiful and charming young lady. It may be that some amorous swain has taken this means of getting you out of the race. No doubt there are many who envy you, Danny."

"Well, that's all right," said Danny. "She has a perfect right to go with anyone she wants to. If she agrees with the writer of this note, I'll step aside, and never say a word. But she will have to tell me that herself, Henry."

Henry rubbed his red nose thoughtfully and looked at the hole in the sand. There did not seem to be a sensible reason for that hole. Around it were plenty of boot tracks, as if several men had stood there. It was only a short distance away to where the two masked men had met Danny Regan. Had the masked men dug that hole?

"Danny, there is something wrong about this ranch," he said.

"Wrong?" exclaimed Danny. "How do you mean?"

"Danny, I hate to say this," Henry lowered his voice, "but I have a feeling that Slim and Frijole were mixed up in that bank robbery."

"No, Henry! You can't mean that."

"Else why are masked men watching the ranch? Danny, can it be that Slim and Frijole in some way got that bank money, and that the men who engineered the robbery are trying to get it back?"

"I can't believe that, Henry. Frijole and Slim are honest men. I'd sooner think that Thunder and Lightning did it."

"Hmmm. Danny, you might have hit the nail on the head. Those two are just—But wait. We will go back to the ranch, take them off their guard and—well, well, I never thought of them."

10

LIARS DON'T STEAL

THEY WENT BACK to the ranch house. Slim and Frijole were not in evidence, but Thunder and Lightning were down at the corral, fixing a post. Henry and Danny went down there.

"*Buenas dias,*" said Lightning. "How am I, you hope and pray?"

"Lightning," said Henry abruptly, "how much money was in that sack you brought back from Scorpion Bend after the bank robbery?"

"How *mucho? Quien sabe?* Maybe meelion dollar."

"You did not count it?"

"*Por Dios,* no! Too much."

"I see. Where is that money now, Lightning?"

Lightning shrugged his shoulders. "*Quien sabe?* We bury heem, but somebody deeg heem up."

"Where did you get the money, Lightning?"

"Firs'," explained Lightning, "I see Sleem and Frijole bury heem. Then we deeg heem up and bury heem again. Een copple day Sleem and Frijole say they cut your ears off eef we do not show them where we bury heem. *Por Dios,* you do not wan' for losing ear, so we show heem—but those money ees gone."

"I'll be a liar!" gasped Danny.

"Was the money gone before Danny shot the man?"

"We deeg for heem about that time, but there ees no money."

"Are you sure that Frijole and Slim did not get it?"

"They never get heem. They are sore like hell."

"A fine, law-abiding outfit, I must say!" exclaimed Henry. "Let us question Slim and Frijole."

They found Slim and Frijole in the kitchen, sampling a new batch of prune whisky.

"Well, what didja find out?" asked Frijole.

"Too much," replied Henry sharply. "It saddens me to think that I cannot trust anyone."

"You mean Thunder and Lightnin', Henry."

"I mean Frijole and Slim."

"Oh, m' God!" exclaimed Slim. "Don't say that, Henry. Why, me and Frijole would lay down our lives for you."

"I do not want your lives, Slim, but I do want the money you two got in that Scorpion Bend bank robbery."

Slim and Frijole stared at each other in amazement. Then Slim whispered, "Lightnin'!"

"Yes," said Henry quietly, "Lightning told us."

"I'll be a liar!" sighed Frijole. "I jist will be a liar."

"Without a doubt," Henry agreed. "I expect you to lie, Frijole. But I want it as near as you can come to the truth."

"I'll do m' best, Henry. We didn't steal the money. You know we wouldn't do that. Personally, I believe in livin' every day so I can look any man in the face and tell him to go to hell."

"I believe the latter statement, Frijole. Proceed."

"Yuh better make it sound good," said Danny.

"Yuh see," continued Frijole miserably, "I had a quar-ter-sack of oats in my hand, when I chased in behind that bank, trying to see who Oscar was chasin'. Well, somebody ran into me and knocked me down, I got up, picked up m' sack and took it back to the buckboard. The only thing I figure is that I got the sack of money instead of the oats. Anyway, it was there in the buckboard next mornin'. And that's the truth."

"I'll swear to that, too," added Slim.

"It has a ring of truth," admitted Henry. "But what happened next?"

"Well," sighed Frijole, "me and Slim didn't want them robbers to find it here; so we took it out in the wash and buried it."

"Why," queried Henry, "did you not turn the money over to me?"

"Yuh—yuh can't think of everythin' right on the spur of the moment, Henry. Me and Slim was kinda shocked, and our first thought was to hide the stuff."

"With no idea of keeping it, of course."

"Good gosh, that never even entered our heads, Henry."

"I see. Then what happened?"

"Well, we got to thinkin' it over later and I says to Slim that we better dig up that money and turn it over to you. It ain't ours, and we didn't—shucks, we never even thought about touchin' a cent of it for our own use, yuh know. Well, we went out there to dig it up, and it had already been dug up."

"Why did you not come and tell me about it?" asked Henry.

"Well, we—uh—hell, it was gone, Henry. We kept still,

hopin' to nab the thief which got it. Me and Slim framed up for to scare Lightnin' and Thunder into admittin' they took it; so we put on masks and came in on 'em.

"And while we're scarin' them two Mexicans, in comes three masked men and tried to scare all of us. But I tricked 'em into thinkin' that Oscar was outside with a shotgun, and they fanned their tails out of there. Them masked men figured we had the money.

"Later on we got Thunder, and Lightnin' to show us where they hid the money, but it was gone again. We was jist finished diggin' when Danny had his gun fight with the two masked men. We all beat it for the house and was there when Danny showed up."

"I lose," muttered Slim.

"You lose what?" asked Danny.

"Well," replied Slim, "I bet m'self a month's wages that Frijole couldn't tell the truth—and he has."

"BUT WHO GOT that money?" asked Henry. "One of you four knows where the money is right now."

"We don't," denied Slim quickly. "Mebbe Thunder or Lightnin' know, but I doubt it."

"Do you realize that it is an enormous amount of money?" asked Henry. "Do you realize that the bank is smashed, and that half the people in Wild Horse Valley will lose their money?"

"It's terrible," agreed Frijole, "but we ain't got it."

"If the people of Wild Horse Valley knew that you four had been playin' three-card monte with their money, they would lynch all four of yuh," stated Danny, and added, "And I wouldn't raise a hand to stop 'em."

"Yuh see," remarked Slim, "while this here hold-up was

goin' on, I was up in the dance hall, listenin' to a feller saw on a bull fiddle. Shucks, I wasn't even near the bank."

Henry looked thoughtfully at Frijole. "After that sack was knocked out of your hand, Frijole, did you happen to go into the bank, before the robbery was discovered?"

"Seems t' me like I did, Henry. Yes, sir, me and Thunder and Lightnin' was investigatin' that open back door. We lit some matches and a feller out in front started yellin' that there's robbers in the bank; so we high-tailed it right out of there. I seen Baker, the banker. He said I was a big masked man with a gun in m' hand. Hell, I didn't have no gun in m' hand."

"Mr. Baker was slightly rattled," said Henry quietly.

"Yuh can't blame him for that," said Slim.

"Is there any possible chance that the masked men who shot at Danny dug up that money before you had a chance?" asked Henry.

"That sand hadn't been touched, before I started diggin'," replied Frijole. "We'd been a-diggin' ten, fifteen minutes before they fired the first shot. If they had the money, what was they hangin' around for?"

"Very good logic," agreed Henry. "For some silly reason, I am inclined to feel that you have told me the truth. I do not refer to the statement you made concerning the fact that you were going to dig up the loot and turn it over to me. That is too large and has too many spines for me to swallow, Frijole. However, I am willing to believe part of the rest.

"In your ignorance and cupidity, you have put me in a terrible position, if the truth of this leaks out. We shall all be blasted. Our only salvation is to keep silent, keep our eyes open, and try to locate the money. If it is not here, and if the masked men did not get it, we must make every effort to discover who has it. I have a feeling that the men who robbed that bank did not get the money. I trust that you boys will keep still about this incident."

"You can shore trust us!" exclaimed Frijole. "And I'll scare them two Mexicans so bad that they won't even remember their own ages."

IT WAS JUST past four o'clock that afternoon when Danny Regan tied his horse in front of the Corcoran home, where Nellie Adams the school teacher lived. Mrs. Corcoran was a large, red-faced, jolly woman, and she gave Danny a welcoming handshake.

"You're a little early, cowboy," She laughed. "Nellie ain't home yet. But come right in and make yourself at home."

"Thank yuh very much, Mrs. Corcoran," Danny smiled. "Nice weather."

"Yes, it is nice. Let me take your hat?"

"Thank yuh, I'll hold it. Yo're lookin' well."

"Feelin' fine. Feel better if your boss would find that missin' money from the Scorpion Bend Bank. But I suppose that is impossible. That just about broken Harry Corcoran." She sighed.

"I'm shore sorry about that, Mrs. Corcoran. Henry's doin' everythin' he can."

"I saw that in the *Clarion*, which came today."

"So he finally printed it again, did he?" Danny grinned.

"And strewed Henry Conroy's remains all over the front page."

Danny nodded. "I reckon he hates Henry. Too bad,

because Henry is the finest man I ever knew, Mrs. Corcoran. Yuh see—"

Danny's eyes had strayed to the organ, on which there was a photograph of a man. Mrs. Corcoran's eyes followed Danny's, and she smiled.

"Good lookin' feller, eh, Danny?" she said. Danny turned and slowly looked at her, a queer expression on his face.

"Who—who is that man?" he asked huskily.

"Don't worry about him," Mrs. Corcoran laughed. "That's Nellie's brother, Steve Adams."

"Her brother?"

"Why, sure, her brother. She can have a brother, can't she? What's the matter, Danny, yuh look kinda green?"

"Must be close in here," said Danny. "I—I'll wait for her on the porch."

Danny stumbled out on the porch as Nellie Adams came through the gate, and he met her a short distance away from the house.

"I—I wanted to see you," he said, searching his pockets for the note he had received. He found it and handed it to her. Quickly she read it and handed it back to him. From her bag she took a folded envelope and took out the enclosed sheet of paper, on which was written:

> *If you want to continue teaching school here, have nothing further to do with Dan Regan.*

The writing was the same as on Danny's note, and there was no signature. They looked at each other curiously.

"Who wrote them notes?" asked Danny.

Nellie Adams shook her head slowly. "Who knows, Danny?"

"Big Jim Harris?" he asked.

"It isn't his writing. I thought of that, too."

"Well, what's to be done about it?" he asked.

"I don't know, Danny. It made me feel spooky."

"Yeah, I'll betcha. You don't want to lose yore job. I haven't much of anythin' to lose—except my life."

"Danny," she said quietly, "let's follow their orders. Maybe we can find out who wrote them. You can't afford to take a chance, and neither can I."

"That's right. If you learn anythin', you can find a way to let me know and I'll do the same for you. I'll pull out now, before somebody sees me down here."

Danny's face was still gray as he rode up to the main street of Tonto. He went straight to the sheriff's office. Henry was there alone. Danny closed the door and leaned across Henry's desk.

"I was down to see Nellie Adams about that note," he said quietly. "She got one, warnin' her to keep away from me."

"Interesting," said Henry. "Very interesting."

"And somethin' else," said Danny huskily. "On the organ in the Corcoran's house is a picture of Steve Adams, Nellie's brother."

"Steve Adams?" queried Henry curiously. "I have never heard of the gentleman, Danny. What about *him?*"

"He is the masked man I shot out at the ranch, Henry."

Henry's eyes opened wide for a moment, but went back to their habitual squint.

"Ain't that hell?" queried Danny huskily.

"And Steve Adams is Big Jim Harris' nephew," said Henry.

"And Nellie's brother," reminded Danny miserably.

"Eh? Oh, yes, her brother."

"And I think I killed him, Henry."

Danny turned away. He went to the door and opened it and stood in the doorway. Henry came over and put a hand on his shoulder.

"You think you killed him, Danny," he said. "There isn't anything in the world to prove it. You may have been mistaken in the man, too. However, should it all be true, you were justified. Say nothing to anyone about this, Danny. I am doing everything I can to clear up this mystery."

"Thank yuh, Henry. Where is Judge?"

"Buckshot is taking his afternoon siesta, and Judge is with him—reading the *Clarion*, which came today. He always takes it with him to a secluded spot, in order to digest carefully everything that Mr. J.W.L. Pelly has to say about us. I surmise he has plenty of spleen to vent this time. It will be interesting to hear Judge's reactions."

"Well, I reckon I'll go back to the ranch, Henry."

"And do not worry, my boy. Old Sherlock Conroy is on the loose."

11

NEVER GAG THE JUDGE

SHORTLY AFTER DANNY left the office Big Jim Harris
sauntered in. Henry greeted him cordially, and Big Jim
sat down.

"If you came to ask me about what is in the *Clarion*,"
remarked Henry, "I can truthfully say that I haven't seen
a copy today."

Big Jim laughed and shook his head. "Our friend Pelly
was kinda vicious this time."

"Not my friend, sir," said Henry. "How much are you
paying him for attacking me, Harris?"

"Payin' him? I never paid him a cent. The man works for
the interests of the tax-payers."

"That statement," said Henry, "is very amusing."

"Well," drawled Big Jim, "I'm not interested in the
Clarion. Have you any news on the bank robbery? The
Commissioners are anxious for action."

"How is your nose?" countered Henry.

"To hell with that!" snapped Big Jim.

"I second the motion," said Henry. "By the way, haven't
you a nephew named Steve Adams?"

Big Jim looked keenly at Henry for several moments. "I
have. What about him?"

"Do you know where he is at present, sir?"

"Right now," replied Big Jim slowly, "he may be in Wyoming, Nevada, or possibly in New Mexico. I am not positive."

"He was working for you at Silver City, was he not?"

"Why, yes, he was there for a while. What is this all about, Conroy?"

"Oh," replied Henry quietly, "I am merely following my latest hobby."

"Hobby? What do yuh mean? What is your hobby?"

"Oh, picking up a loose end, here and there."

"Don't make sense," growled Big Jim, getting to his feet.

"They never do, until you get them all together, Mr. Harris."

"All right, all right." Big Jim walked back to the doorway. "I came here to ask a question and get a civil answer—and all I get is a lot of foolish talk."

"Ghastly, isn't it?" said Henry soberly.

Without replying, Big Jim left the office and went up the street. Henry was chuckling and rubbing his nose when Judge came in, leading Buckshot by the hand, and carrying the latest edition of the *Clarion*.

"Hello, Uncle Henry," called Buckshot, as he climbed up on a corner of the desk. "How are yuh today?"

"Bless your heart, I am fine, Buckshot."

"Uncle Judge ain't—he's mad."

"My goodness! And why is Uncle Judge mad?"

"Look at that front page!" snorted Judge, flinging the offending paper on the desk. "That editor rates a horse-whipping, Henry."

There in the saloon, Henry, tattered and
weary, confronted the murderer.

Henry spread the paper on his desk. Across the top of
the page in huge block type was the following heading;

CRIMINALS RULE WILD HORSE VALLEY!
Futile Efforts of Sheriff's Office Are an Insult to Decent
Men; Editor Assaulted and Manhandled in Retaliation
for Revealing the Truth; Newspaper Office Wrecked by
Vandals

"Not bad," murmured Henry. "Not bad at all, Judge Only
a declaration of war could have carried a bigger heading."

"Damn it, Henry, do not jest," snapped Judge. "Read
what he says."

Slowly Henry read the two column front-page editorial, an amused smile on his moon-like face. At times his
brows lifted slightly, and he thoughtfully rubbed his nose.

Finally he put the paper aside and smiled up at the gold-en-haired boy.

"Did you have a nice sleep, son?" he asked.

"Oh, sure," grinned Buckshot, but added, "Until Uncle Judge swore and woke me up."

Judge snorted, got out of his chair and walked to the doorway.

"I never can understand you, Henry," he said wearily. "You can read *that*—and still smile. I can't. Damme, my blood boils!"

"The acid in it, Judge, said Henry. "That is why you have rheumatism."

"Acid! Henry, are you a man or a mouse? A man would ride to Scorpion Bend and shoot the hide off the writer of that article."

"I," said Henry quietly, "must be a mouse, sir."

"Damned if I don't believe you are! Why, that editor would not dare write a thing like that about any other person in this state."

"Very likely no other person deserves it, Judge. Most of the article is true. Of course, it could have been put in better English. The man is crude in his wrath. He repeats himself.

"In no less than five places in that single article he says that I am without enough brains to know good from evil. One statement of that kind should be sufficient. In three separate paragraphs he calls you a doddering old imbecile, creaky of joint and rheumy of eye. Once should have been enough. He really should have an intelligent person edit his stuff."

"My God, Henry!" snorted Judge. "You only criticize

the writing—not the gist of the thing. Hundreds of people are reading that right now. They will believe it, too. If you allow that man to live and not make a published apology, we shall all be laughed out of the state. You will not get a single vote in the election. And you—you laugh!"

"Uncle Judge acts mad," said Buckshot.

"Uncle Judge," said Henry quietly, "is not acting, son."

HENRY KNEW THAT Tonto City was reading that paper, and he also knew that in the minds of many people he had lost all chance of ever being reëlected. They were watching and waiting to see what he might do about it. Western editors had been horsewhipped for much less.

But Henry's pokerface told them nothing. Outwardly he was smiling, genial, bowing to the bartender at the King's Castle, as he took his drink. Henry was too much of an actor to show the world his feelings. Judge was bitter over the thing; so bitter, indeed, that Henry kept away from him.

Instead of going to supper with Judge and Buckshot, he saddled his horse and rode out to the ranch. Neither Frijole, Slim, nor Thunder and Lightning had read the paper. In fact, Thunder and Lightning could not read, and Slim and Frijole were only able to do so by hard labor.

They discussed the missing money. The four men were eager to find it and turn it over to Henry, but they had no ideas on the subject. They went into detail as to how they had hidden the money, trying to figure out who could have seen Lightning and Thunder bury it. Henry had already questioned Oscar closely over the events at Scorpion Bend, and what Frijole, Thunder and Lightning told fitted in with Oscar's story.

It was nearly midnight, when Henry rode back to Tonto City. He stabled his horse and went to the hotel, where a lone kerosene lamp burned on the hotel desk. Slowly he went up the stairs and down the dark hall to their room. The room was unlocked. He carefully closed the door behind him, lighted a match and went straight to the table where the lamp stood.

As the light flared up he looked around. On the bed, without any covers over him, lay Judge, roped and gagged, flat on his back, blinking painfully at Henry. Buckshot's little bed was empty, the covers flung aside.

With trembling fingers Henry managed to get the gag out of Judge's mouth. He had been struck on the head, and there was a swelling the size of a small egg. Judge lay there, working his lean jaws, while Henry cut the rope loose.

"What happened?" Henry demanded. "Where is the boy?"

"Boy?" muttered Judge: "Boy? You mean Buckshot? Why—"Judge sat up and looked at the empty bed.

"Who was here?" asked Henry.

Judge felt of his sore head and shook it gingerly. Finally he said: "Henry, I don't know."

"You don't know?"

"I do not, sir. I put Buckshot to bed, and went to bed myself. I have a faint memory of someone being in the room; I thought it was you. Then I must have been hit over the head. Later, I must have awakened and believed I was in the grip of a terrible nightmare, in which I was gagged and bound. But the boy—"

Henry looked blankly at him, his mind a whirl. Then he began to stare around the room, and his glance went to the tumbled clothes on Buckshot's bed. Against the blue of a blanket was an oblong of paper—an envelope. Quickly he seized it, tore it open and took out the folded sheet of paper, which he held closer to the lamp. The note was printed in pencil, and read:

WE'VE GOT THE KID. DO NOTHING. ANY FURTHER INVESTIGATION BY YOU AND YOU'LL NEVER SEE THE KID AGAIN. DO NOTHING. WAIT FOR ORDERS.

IT WAS UNSIGNED. Henry read it aloud to Judge, who sank back on his pillow, staring at the ceiling.

" 'We've got the kid,'" he muttered. "My fault. I should have locked the door. Damn their souls to hell!"

"We have never locked the door before," said Henry huskily. "Who would suspect that they would harm Buckshot? You are not to blame."

"But how could they come right into this hotel and do a thing like that, Henry?"

"Simple, Judge. They came up the rear stairway and entered this room quietly. They knocked you out, very likely gagged the child, and went back the way they came, when the coast was clear. It is a dark night. By now they are far away. There was little danger of being seen."

"I can see that now, Henry," groaned Judge. "But what do they mean when they order us to do nothing, and say that any further investigation by you—what investigation, Henry?"

"Investigation of that Scorpion Bend robbery—and the murder of Tony Dunham, not overlooking the murder of

Fred Langley. Judge, they are so frightened right now that they have stooped to kidnapping, hoping we'll drop everything in order to save that boy."

"Wouldn't you, Henry?" asked Judge.

"To save Buckshot," replied Henry seriously, "I would agree to stand on my head for the rest of my life. Judge, we must play the game their way and wait for something to develop."

"You mean—not make any effort to find him?"

"Do you want them to kill the child, Judge?"

"Henry, are you so gullible that you can believe that they will ever return that boy to us? His life means nothing to them. If the men who took him are responsible for the killing of Fred Langley and Tony Dunham, do you think they would hesitate to kill that boy?"

"I do not want to think along that line, Judge. Do you want to have Doctor Knowles examine your head?"

"My head is all right, sir. I shall use a hot towel and a little patience. And further than that, sir, an examination of *my* head should be conducted by a number of psychologists, rather than by a country doctor."

"I merely meant the exterior, Judge. Well, there is nothing we can do tonight. The die is cast, as they say. We must face tomorrow with a smile."

"I do not believe I shall ever smile again," said Judge.

"Few, if any, will notice the change, Judge. Brace up, man! Those men are so frightened that they will do anything to stop us."

"Frightened of *you*, Henry?"

"Judge," said Henry, "you must not believe everything you read in the *Clarion*."

12

CRAZY WOMAN CANYON

WORD QUICKLY SPREAD next morning about the kidnapping of Buckshot, but neither Henry nor Judge said anything about the note. The office was besieged by people who wanted to help find the boy. John Campbell, the prosecutor, together with the three commissioners, came to the office for a consultation.

"Hangin' is too good for them," declared Big Jim Harris. "This valley is goin' to get such a bad reputation that nobody will want to live here. I suggest that we make up a posse of a hundred men and search every possible place in the valley. What do you think of that idea, John?"

The prosecutor shook his head. "No, I'm afraid not, Jim. We might be riding with the men who did it. There must be a reason behind this. Men don't kidnap a child just to be kidnapping. There must be a ransom reason for it. Even if it were revenge against Henry or Judge, those men will let it be known. My suggestion would be to wait for a word from them. How do you feel about it, Henry?"

"I believe you are right, John."

"Well, all right," sighed Big Jim. "I'm a man of action, myself."

"I believe they will communicate with us," said Judge

wearily. "It is difficult to analyze their reasons for taking the little boy, unless they are trying to force us to do something against our will."

"Do something?" queried Big Jim. "Well, I don't know about that, but I do know that everyone in this valley has asked that you *do something*. A bank is ruined by theft, murder is committed, but nothing is done about it. And now, a little child is kidnapped—and I suppose nothing will be done about that."

"We are not in the habit of issuing bulletins on our daily findings, Mr. Harris," stated Henry coldly. "You merely suspect that we are and have been idle all this time."

Big Jim laughed shortly. "I'll believe different when I've got proof."

"I wonder if a reward would do any good," said the prosecutor. "The county hasn't much money for such things."

"A suitable reward would be out of the question," said Big Jim.

"I do not believe we need a reward," said Henry.

"Why not?" asked Big Jim quickly.

Henry smiled thoughtfully. "We will not go into that at present, Mr. Harris. Just give me a few more days."

"That suits me," said John Calvert, one of the commissioners. "Henry has surprised us several times, and I'm willing to be surprised again. How do you feel about it, Al?"

"The same as you do, John," replied Al Rose.

"Thank you for your confidence, gentlemen," said Henry. "I am very sure that in a few days Mr. Harris will agree with you."

"I'm not," growled Harris, "but I'm outvoted."

After they were gone Judge looked dismally at Henry.

"Poker," he said, "Just plain poker, Henry. You haven't a damn face, nor an ace, and a pair of deuces would look like a royal flush in a hand like yours. And yet you sit there and bluff them into believing you have something to work on. Henry, I take off my hat to you. But what is the use?"

"I guess I am just a born liar, Judge. Perhaps it is my sense of the dramatic, or the fact that a Conroy never admits defeat. And," Henry paused for a moment, "And still, I may be right. By Jove, I may be on the brink of a great discovery."

"And," said Judge, "do not forget that every moment you totter on the brink, Buckshot is in those scoundrels' hands. Last night, when he said his prayers, he said 'God bless Uncle Judge, and God bless Uncle Henry.' Then he said, 'Uncle Judge, where is Uncle Henry?' I said, 'God knows, I don't.' Then he said, 'You know where he is, God. Amen.'"

"A grand, little lad," said Henry quietly. "I wonder if we shall ever know his right name. A swell little trouper, Judge. Nearly old enough to go to school, too. We must provide for him—for the future. Neither of us have anyone to inherit our earthly belongings."

"Mine?" queried Judge.

"At least, you might leave him a memory of a smiling face, Judge."

"I've got along with this face for over sixty years, sir."

"And show the effects of it, Judge."

HENRY WALKED UP to the new bank, where Charles Baker, who was to take charge, was directing the work of reconstruction. He greeted Henry cordially and expressed his sympathy over what had happened. Henry seemed rather indifferent, and evaded Baker's questions regarding his opinion of the kidnapping mystery.

"Do you suppose they will ask a cash ransom for the return of the boy?" he asked.

"No, I do not," replied Henry.

"Well—uh—why would they take him?"

"A cash ransom idea is out of the question, Mr. Baker. In the first place, he is not my son, not even by adoption. In fact, he is not even related to me. We do not even know his right name. Would any man pay a large sum of money for the return of the child under those circumstances? True, I am fond of the little boy. But if the kidnappers expect a large sum of money for his return, I am very much afraid they are doomed to disappointment."

"I see," mused Baker thoughtfully. "They haven't made any demands yet?"

"Not yet, sir."

"Have you made any attempt to find him?"

"Not physically. How soon do you expect to open this bank?"

"In about a week, I believe."

"I was just wondering," remarked Henry, "just how much faith the public will have in this institution. You must remember that this bank has failed twice, and the recent failure in Scorpion Bend may have a bad effect on depositors."

"I believe the people will have absolute faith in this bank," declared Baker. "They will know that Jim Harris is behind it."

Henry's brows lifted slightly, but he made no comment.

He went back to the office, where he rummaged in his

desk, until he found an old letter written to him in long-hand by Big Jim Harris. It was merely a communication regarding county business, and was signed by Jim Harris, as chairman of the commissioners. Henry put the letter in his pocket and leaned back in his chair, his brow furrowed.

Danny Regan, Frijole Bill, Slim Pickins, together with Thunder and Lightning, came to town. They had heard about the disappearance of Buckshot, and were anxious for more news.

"Lemme at 'em!" roared Frijole. "I done heard about it, Henry, and I'm ory-eyed. Of all the danged things I ever heard about! Where do yuh reckon they're holdin' that kid, huh?"

"Calm down, Frijole," advised Henry quietly. "We have no idea where they took him."

"I like to keek heem in your pants," declared Lightning. "Those damn leetle keed, I'm like heem too much."

"Thank you very much," said Henry. "I know you are all loyal."

"Loyal—hell!" snorted Frijole. "I'm jist sore."

"Ain't there anythin' we can do, Henry?" asked Danny.

"Just wait, Danny. Nothing can be done—not at present."

"Well, you jist turn me loose," said Frijole. "I'll turn this whole valley upside down, and I'll betcha I'll shake out that kid. Old Frijole ain't been on the warpath since Geronimo was a pup, and I kinda hanker to open m' tonsils and howl like a wolf. Didja ever hear me howl like a wolf, Henry?"

"Thank you—no, Frijole. Your word is sufficient."

"I can shore do her. Learned it from an Apache."

"Has Oscar been out at the ranch?" asked Henry.

"He was out there last night," replied Frijole. "Somebody told him what was in the *Clarion,* and he's goin' around mumblin' to himself about what he's goin' to do to that editor."

"My goodness, he did plenty!" exclaimed Henry. "I hope he keeps away from there."

"When it comes to Oscar Johnson," said Slim, "the best you can do is to hope."

Judge came to the office a little later. He seemed in a nervous frame of mind.

"I get the fidgets, sitting around, Henry," he declared. "There is not enough action to suit me."

"Good!" exclaimed Henry. "We are going to saddle our horses and take a ride."

"A ride? On horses, Henry? My rheumatism has been—"

"To horse!" interrupted Henry. "And do not talk to me about your rheumatism, sir."

"I merely mentioned it, Henry. Naturally, with the pain I suffer, it is always uppermost in my mind. And riding—a saddle—"

"Will do you a world of good, Judge. Come with me."

FOR THE NEXT ten minutes their little stable was filled with grunts and groans as they saddled their horses, but they finally rode forth. Judge detested chaps and boots, and in a short distance his overalls had pulled up to his knees, exposing his lean shanks, his feet clad in elastic-top gaiters. No two men ever looked less like peace officers.

"Whither?" queried Judge, after they left the road and headed into the hills.

"Oh, just hence," replied Henry, leading the way.

"Have you—er—developed an idea, sir?" asked Judge, fending a mesquite limb away from his head.

"I have the small beginnings of one, sir," replied Henry. "One would have to use a powerful magnifying glass to identify it, but it is all I have. Judge, do you remember the old El Segundo mine?"

"Yes, I remember it. I believe it now belongs to Jim Harris. It is out near Crazy Woman Canyon. But what has that to do with your idea?"

"Very little, I am afraid, Judge. Still, one must start somewhere, mustn't one?"

"I give up!" snorted Judge. "What has an abandoned mine got to do with things? Henry, you don't suppose that Buckshot is there, do you?"

"Nothing as simple as that, my friend. I merely ask about an old mine, and you get hysterical."

"Well, all right. I still do not see the idea."

"As I said a while ago, sir, it is microscopic."

They followed an old trail that led to the mine, and both riders were weary when they reached the huddle of decrepit shacks. Smoke was trickling from an old stovepipe, as they came into the opening on the side of the hill.

"By gad!" exclaimed Judge. "Someone living here, Henry."

"Yes, I knew there was. It is a Mexican, but I do not know his name. Harris hired him to look after things."

Two little Mexican kids appeared in the doorway of the shack as the two men rode up, and a moment later a middle-aged Mexican stepped out. He did not seem friendly, but he managed to smile.

"Mucho caliente," observed Henry. It was indeed warm out there.

"Si, si," replied the Mexican. "W'at you want, eh?"

"Have you any water?" asked Henry.

"Sure." The Mexican dipped a gourd into a barrel, just inside the shack, and one of the children brought it out to Henry.

"Gracias," Henry smiled. "What is your name, my little man?"

"Chico," said the youngster. Henry tossed him a half-dollar, and he pounced on it like a hawk on a quail. Henry tossed another half to the little girl, who almost fell off the rickety steps to get it.

"Gracias, señor—gracias." The Mexican smiled widely now.

"So your name is Chico," said Henry. "What is your last name?"

"Hernandez," said the youngster. "My seester ees Chiquito."

"Nice names," Henry told them heartily. "And what is your father's name?"

Both children looked to their father to answer that one.

"I am Juan Hernandez, *señor,*" he said.

"Thank you. You are the caretaker of the El Segundo mine?"

"Si, señor. I leeve here."

"Well, that is nice. Thank you for the water, and *adios.*"

As they rode away, the two little Mexicans were still standing on the porch, waving to them.

"OF ALL THE asinine missions!" snorted Judge. "You order me to ride with you in all this heat and over all these damnable hills merely to borrow a drink of water from a Mexican."

"Borrow?" queried Henry. "I paid well enough for it."

"Fifty cents a swallow. But what good came of it?"

"My dear Judge, I cannot answer that question. I merely wanted to know the name of the Mexican."

"Good gad, you could have found that out in Tonto City!"

"Granted, sir, granted. But I wanted firsthand knowledge."

"Well, I hope you are satisfied, Henry."

"Oh, perfectly. In fact, I feel that the trip was well worthwhile. The next thing I must find is a Mexican I can trust."

"Why not use one of your own—Thunder or Lightning? Or don't you trust them?"

"Thank you for the suggestion, Judge. I trust them perfectly, but for obvious reasons they will not do. Better than an honest Mexican would be one so dumb that he could not answer a question."

"Poco Vasquez," said Judge.

"Poco Vasquez! The very person!"

"Dumb enough," said Judge. "A perfect example of a singletrack mind, if there ever was one. I saw him this morning, helping swamp out the King's Castle Saloon. He does odd jobs for Big Jim Harris."

"Excellent, Judge—excellent. You take a load off my mind. Poco Vasquez it shall be."

Judge examined his companion narrowly and in silence for a moment or two.

"But what in the world is your idea, Henry?"

"The idea," said Henry, "has grown until it is nearly visible to the human eye, but not quite, Judge."

"I hope it is more sensible than it sounds."

"It positively is not, Judge. It is hair-brained, full of flaws, and might blow back and ruin me. But, as I said before, it is the only one we have. My old friend, I dare not tell you what it is. You would never be a party to it; so it is better that you do not know."

One of the first persons they saw after stabling their horses was James Wadsworth Longfellow Pelly. He was with Charles Baker, inspecting the new bank. No doubt, he was going to give it some much-needed publicity.

Oscar was half-asleep on the office cot. He said:

"Yah, su-ure, Ay saw de editor. He came down ha'ar. He say he vants some trut' about de kidnapping of Bockshot. Va'al, Ay got oop and Ay said to him, 'Ay vill give you something to print,' and den he vent avay yust like a yackrabbit."

"No wonder," said Judge dryly.

"Ay vill say he ain't," agreed Oscar. "Ay saw Eric today. He vars limping around, vit two black eyes."

"Limping with two black eyes?" queried Henry.

"Yah, su-ure," Oscar laughed. "He apologized to me. He say he is sorry he took Yosephine from me, and Ay can have her back vit his blessing."

"Well, will you be fool enough to take her back?" asked Judge.

"Only on an agreement," declared Oscar warmly. "Ay am no fool."

"What sort of an agreement?" asked Henry curiously.

"An agreement," said Oscar soberly, "that she vill vistle before she svings."

"True love—but with reservations," chuckled Henry.

"It is clear," Judge remarked, "that romance often differs from the poet's conception of it. It is not altogether bliss. It is even dangerous."

"Free-holey left a yug in de back room," suggested Oscar.

"Well, my goodness, what are we waiting for?" asked Henry quickly. "Bring the cups, varlet."

"This is no time to celebrate, Henry," said Judge.

"Bring only two cups, Oscar," called Henry.

"Never mind!" called Judge. "Bring all three, Oscar!"

13

THE BIG GUN

POCO VASQUEZ WAS a little and skinny half-Mexican, half-Yaqui, and usually half-starved. He only had two ambitions in life. The first was to earn enough money to buy some tequila, and the second was to make enough money to buy some more tequila. He squatted beside the stable doorway, while Henry explained just what he was to do. Poco had a pinto horse, nearly as thin as its owner.

"I want you to get this all clearly in your mind, Poco," explained Henry. "You will ride to the Circle H ranch. You will find Cash Silverton and give him this letter. For this I will give you five dollars."

Henry showed him the five silver dollars and the Mexican's eyes sparkled. That was a lot of money to Poco Vasquez.

"Geeve now?" he asked.

"I will give you the money when you come back. Ride to the Circle H ranch, give the letter to Cash Silverton, and come back here. If Cash Silverton asks you who sent the letter, what will you tell him?"

"*Qien sabe?*"

"All right. If he asks you if Big Jim sent it, what will you say?"

"*Si, si.* Beeg Jeem. You Beeg Jim."

"You are almost letter perfect, Poco. Come right to the office when you get back."

"*Muy pronto. Adios.*"

Henry watched the Mexican ride away, sighed and leaned against the stable wall. "I wish," he said aloud, "I knew a Yaqui god I could pray to for the safe delivery of my message—but I don't."

James Wadsworth Longfellow Pelly stayed all night in Tonto, and when Henry went back to the office he found him in there, talking with Judge about the kidnapping of Buckshot.

"You have met Mr. Conroy, have you not, Mr. Pelly?" queried Judge.

"I have," said the editor.

"He has," Henry agreed.

"Mr. Pelly wants the story of the kidnapping, Henry."

"You may tell him, sir," replied Henry. "I was not there."

"Just what do you wish to know, Mr. Pelly?" queried Judge.

"I want a complete story of the kidnapping, together with any clues left by the kidnappers. I mean, of course, a description of the clues. I want your opinions as to why it was done, too."

"Wouldn't you like to know who did it?" asked Henry.

"Why—er—yes, of course!"

"So would we," Henry told him. "Judge can tell you the story, but there were no clues. I—"

HENRY HESITATED. ON the floor, nearly behind the half-opened door, was an envelope. Slowly he got out of his chair and picked it up. On it was penciled: HENRY CONROY, SHERIFF.

Judge and Pelly were watching Henry. He opened the envelope and examined the one sheet of folded paper, on which was printed:

WE WANT THE MONEY FROM THE SCORPION BEND BANK. THAT MONEY IS ON YOUR RANCH. DIG UP THAT MONEY. WRITE YOUR RESIGNA- TION AS SHERIFF. AND WE WILL BE READY TO MAKE THE TRADE. YOUR RESIGNATION WILL MEAN THAT YOU HAVE THE MONEY FOR US. THEN WE WILL COMMUNICATE WITH YOU AGAIN. DISOBEY THIS ORDER AND THE KID DIES.

Henry read the note, without a change of expression, and went back to his chair. "Sorry to interrupt, gentlemen," he said quietly. "Go ahead with your story, Judge."

"The story is common knowledge," said Judge. "Mr. Pelly has heard it a dozen times, and I have nothing to add."

"Then," suggested Henry quietly," suppose we talk about Mr. Pelly's editorial in the last *Clarion*."

"I do not care to discuss it," said Mr. Pelly quickly, getting to his feet. "I am here merely to write up a story of the kidnapping and the opening of the new bank. Good day."

James Wadsworth Longfellow Pelly lost no time in getting away from the office. Henry took the note from his pocket and handed it to Judge.

"It must have been put under the door last night," he said, "and when you opened up, it was shoved back."

"My God!" gasped Judge.

"Rather interesting, don't you think?" asked Henry. "All they want now is that money and my resignation."

"But we haven't the money, Henry!"

"And so," added Henry dryly, "the joke is on them."

"Joke? They will kill Buckshot, and we cannot do a single thing to prevent it. Don't you realize that, man?"

"Perfectly, Judge. They want that money, they want my resignation, and then they will return Buckshot—we hope. But above all things, they want that money, and that is the one thing we cannot furnish."

"Damn 'em!" muttered Judge. "I knew they would ask the impossible."

"The only thing we can do now," said Henry, "is to get Buckshot back—without the money or the resignation."

Judge, pacing up and down the office, halted and scowled. "You think of the most impossible things, Henry."

"Very well. If you can show me how we can get that money, Judge, I will not try to get him back otherwise."

"One of us must be crazy!" snorted Judge, and went striding out of the office. Henry leaned back in his chair. The poker face was gone now. There was no one to bluff, except himself, and deep in his heart he felt that he had been bluffing all along. He still had his one slender thread of hope, but it was mighty weak. It all hinged on his hunch.

He went out to the stable, saddled his horse and rode out to the ranch, without saying a word to Judge. It was Saturday, and everyone in the valley would be in Tonto City. By going to the ranch he could avoid questions and conversation. Henry Harrison Conroy wanted to be where he could think. But for this trip he had belted on his forty-five Colt, and had taken a liberal supply of ammunition.

BIG JIM HARRIS sauntered down to the Corcoran home that afternoon. He had seen little of Nellie Adams since she started teaching school in Tonto City. After all, she was his niece, a very pretty young lady, and it was time for him to make a few plans for her.

He found her under an old oak in the front yard, reading a magazine, and he felt that her greeting was none too cordial. He sat down beside her.

"Everythin' going good at the school?" he asked.

"Very good, thank you, Mr. Harris."

"Why not call me Uncle Jim?" he queried.

Nellie produced a folded piece of paper and handed it to him. "Will you tell me why you wrote that, and were ashamed to sign your name?" she asked.

It was the note she had received, warning her not to have anything more to do with Danny Regan. Big Jim flushed slightly, started to deny it, but Nellie stopped him.

"It is your writing," she said.

"Well, I'll tell yuh—" He looked closely at her. "Have you seen Regan lately?"

"If you mean, did he show me the note he got—yes."

"You told him I wrote it?"

"I told him it was not your writing."

Big Jim sighed with relief. "Regan is one of Conroy's outfit," he said, "and I won't have you trailin' with any of that gang. I'm goin' to put them out of business, and I—well, I figured you was seein' too much of him, Nellie."

"Is that any of your business?" she asked coldly.

"Yo're my niece, and Regan is my enemy. The two don't mix."

"After all," said Nellie quietly, "I am of age, and I have no reason to feel that you are my guardian."

"I got yuh this job, didn't I?"

"Yes, that is true. Still, that does not give you the right to warn me against seeing a young man, just because you do not like him. You even threaten to take my job away from me."

"Yes, I can do that, too, young lady. But not if you are reasonable. Maybe you have overlooked the fact that Big Jim Harris is goin' to boss this valley. Before I get through with my plans, my word will be law around here. I've got plans for you, too."

"Oh, you have? That's fine!"

"Gettin' sarcastic, eh? You don't need to take that attitude. If you don't believe I can do what I say, go right ahead and see Regan."

"Perhaps I will. But if I do, I shall tell him you wrote that note."

"What good will that do yuh? What can Regan do about it?"

"He might," she suggested, "make you sign your name to it."

"Is that so? Go ahead and tell him."

Big Jim got to his feet and looked down at her. "Yo're a foolish girl, if yuh ask me, Nellie. Maybe yo're just ignorant, I dunno."

"Maybe it runs in the family, Mr. Harris. But before you go, tell me where I can get in touch with Steve."

"Steve?" Big Jim's face hardened. "I dunno where he is.

Wyomin', New Mexico, Colorado—mebbe. What do yuh want him for?"

"I thought he was working for you—at the Circle H."

"He was. Steve is pretty much of a wild devil, and he don't stay long in one place. You may hear from him some day."

"Was Steve ever around here?" she asked.

"You mean here in Tonto City? No, I don't think so. Why?"

"Oh, nothing—I just wondered."

"What are you drivin' at, Nellie? What about Steve bein' here?"

"I don't know," she replied. "Mrs. Corcoran told me that the other day when Danny Regan came here to ask me about that note, he saw Steve's picture in the house. Mrs. Corcoran said his face turned white, and he acted as if he had seen a ghost. She said his voice was hoarse, when he asked her who that man was. Then he hurried outside, and I met him at the gate."

"Seen a ghost, eh?" muttered Big Jim. "Why would Steve's picture look like a ghost to him? Foolishness. Steve never was down here, not as far as I know. Forget it. Well, I'll be seein' yuh."

BIG JIM TURNED and walked out through the gate, and headed back for the King's Castle, grim-faced as he strode along. He needed a big drink of whiskey and a chance to think things over calmly.

The town was crowded with people, the hitch-racks filled. All the games were wide open at the King's Castle, and the long bar was jammed. Business was good, but Big

Jim was not happy. Down in his heart was a feeling that everything was not all right.

Many people visited the new bank, watching the finishing touches. Charles Baker was there, pointing out the improvements, boasting that at last Tonto City would have a real banking institution, where the money would be safe.

Oscar Johnson and Slim Pickins, followed by Thunder and Lightning, roamed the town, having a drink here and there. James Wadsworth Longfellow Pelly was still in town, but he managed to keep away from the quartet from the JHC. There was plenty of conversation regarding the editorial in the *Clarion,* and Mr. Pelly was not exactly flattered by some of the outspoken criticism of his masterpiece. He would be glad when it was time for the stage to leave for Scorpion Bend.

He sought Big Jim Harris in the King's Castle Saloon and told him he was just a little afraid of Oscar Johnson & Company.

"They follow me around all the time," he complained.

"Yo're pretty much of a coward, ain't yuh, Pelly," remarked Big Jim. "You can write things all right, but yuh ain't got the nerve to back 'em up."

"You told me that I would have protection," reminded the editor.

"Then yuh better crawl into a hole, until stage-time," snarled the big man. "I can't be bothered with you now." James Wadsworth Longfellow Pelly was sensitive. At least, he thought he was, and this debuff was too much. He had promised Big Jim full support of the *Clarion* in this campaign to defeat Henry Harrison Conroy; but if this was the way Big Jim felt about it...

So J.W.L. Pelly, feeling rather heartsick, went to the bar and ordered rye whiskey. It was the first drink he had ever bought over a bar, and after the strangulation period was past, he felt quite elated.

14

THE SHERIFF RIDES ALONG

FRIJOLE BILL CULLISON could hardly figure Henry out. Henry had planted himself in an easy chair on the old porch, where he sat most of the afternoon, saying nothing, even ignoring the fact that a jug of prune whiskey and an empty cup were within reach.

"The man needs a doctor," decided Frijole. "Ain't normal a-tall."

Old Bill Shakespeare, the rooster, minus most of his neck feathers, and with only one tail feather left, perched on the porch railing, but failed to elicit a smile from Henry.

"Mebbe he's mournin' about the red-headed kid," suggested Frijole to himself, as he went about cooking supper. "I shore don't blame him a bit. What wouldn't I give to git my hands on that kidnapper! I'd shore bust his mainspring real quick."

Henry answered the call to supper, but he had little to say. Frijole watched him, a scowl between his eyes, but he did not speak either. Henry went back to his seat on the porch as soon as supper was over. Frijole remarked to his pots and pans:

"He acts jist like a man who was fixin' to kill somebody. I've seen gunmen act thataway, jist before they cut a six-shooter swath. But if I was him I'd spend my time practicin' shootin', less'n I was aimin' to do the job with a shotgun."

The old clock over the fireplace had just struck eight o'clock when Henry came back into the house. He buckled on his gunbelt and turned to Frijole.

"Which is the best way to get to the old El Segundo mine on Crazy Woman Canyon?" he asked.

Frijole looked curiously at him. What on earth did Henry expect to find in Crazy Woman Canyon, he wondered?

"Well," he said thoughtfully, "I'd go up the old wash, back of here, cut over to the rim of Smoke Tree Canyon, foller that around to that open ridge and foller that ridge until yuh cut what's left of the old road to El Segundo. I dunno what in hell you'd—"

"I wish you would saddle my horse, Frijole."

"Yo're danged right. But if yo're goin' over there, I'd shore like to go with yuh, Henry. You act like you've been stewin' up somethin', and I'd—"

"No, Frijole, I shall go alone."

"Well, yeah—course, yuh know what yuh want best."

"Thank you, Frijole."

"Oh, yo're welcome. I'll have the hull on that bronc in two minutes. But I don't see—" Frijole hesitated. Henry smiled for the first time that afternoon, as he said:

"Neither do I, Frijole."

"Uh-huh, I see. Well, if you ain't comin' back this-away, I figure I'll go to Tonto."

"Why, of course. By all means. No, I—I very likely will not come back this way."

Frijole watched Henry mount and ride past the corrals and into the old drywash, where Thunder and Lightning had hid the money. There was plenty of starlight. Frijole saw him disappear at last.

"I dunno," he said. "Beats me—him actin' thataway. Goin' to Crazy Woman Canyon at night. I wonder if he's lost his mind—or is jist losin' it. Looks spooky t' me. Well he's old enough to know what he wants—or he's gone loco over the loss of that kid. Mebbe that's it. Dawgone it, I better go to town and tell Judge and the boys."

IT WAS A long, hard ride to the old El Segundo mine from the JHC. Henry had never been over that route before which made it doubly hard. In the darkness he had trouble in finding the open ridge but once on it he was able to follow it to the nearly obliterated road to the mine. It was nearly eleven o'clock when he was able to discern the old mine buildings.

There were no lights. He rode in close, tied his horse in a thicket of piñon pines and made his way to a point about a hundred feet from the cabin occupied by the Hernandez family. There he sat down behind some brush. A crescent moon peeped over the hills casting only a feeble brightness.

Henry stretched his cramped legs and wondered just what degree of damn fool he qualified for. With only a hunch so far-fetched that he even marveled at his own foolishness, here he was, sitting behind a brush-heap watching a shack in which every occupant was peacefully sleeping. Somewhere a coyote lifted its voice in cackling protest to the moon and Henry's reflections went back to his days and years in vaudeville when he knew only the paved thoroughfares of cities.

With his back against the bole of a piñon, he alternately dozed and watched the shack.

"What a fool, what a fool!" he told himself. "Thank the Lord, I am the only one to know what I am doing."

Midnight passed, one o'clock, two o'clock. It was colder now. A breeze swept across the hills. Judge would be in bed sleeping warmly. He would suppose that Henry was out at the ranch. Everyone in the world was probably comfortable, except Henry Harrison Conroy, the fool who had a hunch.

Henry's eyes scanned the star-lit skyline, and his shoulders suddenly jerked away from the piñon. It might have been a deer. Too large for a coyote or a lobo wolf. Something had come over that ridge. He crouched forward, ears alert for the first sound. It came a few minutes later, the sound of hoofs on hard ground. Then he saw the dark bulk of two riders, coming up to the front of the shack.

He heard the creak of a saddle as a man dismounted, followed in a few moments by the sound of someone knocking on the door. After a time there was a light in the window, and he saw more light as the door was cautiously opened. He was unable to hear the conversation. Evidently both men had gone inside. Henry crawled closer.

Finally the door opened and he heard a man's voice say:

"You go to Tonto and tell Big Jim that everythin' is all right."

Then one of the men came out, mounted his horse and rode away.

Henry got to his feet, stretched his cramped muscles and began moving toward the lighted window. As he came up close to the house he could hear voices in the shack. Juan

Hernandez was arguing in a high-pitched voice, while the replies of the other man were merely low mumbles.

Henry had had plenty of time to plan out his attack. Gripping his forty-five Colt in his right hand, he stepped gingerly up on the rickety porch. His very weight seemed to jar the shack, and with two quick steps he reached the door, intending to kick it open. But he stepped on a round object, throwing himself off-balance, and he pitched forward, hitting the door solidly with his left shoulder.

The flimsy door crashed open and Henry went sprawling across the threshold. He heard a woman scream, and caught a flash of the two men in the lamplight. A man yelled out a curse, and a bullet ripped across Henry's left shoulder as the man backed against the wall, shooting down at him.

Henry was unable to get in position to shoot at the man. He merely lifted the gun in his general direction and pulled the trigger, just as the man fired his second shot. But Henry was lifting from the floor, and that bullet tore into the floor under his right knee.

Henry heard the crash, as the man went down, and the woman was crying, *"Madre de Dios! Madre de Dios!"*

Henry got to his feet, choking a little from powder fumes. Juan Hernandez was backed against the wall, holding his wife behind him. On the crude bunk, along with the two Mexican children, was little Buckshot, dirty of face and wide-eyed.

"Uncle Henry!" he cried. "Uncle Henry, I knew you'd find me!"

Then quite suddenly his face broke into wide grin.

"My little man," said Henry quietly, "I thank you for such faith."

Henry took the lamp and stepped over to look at the man. One glance was sufficient for him to realize that the man would never get up again. It was Cash Silverton, candidate for sheriff.

Henry put the lamp down and looked at Hernandez.

"*Por Dios*, I know notheeng," wailed the Mexican. "Those men breeng the leetle one and say we mus' keep heem for w'ile. I am only poor *Mejicano, señor.*"

"You have nothing to fear, my friend," said Henry.

"*Gracias, gracias, amigo*. I am only poor—"

"I believe you said that before, Mr. Hernandez. Buckshot, your face is very dirty, but it is the finest sight I have ever seen. Are you all right, my boy?"

The child nodded.

"I'm all right, Uncle Henry."

"All right, Buckshot; we are going back to Tonto City. Come."

Juan Hernandez and his wife stood in the doorway of the shack, watching Henry mount his horse, with Buckshot in his arms.

"*Vaya con Dios!*" called Juan Hernandez.

"Go with God," translated Henry. "Judging from my luck, I came with Him, too."

IT WAS WELL after midnight when Judge stumbled into the office and lighted a lamp. Judge was well liquored, but not inebriated. His face was lined with worry as he flopped in Henry's chair. All evening he had watched and waited for Henry, not having any idea where he had gone. Just a few minutes ago Judge had accosted Frijole, who had confided—rather thickly, of course—that Henry was somewhere in Crazy Woman Canyon, probably hunting for owls.

Judge looked up as John Campbell, the prosecuting attorney, came in.

"Have you seen Henry?" he asked. Judge shook his head.

"Where do you suppose he can be, Judge?"

"John, I have no idea. I'm worried, I tell you; more worried since Frijole said he was out at Crazy Woman Canyon. Damn it, John, a man of Henry's age has no business out there at night. Hunting for owls, indeed!"

"Who said he was hunting for owls?"

"Frijole Bill. The idea is ridiculous!"

"Judge, what on earth happened to Pelly, the *Clarion* editor?"

"Has something happened to him?"

"Didn't you hear them—or are you deaf? Oscar Johnson got an accordion, Slim Pickins has a violin with only one string, and they are playing the music, while James Wadsworth Longfellow Pelly campaigns for Henry Harrison Conroy."

"No, John!"

"They have visited every saloon and store in Tonto City tonight, except the King's Castle. Big Jim is wild about it."

"But Pelly, John!"

"Pelly," said the big lawyer, "is drunk as a fool and steady as a clock. He says that Big Jim turned him down; so from now on he is going to work for Henry Conroy."

"It sounds impossible, John. But they surely will not go into the King's Castle."

"With Oscar Johnson leading, Judge? That Viking

would go into Hell and defy the Devil, especially with that accordion. I am naturally all for peace and order, but I should hate to miss seeing them invade that place. Right now Big Jim is running a big draw poker game, and there is plenty money on the table. Mr. Charles Baker is also in the game, and, judging from his handling of a poker hand, the man has not always been dealing through a cashier's window."

"If we only knew where Henry was," complained Judge. "John, I am afraid something has happened to him."

"Judge, I feel that I am being kept in the dark on this kidnapping deal, and I believe it is time for you to tell me a few things."

"You promise to not tell, John?"

"I'll do my very best, Judge."

It did not take much time for Judge to give Campbell an outline of things, including the ransom demand.

"But that money isn't on the ranch, John," declared Judge. "We have no idea where it is. They demand Henry's resignation and the money. If you can see a way out—God bless you. I can't."

"Queer doings," muttered the lawyer. "I had no idea. Then the kidnapping connects up with the bank robbery. Hmmm."

"And the murder of Tony Dunham," added Judge. "They meant to kill Henry. And Henry thinks the same gang killed Fred Langley."

"Well, well! And do you think that Henry, single-handed, is trying to best that gang, Judge?"

"He is just that sort of a fool, John."

"No wonder you are worried. But what can be done

about it, when we don't even know where he went? Going to Crazy Woman Canyon doesn't make sense, Judge. There is nothing out there, except the old buildings of El Segundo mine."

"I know it. Henry took me out there with him yesterday. Went clear out there to merely find out the name of the Mexican living there."

"To find out his name? Why did he want to know the Mexican's name?"

"By gad, I'll bet that is where he went again tonight, John!"

"But why would he go out there again?"

"I—I don't know," confessed Judge wearily, "unless he forgot the name and went back to learn it again."

"Big Jim Harris still owns El Segundo, doesn't he?"

"Yes. This Juan Hernandez is the caretaker."

"Judge, you don't think that Big Jim Harris—"

"Our leading citizen?" queried Judge soberly.

John Campbell shook his head and walked to the doorway. Up the street came Oscar, Slim and Pelly, with Thunder and Lightning bringing up the rear. Their music was scarcely melodic, but they surely made enough noise. Lightning was carrying a cardboard sign on a broomstick, on which was crudely lettered in shoe polish: WE WANT HENRY!

Judge came to the doorway and watched them. Oscar started singing:

"Ay vars born in Minneso-ta, den Ay came to Nort' Dako-ta, ridin' Yim Hill's big, red vagon, Yudas priest, Ay feel for fight!"

"Viva Enrique!" shrilled Thunder and Lightning in unison. *"Viva Enrique."*

"Heading for the King's Castle, Judge," said Campbell. "We should be in at the kill."

"The law *should* be represented," said Judge wearily.

There was quite a crowd following Oscar Johnson & Company. Most of them had heard that the *Clarion* had gone pro-Conroy, and they wondered what Big Jim Harris would do about it.

BUT JIM HARRIS was not in there to meet them. Just ahead of the procession, entering the saloon, was Sid Mercer, the man who had come to the Hernandez shack with Cash Silverton and Buckshot. He flashed a signal to Big Jim, who dropped out of the game and took Mercer to his private office at the rear of the saloon.

Big Jim closed the door and faced the tired cowpuncher.

"We're all set, Jim," said Mercer. "Cash and the kid are at the shack, waitin' for further orders."

"Cash and the kid are what?" gasped Big Jim.

"Like you ordered in that letter," explained Mercer, "we brought the kid to the Hernandez shack tonight, and Cash is—"

"Good God man, what are you talkin' about?" demanded Big Jim.

"Why, the letter you sent to Cash today by that dumb Mexican. The kid is at El Segundo."

"Letter by a dumb Mexican—the kid at El Segundo? Sid, I don't know what yuh mean. I never sent any letter to Cash Silverton."

"Yuh didn't? Cash said it was yore writin', Jim."

Big Jim's usually florid face was gray in the lamplight. "This letter—what did it say, Sid?" he panted.

"Why, it said somethin' had gone wrong and for Cash to take the kid tonight to the Hernandez shack at the old El Segundo mine, and for Cash to stay there until yuh got in touch with him."

"And you took the kid there?"

"Sure. We thought it was all right, Jim."

"We've been tricked!" gasped Big Jim. "I never wrote any note. Wait! Conroy! That's who done it! Sid, we've got to do somethin' mighty quick!"

"Want me to go out there and warn Cash?"

"Too late! You don't think they'd wait for that, do yuh? No, we've got to frame somethin'—fast. If they get Cash, he might talk to try and save his own neck. That kid might recognize—"

"We all wore masks around him, Jim. You know that. Tonight me and Cash didn't wear any. He said he'd dump the kid over the edge of the canyon if anythin' went wrong. Our best bet is to hightail it out of this country."

"And leave everythin' I've built up here?" snarled Big Jim. "I'll beat 'em. They can't put any deadwood on me. Nobody can prove that I done anythin'. That kid couldn't have recognized me at the ranch. Listen!"

Oscar Johnson & Company had taken over the King's Castle, and James Wadsworth Longfellow Pelly was on a table, addressing the crowd in favor of the reëlection of Henry Conroy. Pelly was crosseyed from liquor, but his speech was straight, mainly intelligible.

"Who's that, makin' the speech?" asked Sid Mercer.

"A dirty skunk who turned against me," snapped Big

Jim. "I'll make him wish he'd never turned. But to hell with him. We've got somethin' bigger than a drunken editor to figure out."

Big Jim was without a coat, and now he picked up his gunbelt from the desk and buckled it around his waist. It was heavily studded with silver ornaments, and the buckle was a huge wolf's head, done in silver and gold.

"You can't shoot yore way out of this, Jim," warned Mercer. "If we had some of the boys from the ranch—"

"I know. I should have kept a bunch of 'em down here. Hell, yuh never know what'll happen. Listen to that damn fool out there, makin' a speech for Henry Conroy, right in my own saloon. I've got a good notion to go out there and wring his neck!"

Suddenly everything went quiet. There was not a sound in the saloon. Big Jim, tensed against his desk, stared at the closed door. Then a big cheer went up; a cheer that fairly rocked the Kings' Castle, followed by a flurry of voices.

"What's goin' on out there?" Big Jim muttered. "C'mon, Sid!"

15

WHO GOT ELECTED?

BIG JIM FLUNG the door open and went crashing into the crowd. Still he could not see what was going on, so he clawed and shoved his way ahead. Finally, by main strength, he reached the center of the roaring mob, just as Henry Conroy, hatless, his shirt torn, face scratched and bleeding, lifted Buckshot to the top of the bar.

Big Jim and Henry were not six feet apart, facing each other. Men were jostling, asking questions. James Wadsworth Longfellow Pelly was still on the table, crouched over and trying to balance himself, as the crowd jostled against his platform.

"You found the kid, eh?" Big Jim's voice was husky.

"Yes, sir," said Henry quietly. The crowd was silent now.

"Good!" croaked Big Jim. "Good work, Conroy."

"Cash Silverton is dead—out there in Juan Hernandez's shack, Jim," said Henry.

"Silverton—dead? Who killed him?"

"I killed him," replied Henry flatly. "We shot it out, Jim."

"Why—I—" Big Jim's lips twisted, but no sound came.

"And yellow enough to talk, before he died," lied Henry.

"Talked? Talked about what? I don't know what yuh mean."

"Talked about the robbery of the Scorpion Bend Bank, the murder of Tony Dunham. Dying men say things, trying to clear their conscience, I suppose. He said you were the ringleader, Big Jim Harris."

"Me?" Big Jim laughed, but without mirth. "You can't prove a damn thing, Conroy. You know you can't. I don't believe Silverton talked. You damned red-nosed bluffer, you're lyin'."

"Am I?" asked Henry quietly. He shifted his eyes and looked at little Buckshot, who seemed to be very weary, but alert.

"Buckshot, you spoke about a big man who was with the gang that stole you from your room. Do you see that man in here?"

"That man," replied Buckshot, pointing at Big Jim.

"The kid lies! He never seen me in that gang!"

"Had a black mask on his face," said Buckshot. "I cried and he slapped me."

"Crazy talk," said Big Jim hoarsely. "Kids imagination. How could he identify a masked man, anyway?"

"That belt buckle," shrilled Buckshot. "That big dog's head, Uncle Henry; I remember that."

BIG JIM'S NERVE broke then. With a surge of his huge body he threw the crowd back, as his right hand flashed to his holstered gun. In the same instant the table crashed over, flinging James Wadsworth Pelly on top of Big Jim; and the editor's clawing arms caught the big man around the neck and his flailing legs prevented Harris from drawing his gun.

Then, right over the upset table, dived the huge figure of Oscar Johnson. His mighty arms flung Pelly aside, and he seized Big Jim in a bear-hug. The surge of the crowd tore the long bar from its moorings, glasses crashed to the floor, and the bartender came over the top, like a white-aproned monkey.

"A rope!" yelled somebody. "Get a rope!"

Henry grabbed Buckshot off the bar and quickly passed him to the dazed Judge, over the heads of the milling men. A moment later Oscar came to his feet, and he stood looking down, his huge shoulders hunched, arms flexed.

"Pick him oop!" he yelled. "Back oop, you fallers, before Ay bust you von!"

The crowd shoved back. Henry managed to get in beside Oscar. Big Jim was lying senseless on the floor.

"Ay yust skveesed him, Hanry," said Oscar, panting a little. He had Big Jim's heavy belt in his hand. It had been torn in two like a piece of cardboard.

"All right, men!" snapped Henry. "Pick him up and carry him down to the jail. Will someone please get Doctor Knowles?"

"Let's hang the dirty pup!" roared a voice. "No use wastin' money on a feller what's done what he done, Conroy."

"There is still law in Wild Horse Valley," replied Henry.

"I'd tell a man, there is!" yelled a voice, "and we've still got a hell of a sheriff! You get my vote, Conroy."

The crowd moved back, giving the men room to take the unconscious Big Jim Harris to jail. James Wadsworth Longfellow Pelly was leaning against the bar, a trickle of blood from his chin and cheek, his shirt nearly torn from his body.

"What a story!" he breathed. "What a story!"

Charles Baker, the banker, disheveled from the crush of the crowd, came to Henry, panting.

"Terrible!" he gasped. "All my hopes and future gone! I had no idea what sort of a man he was. Believe me, I have had my lesson. But thank the Lord, it is all over. Right has prevailed."

"Mr. Steve Elkins," said Henry quietly, "you seem a trifle upset."

THE BANKER STARED at Henry, his eyes quivering as if he were looking into a bright light. His tongue licked at his dry lips, and the muscles of his jaw tightened.

"Elkins?" he whispered. "No—no, my name is Baker. You know my name is Baker. Everybody—"

"Everybody, except me, knows you as Baker. But your name is Steve Elkins, and you murdered Fred Langley in my office."

"No, no, I—"

Henry had his Colt .45 in his hand. "Danny," he said quietly, "will you take the guns off Mr. Elkins? You will likely find one in each coat pocket, and there is a possibility that you will find one up his right sleeve."

A moment later Danny said, "Henry, you must be a mind-reader."

"No," smiled Henry, "I am merely a practical magician. Now, if you will kindly remove Mr. Elkins' collar, you will find a triangular scar on the back of his neck. It happens that the other day I saw the gentleman working in the new bank, and the day was so warm that he had removed his collar. Thank you, Danny."

"Henry!" snorted Judge. "Do you mean to say that you

have known for several days that Baker was Elkins—and did nothing about it?"

"You mean, I presume—*said* nothing about it," said Henry dryly.

The prisoner was white-faced and his body wavered. He said:

"If I—if I talked, would it help me?"

"It usually does, Elkins," replied Henry. "No doubt you know most of Big Jim's activity. For instance, you and Big Jim framed to break the Scorpion Bend Bank. You *had* to be in on the deal, or they would never have known about that payroll. You had been stealing from the bank, and you had to do something before the bank examiner arrived.

"Big Jim wanted that money to open this bank. But circumstances ruined that, when your men lost the money. Who was the man who was selected to murder me, but got the stage driver instead?"

"Cash Silverton," whispered the prisoner. "Big Jim wanted you out of the way. Big Jim framed the kidnapping of the boy. He wanted to force you to resign. He believed the money was hidden on your ranch."

"You wrote the ransom notes?" asked Henry.

"I was not implicated in any way, except that I knew the details. I killed Langley because I knew he was going to kill me, if he could."

The men came trooping back from the jail, headed by Oscar. "Doc is trying to fix him oop," announced Oscar.

"Well," said Judge," everything is cleared up except finding that money—and I do not believe it will ever be found."

"What money, Yudge?" asked Oscar.

"The money that was stolen from the Scorpion Bend

Bank, Oscar. A grain-sack, containing thousands of dollars, mostly in currency."

"A grain-sack?" queried Oscar. "Va'al, Yumpin Yimminy! Ay have got it, Yudge! It is in my var-sack, onder my bonk at de ranch. By Yudas Ay vondered what it vars."

"You have that money?" gasped Henry. "Oscar, you—why didn't you say something about it?"

"Ay didn't know what to say," replied Oscar. "Ay knew it vars a lot of money, and Ay wondered why de owner didn't start yowling about it."

"Where did you get it?" asked someone.

Oscar's eyes slowly scanned the faces around him. Against the wall were Thunder and Lightning, and over to his left stood Slim and Frijole, listening anxiously. Oscar grinned slowly, as he said:

"Ay just found it in de road."

"You—you wonderful Viking!" breathed Judge.

"Big brute," observed Buckshot. "I like him, too."

STEVE ELKINS WAS staring at the little boy, his jaw tightly shut. Henry took him by the arm and said, "We better be going, Elkins."

They walked past the crowd and out into the clean, cool air of the street. Elkins said quietly:

"Conroy, I—I don't know what you know, but if you know anything—don't ever let the kid know."

"Elkins," said Henry, "I rarely tell things that affect anyone. You need not worry—the boy will have his chance. Did you know Steve Adams?"

"Yes, I know him, Conroy. Big Jim said he was afraid you might connect him with Steve—after that incident at the ranch. Steve is all right. Danny Reagan's bullet didn't kill him. I—I hope that will close the incident. It was the only one Steve was mixed up in."

"Who was the man with Steve?"

"Cash Silverton."

"Quite a man," sighed Henry, as they reached the office.

Doctor Knowles was working over Big Jim Harris, who had several broken ribs and a dislocated shoulder. He swore at Henry, who nodded pleasantly and locked Elkins in a cell. Danny was there. He met Henry in the hallway.

"Steve isn't dead," whispered Henry. "He will be all right; so we will forget it."

"That's awful nice of yuh, Henry," said Danny with feeling.

"Yes, I'm a nice man," agreed Henry wearily. "I am just what that man in the King's Castle said about me—a hell of a sheriff."

"And you'll keep right on bein' a hell of a sheriff, Henry. Nellie won't even have to know what happened."

"True, my boy—unless you tell her. Ah, who have we here?"

It was James Wadsworth Longfellow Pelly, at least partly sobered. He looked at Big Jim, looked at Henry and sighed deeply.

"I am staying for another day," he said quietly, "in order to get all of the story. I have been so busy campaigning, you know—"

"Sorry I was not here to see it all, Mr. Pelly," said Henry, "but I had a job of work to do."

"I understand, Mr. Conroy. Wild Horse Valley will build a monument to you for this night's work."

"Ghastly, isn't it?" Henry smiled.

"Conroy!" called Big Jim painfully. "If you'll loan me a gun, I'll do the county a big favor."

"Sorry, Mr. Harris," replied Henry, "but suicide is not my idea of enforcing the law."

"Suicide, hell! I want to kill that damn editor!"

OVER AT THE hitchrack Frijole, Slim Pickins, Thunder and Lightning mounted their horses. In a couple of hours it would be daylight. As they rode out of town, Slim said:

"Damndest thing I ever seen, Frijole!"

"Not me," replied Frijole quickly. "I 'member one time down in the Injun Territory, me and Paw-Paw Bill was runnin' a freightin' outfit. One mornin' I says to Paw-Paw Bill, I says—"

"I know exactly what yuh said," interrupted Slim. "I've heard that story so many times that I even know the names of every horse yuh had in the outfit. Yo're jist tryin' to belittle Henry, and yuh can't do it. Nossir, I take off m' hat to that red-nosed rannahan—he's top-hand in my outfit."

"Belittle Henry?" snorted Frijole. "Beelittle *him?* Slim, you know that ain't true. Gimme a couple weeks with Henry, and I can make him the saltiest gunman in Arizony. And the smartest, too, I'll betcha. Why, we thought he didn't know nothin'—and look what he done."

"I'm like for asking one question," said Lightning.

"Well, Lightnin', I reckon yo're entitled to one question," said Slim quickly. "Cut her loose, feller—we're ready to answer."

"Mucho gracias," said Lightning. "Een those saloon ees too much noise for leestening. I'm onnerstand that Henry keel those Seelverton and find those leetle keed, wheech ees name from Bockshot. Then he ees put those Beeg Jeem

een jail for sometheeng—I hope. Then he ees poke hees gon in those man's belly and tak' heem to jail—I theenk. All that ees all right weeth me, but I'm like for know what happen."

"What happened?" snorted Frijole. "Why, yuh just said what happened. What else is there that yuh don't understand?"

"I'm like for know theese. Who got elected sheeriff?"